The Angel Scroll

Prophecy. Destiny. Love
A Novel

The Angel Scroll

Prophecy. Destiny. Love
A Novel

Penelope Holt

ROUNDFIRE
BOOKS

Winchester, UK
Washington, USA

CollectiveInk

First published by Roundfire Books, 2024
Roundfire Books is an imprint of Collective Ink Ltd.,
Unit 11, Shepperton House, 89 Shepperton Road, London, N1 3DF
office@collectiveinkbooks.com
www.collectiveinkbooks.com
www.roundfire-books.com

For distributor details and how to order please visit the 'Ordering' section on our website.

Text copyright: Penelope Holt 2023

ISBN: 978 1 80341 569 7
978 1 80341 573 4 (ebook)
Library of Congress Control Number: 2023937514

A CIP catalogue record for this book is available from the British Library.

Design: Lapiz Digital Services

UK: Printed and bound by CPI Group (UK) Ltd, Croydon, CR0 4YY
Printed in North America by CPI GPS partners

We operate a distinctive and ethical publishing philosophy in all areas of our business, from our global network of authors to production and worldwide distribution.

Contents

For Richard, Matt, and May
And for Sue

"The eye altering, alters all."
William Blake

Chapter One

Dreams

In Benares, India, the sweltering night dragged on. Moonlight slid through the bedroom window and bathed the young, Christlike figure who sat cross-legged on the floor. Only a loincloth covered his slender hips, and his long, coarse hair was coiled in a topknot on his crown. He'd been watching the young woman on the low bed for hours. She was feverish, her breathing shallow, as she squinted at him now through half-closed lids. Her husband held her hand and shot the young man a pleading look. "Please let her live. I'm a rich man. I can pay you. I can help the poor of Benares, the poor of India."

"To thwart death is not to conquer it," the young master said, and the husband buried his head in the bed's embroidered cover. In a single, fluid movement, the holy man rose and stroked his host's bent head, His long, graceful fingers raking the dark hair, slick with perfumed oil, revealing a channel of pale, moist scalp.

Beyond the bedroom, in the narrow hallway, the master found his three companions propped against a wall and dozing. He tapped the closest with a calloused foot, and one by one the sleeping men awoke. "Is she well now?" the tall one asked, stretching.

"She will be dead come dawn," his master whispered, as the four men stepped into the dusty and deserted Indian night.

The phone rang. Claire woke up and realized her face was wet. She'd been crying again. She eyed the clock. 9 a.m. She cleared her throat, picked up the phone, and tried to sound awake. "Hello?"

"You still sleeping?" Claire held the phone away from her ear to stop Deirdre Vetch's whine from piercing her brain. "You're coming to the gallery to talk about the painting, right? We must talk." Deirdre's verbal pummeling began.

"It's not for sale. Sell something else." Claire pulled herself into a sitting position on the bed.

"The buyers don't want anything else. They want the *Miracle*."

"*Absent a Miracle*," Claire corrected her agent—again. "The name of the painting is *Absent a Miracle*."

"I know what the painting is called, Claire. I also know it's the best thing you've done, and we could retire on what this latest buyer is offering for it."

"Sell the others."

"They're no good," Deirdre blurted out and then caught herself. "I didn't mean that. Your work is good...all of it...most of it...but *Absent a Miracle* is unique. It shows the others up as..."

"As what, amateurish?" Claire winced. Talk about not pulling your punches, Deirdre could be brutal.

"No, not amateurish." Deirdre groped for the right words. "They're good abstracts, very promising, but you know, *Miracle*, I mean *Absent a Miracle* is powerful, a modern masterpiece."

"I have to go." Claire felt exhausted, disoriented by the recurring dream that had been disrupting her sleep and upsetting her for months. How many times had it come? She'd lost count, but enough for her to memorize it and depict it perfectly in her painting, the one Deirdre was itching to sell. The dream always made Claire sad for the husband and wife she didn't know. They needed a miracle from the young holy man, but he just watched their ordeal and did nothing.

Deirdre kept pressing her. "You've got to come to the gallery."

"I'll come later," Claire relented. "I can't talk now, I'm expecting someone." She glanced at the clock. "In thirty minutes. I have to go." She hung up without saying goodbye. It wasn't like her to be rude, but boy, was Deirdre annoying.

At 9:30 exactly, Claire heard the buzzer announcing a visitor to her Upper West Side apartment. She buzzed him into the building and checked her face in the hall mirror. She looked pale and had puffy bags under tired eyes. "I look like a wreck," she groaned, as she tucked wayward ringlets behind her ears. She glanced at a framed photo of Jake taken on a friend's sailboat. He grinned up at her, windswept and rosy in a sunshine yellow slicker. Gently kissing the tips of her fingers, she touched them to her husband's smiling lips, a daily caress that left fingerprints on the glass. Pressing her ear to a crack in the front door, she heard the click of footsteps on the tiled corridor and squinted through the door's peephole. Like a fun house mirror, it distorted the stranger who was now standing on her doorstep. Claire opened the door.

"I'm Richard Markson," he said. He was tall, at least six feet two, reserved and perhaps a little shy. The type that can tolerate pauses in conversation and never feel the urge to fill them.

"Come in, please." Claire stepped aside to let him enter and experienced the familiar and pleasing sensation of feeling feminine in the presence of a tall man. Jake had been tall, as tall as this guy Markson, who smelled of fresh air and a subtle cologne. "Please come into the kitchen. I just made some coffee. Want a cup?"

"No thank you."

Claire heard the chill in her guest's refusal. Dressed in slightly wrinkled khakis, and a tee shirt embroidered with the symbolic third eye, she led the way, barefoot, down the apartment's long, narrow hallway that acted as a gallery for her soft abstract paintings. Her visitor followed. "Just have a seat in here, please, while I get some coffee." Claire pointed to a chair in the small, casual but stylish living room. Two walls were covered with her artwork. Two more had the floor-to-ceiling bookshelves Jake had built. Their oak shelves were overloaded with rows and stacks of books, with the spines of her oversized art books jutting out. Rays from a fall sun pierced the apartment's windows and bounced off a vase of wide-awake white daisies, as dust motes danced in a shaft of light. The aroma of fresh-ground coffee snaked in from the kitchen, and as she left to go grab a cup, Claire noticed her guest take in his surroundings. When she returned, she brought the wrinkled flyer she had torn days earlier from the bulletin board at her local grocery store. Markson perched on the edge of an easy chair, as Claire sank into the cream, overstuffed couch opposite. His eyes flicked over the flyer on her lap, and she saw him press his mouth into a grim line. "Who's the artist?" he asked.

"I am." Claire scanned her paintings, trying to see them through a stranger's critical eye. Markson nodded, noncommittal. I hate it when they silently judge the work, but make no comment, she thought. She ignored an eruption of artistic insecurity, ignited by her earlier spat with Deirdre, and fueled now by her aloof visitor. "Your phone number is on here. I assume you know the young woman on this missing-person flyer?" Claire pointed to the wrinkled paper.

"She's my sister." Markson flexed the fingers on both hands.

"I'm not sure how to say this, but I've been seeing images of this woman," Claire said, taking a sip of coffee.

"Really?" As Markson stared at her, Claire saw both annoyance and sadness in his blue eyes. She reached down to uncurl the fringe of the area rug.

"Ms. Lucas," Markson said.

"It's Mrs. Lucas," Claire corrected him.

"I posted the flyers over eight months ago when Hilde first went missing, before I knew she was dead." Markson looked her right in the eye.

Dead! She was shocked, but why? It made sense that a missing woman might turn up dead. Now she understood his annoyance. He probably thought she'd called him out of morbid curiosity. "I'm sorry, Mr. Markson. I had no idea that this woman was your sister, that she was dead."

Claire wondered if she should explain her strange behavior to her annoyed visitor. Should she tell him about the bizarre occurrences that had led her to call him? He was staring at her, waiting. She touched slender fingers to her left temple. "A few months back, I started having a problem," she began. "I noticed a strange, egg-shaped opening next to the corner of my left eye. At first it was just like a dark spot, but soon I began to see colors, flashes, and flickering lights there. The space gradually grew bigger, until I could make out shapes, fragments of images, faces even. I saw one face repeatedly," Claire hesitated, "a young woman with bobbed blond hair, wearing a striped blue and white shirt with the collar popped. I had no idea who she was until I recognized her on the poster in the store." Claire stared down at the flyer and stroked the image of the young woman.

"Maybe you saw her first on the flyer without realizing it. It was probably the flyer that triggered the images." Markson's voice was even, but his eyes were still sad.

"Maybe." Funny, she hadn't thought of that. "I'm sorry if I've upset you. I recognized your sister as the woman in my..." she struggled for the right word, "my vision. I thought I could help."

"Are you a psychic, Mrs. Lucas?"

Claire saw Markson staring at the mystical third eye on her tee shirt. The top was something she'd picked up on impulse a few years back at the Amsterdam Avenue street fair. "Groovy!" Jake had laughed and paid the vendor for it. A bad choice for today, it was the first thing she'd yanked from her chaotic top drawer in her rush to get ready. "Oh no, I'm not a psychic, I'm a painter. Nothing like this has ever happened to me before."

Markson stood. "I'll show you out." Claire led him back down the hallway past her paintings, feeling self-conscious and certain that her guest disapproved of her, and everything about her, including her artwork. At the door, she was about to say goodbye when her visitor turned to her. She studied his face. He was handsome in a finely drawn, refined way. "The police found my sister's body in the East River," he said. "They think she jumped from the Brooklyn Bridge. There was nothing suspicious. She'd been depressed."

Claire watched him study the photo of Jake on the sailboat and take in her husband's strong, friendly, open face. "Why did you come here?" she asked.

"I'm not sure," he said finally. "Your message wasn't clear. You said you'd seen my sister. I thought you might have known her, had seen her in person before she died, and maybe you had a message from her."

"I'm sorry if I made things worse," Claire said.

"No, not worse." He stood for a moment on her doorstep with his hands in his pockets, then started down the corridor, looking back just as she was about to close the door. "Mrs. Lucas, what was my sister doing when you saw her in your vision?" Claire tilted her head. "She was crying." He nodded. Then, rather than taking the elevator, he headed down the stairs. Claire lingered on the threshold of her apartment, listening until she no longer heard his hurried footsteps echo through the stairwells.

Less than an hour after his meeting with Claire Lucas, Richard Markson arrived downtown at one of the trendier Soho art galleries. Sitting in the middle of a sleek white modern bench, he stared at the canvas hanging on the wall before him. As he contemplated the work, a steady stream of people passed between him and the large, four by six-foot painting. All of them, he saw, even those who clearly knew little or nothing about art, lingered a long while before this particular canvas. Like him, they could feel the painting's strange pull. They stood before the hypnotic work, as he had many times, and allowed its meaning to penetrate their being. They don't realize it yet, Markson thought, but when they leave the gallery, these unsuspecting observers will take the painting's message with them. They will think about it often in the days and weeks to come and feel a strange sense of tranquility and well-being when they do.

Markson continued to scrutinize the work, even though he'd already committed every inch of it to memory. A beautiful young Indian woman lies sick in bed. Her half-open eyes are fixed on a young holy man who watches her. Another man, her husband probably, is weeping, his face resting in the woman's open palm. Even without the help of the title, *Absent a Miracle*, it was easy, Markson thought, to grasp the painting's message. The holy man will not perform a miracle to raise the sick woman from her deathbed. And although her husband grieves, the young woman is accepting. She's in receipt of a more powerful miracle, grace in dying, peace amid suffering. Tears slid down Markson's cheeks, unlocking his own grief, and making it hard to control the medley of pain that tightened his chest and throat. He stood up and reached out to touch the canvas.

"Sir, please step away from the painting." The guard's tone was firm. People turned to look at the tall, well-dressed respectable man, who didn't look like the type to get out of line. Markson pulled his hand away, but not before lightly touching the canvas. He knew from prior furtive touches that it felt warm. Glancing at the guard, he nodded. He'd got the message. He wasn't going to mess with the painting. He squinted again at the imprint on the card pinned next to the work, *Absent a Miracle*, oil on canvas, by Claire Lucas. Released from the pull of the extraordinary work, Markson left the dim interior rooms and spot-lit paintings of the Soho gallery and stepped into the bright sunshine.

Claire was headed downtown, too, and sat lost in thought under the fluorescent lights of the subway car. At 59th Street, she almost missed her stop. Jumping up at the last minute, she elbowed her way through the heavy doors as they were closing. She emerged from the subway into the bustle of Columbus Circle and checked her watch — 10:45. Good, she had fifteen minutes to make the walk across Central Park South to her 11 a.m. appointment.

Out of habit, she swiveled her left eye to check its far corner. This spot where strange visions and light shows routinely appeared was dark; no lights, no activity, and no sign of Hilde Markson. I know her name and what happened to her now, she thought. Her brother thinks the flyer triggered the visions, but he's wrong. I saw his sister crying through the strange opening long before I noticed the flyer in the store. She strolled on, deep in thought, until she reached her doctor's office on East 63rd Street.

Dr. Bentley smelled like peppermints. He shone the light in Claire's left eye and told her to roll her eyeball this way and that. He did the same with the right eye and then the left again. "Well?" Claire asked after he'd examined her in silence for a minute or two.

"I can't see anything out of the ordinary. Is it a floater?" he asked, crunching his peppermint. Claire struggled to explain. "It's not really in the eye itself, it's more in front of the eye, next to the far-left corner."

"Hmm." He switched off his light and slipped it into the pocket of his bright white coat where his name was embroidered in dark blue cotton, "Dr. James Bentley." Claire tried to explain. "It started out like a strand of thick black cotton hanging in front of the eye, obstructing my line of sight, very annoying and distracting."

"And it's getting bigger?"

"Yes, at first it was about the width of fishing line, but now it's much wider, like a dark, egg-shaped spot, like a keyhole or opening that I can see things through."

"What things?"

"Well, at first I saw colors and flashing lights, and then I began to see shapes, and faces."

"Sounds like a problem with the retina." Bentley leaned against a chair.

"You see faces when you have a problem with your retina?" Claire frowned.

"No, bright lights, flashes, distortions, that sort of thing." Bentley began scribbling notes in her records.

"But I saw more than that. I saw the face of a missing woman I've never met. That was more than just a distortion." Claire rubbed her forehead as the strain of the morning returned.

"Sometimes the brain plays tricks, creates optical illusions when there's a problem with the eye, with the optic nerve." Bentley was gentle, reassuring, and Claire felt uncertain again. "So it's my brain and not my eye? Should I be worried?"

"Not really. Stress can mess with the nervous system." The doctor put his head on one side and studied the attractive young woman on his examination table. She looked tired and thinner than when he'd seen her last. She slid off the table and slipped on her beat-up loafers. All I seem to wear these days, she thought. How long since I dressed up? Felt attractive? Desirable? She wanted to head off Bentley's "I know you're under stress and your life is hard right now" speech. "So what now?" She put on her game face.

"Follow up with a specialist and an MRI for good measure. Just a precaution," he added when he saw her pull a worried face.

"Okay then." Claire reached for the door handle.

"I'll give you a referral for Lenny Hill and make sure you get in within a day or so, okay?" He squeezed her shoulder. The gesture made Claire's heart clench, and she wanted to lean against the short, sweet, kind man who smelled like peppermints and admit that yes, life really was very hard right now. Instead, she hurried out through the waiting room, barely managing a smile for Christine the receptionist.

Back at the subway, Claire debated her next move. I'm too spent to go face-to-face with Deirdre Vetch. Maybe I should head home and take a nap. No, I'm sleeping too much. If I don't go to the gallery, Deirdre will only stalk me with more calls. What a lousy morning! Better get all the tough encounters out of the way, so I can relax and hole up for the night. I ignored this problem with my eye for too long. I bet there's a medical explanation. Maybe it'll explain the strange dreams too.

As she hopped on the downtown express, headed for Soho, Claire's relief gave way to embarrassment. Why did I have to go and contact Richard Markson? The poor guy is mourning the loss of his sister under heartbreaking circumstances. I've made it worse, and I look like a weirdo. I should have checked the problem out with a doctor before I bothered him with my bizarre claims. But the truth was that she'd had her fill of doctors, of Jake's doctors, the waiting rooms, the tests, the labs, the treatment rooms, and finally, the hospital rooms. And it was all too fresh in her memory. As the train sped along its underground track, she looked out at the darkness through the car's window and saw the weary face that the glass reflected back to her.

Claire stood before the same chrome and glass doors of the Vetch Gallery that Markson had exited earlier. She ducked inside, deciding to take a quick look at her painting before heading upstairs to Deirdre's office. "Hi there, Manny." Claire smiled at the good-natured guard Deirdre had posted to watch over her canvas.

"People are still coming to see it, Ms. Lucas." Manuel enjoyed being on speaking terms with the artist of this celebrated work. He didn't understand most of the stuff in the Vetch Gallery, but this painting that Ms. Lucas did, it made you feel good inside. "People get a little crazy," Manuel shook his head. "Some of 'em cry, and others want to touch it. I just had to check some well-dressed guy who was trying to paw the canvas. I don't think they mean any harm, you know. They just want to touch it because it makes 'em feel good, I think."

Claire nodded and smiled, turning to look at the painting she still found so hard to believe she had created. Despite her art-school training and many years toiling at her craft, she knew this work was far above her usual level of expertise, and it was in a totally different style than her other work. If she had not lived through the six intense weeks it took to get the evocative tableau on canvas, she would have sworn someone else had done it. But the triumphant work didn't make Claire proud. She felt like a fraud. And the scene that brought serenity to others distressed her. It carried her back to the dream that inspired the painting, and its intimations of death that stirred up feelings of grief. She walked away from the canvas.

Upstairs, she tapped on Deirdre's office door. "Come!" Her agent's voice dripped with the affectation that she poured on when her fanciest clients were around. Claire ventured into the stylish office and saw her agent sitting opposite a slender, middle-aged man, who was dressed head to toe in immaculate charcoal gray cashmere.

"Oh, Claire, great, great, great, you're here!" Deirdre stood and air kissed her on both cheeks, taking in the younger woman's beat-up loafers and chronic Gap uniform. When would this person learn that the art world was about appearances? Deirdre thought. About displaying a high level of taste and flair in all things? Today, as usual, Claire looked worn out and blah. Without a doubt she was striking—gorgeous dark ringlets, pale skin, and green eyes. She was quite tall with an athletic build. There was an intelligent air and strong artsy vibe about her, and when she spoke, she sounded surprisingly seductive. But the young artist seemed to know next to nothing about how to package herself for success.

"Sit down, sit down." Deirdre directed Claire to the sleek Eames chair next to her guest, who was tapping his foot in slow time.

"Your timing could not have been better," Deirdre trilled. "Claire, I'd like to introduce you to Lucien Gray. He is the gentleman who has been trying to buy your work for a couple of weeks!" Deirdre widened her eyes like an aging flirt and wrinkled her nose at Gray.

"You're playing hard to get." Gray smiled at Claire, but under the light tone, she detected that he was more than a little annoyed. Maybe he thinks I'm greedy and just holding out for a bigger payday, she thought. The more she insisted that she didn't want to sell *Absent a Miracle*, the more Deirdre hounded her on behalf of clients who were eager to own it. Claire knew that if she withdrew the painting from the gallery, she could kiss Deirdre goodbye as an agent, and it had taken years of struggle to win Deirdre Vetch's representation. Throughout Jake's illness, and the awful months since, the artist had hung onto it by a thread as fragile as a spider's. She knew that if she hadn't rustled up her celebrated canvas, some months back, Deirdre would have dropped her.

"Claire." Deirdre said her name like she was trying to coax a distracted toddler. "Mr. Gray has just offered us eight hundred thousand dollars for the painting. Isn't that great?"

Oh no! Claire looked from Deirdre, who wore a shaky but determined smile, to this man, Lucien Gray, who was staring at her with thinly disguised contempt. "Thank you for taking an interest in my work" was all she could think to say.

"I'm actually more interested in making it my work," Gray quipped. Then he threw her a look that said he expected her to leg it downstairs and personally gift-wrap the four-by-six-foot canvas.

"Lucien, dear, why don't you leave me and the artist to talk business? I'll call you later." Deirdre stood up, and Claire caught Gray staring at her with narrowed eyes. Deciding not to push it, he rose and extended his hand, trying honey instead of vinegar. "Ms. Lucas, you are very talented. It would be my great pleasure to buy this beautiful work. I would give it a very good home, and of course, you could come and visit. I know how hard it is to let paintings go, like children. So many great artists have told me this." He stressed the word "great" as though it didn't apply to Claire, even though it was her work he was so determined to own. Still, she had to agree with him that she wasn't "great." She felt like a fraud. She did love her real work, the abstracts she'd always created, until the morning she had been compelled to put her powerful dream on canvas with exquisite realism, and had, in the process, transformed herself into a "modern master" as Deirdre called her. "Come and see the Lucas painting, she's a modern master." That's how Deirdre had started the buzz over *Absent a Miracle*, after she had relocated the canvas from Claire's studio, in her apartment's spare bedroom, and installed it downtown in the Vetch Gallery.

Deirdre clicked the door shut after Lucien Gray and rounded on Claire with a scowl. "This is it, Claire, crunch time! No more stalling! What's the most you ever sold a canvas for?"

"Twenty-five hundred for *Raindrops*." Claire smiled as she thought of the painting done in a soft palette of pinks and grays. It was one of Jake's favorites, and he hadn't wanted her to part with it.

"Exactly. Eight hundred thousand is a massive sum for an unknown artist."

"You couldn't retire on a hundred and sixty thousand dollars," Claire interrupted her agent.

"What?" Deirdre looked confused.

"You said we could both retire on what we're being offered. You'd only get a hundred and sixty grand," Claire said.

"I was exaggerating."

"We could get more." Claire was stalling, appealing instinctively to her agent's greed. It worked. Deirdre, rail thin in her immaculately cut, size two Chanel suit, studied Claire for a second and then laughed. "Look at the cojones on you?"

"Ask for a million five. It's worth at least that," Claire said, feeling absolutely and positively sure that the painting would never fetch such a huge amount. To her surprise, she saw Deirdre squint, scrunch up her mouth, and start running mental calculations. Claire maintained her bluff. "Come on, Deirdre, we'll hold out for a million five, and if we don't get it, we can always sell it to Gray for what he's asking now, or a bit more."

"You're gonna piss him off," Deirdre sing-songed, but Claire could see that she liked the angle.

"I'll be bad cop, you be good cop," Claire pressed on. "Take him for nice lunches at the St. Regis and work your magic."

"Okay, let's give it a try." Deirdre sucked in a breath and smoothed her shiny, perfectly highlighted hair, suddenly exhilarated by a sense of risk and relief that Claire Lucas had gone from being a brat to a savvy partner in crime. "Which brings me to my next question. Why aren't you painting more *Miracles?*"

Claire had barely picked up a brush in weeks, and any new work would be nothing like the extraordinary canvas hanging in the gallery below. *Absent a Miracle* was a one-off, an inspired work for sure, and she doubted that there would be others like it. But this was not the time to break the bad news to Deirdre Vetch.

Done with her meetings for the day, Claire hopped off the subway, twenty-five blocks south of home, and grabbed a hotdog and juice from a stand on the corner of 72nd Street and Broadway. She squirted mustard on the frank and bit into the bun. Usually health conscious, she had let her diet go to pot lately, but the walk home would burn off the junk food, give her time to think, and hopefully tire her out so she could sleep.

The late-afternoon sights and sounds of the Upper West Side soothed her feelings of isolation. Whoever said that New York was unfriendly didn't know the city the way she did. She squeezed past kindergartners in hats festooned with tassels and pompoms, as they meandered down the sidewalk, in what looked like a small child's conga line. Each kid held onto a length of rope, attached on either end to frazzled caregivers, who herded the tykes along.

Claire's thoughts returned to the eight hundred thousand dollars that Lucien Gray had offered for her painting. I could use the money, she thought. Jake had died a young New York City schoolteacher with barely any savings and no life-insurance policy. But selling her painting seemed out of the question. Tomorrow I'll come clean with Deirdre, tell her I'm withdrawing the work altogether, even if it means losing her as an agent and getting blackballed at every gallery in Manhattan.

Claire was not sure why, but she knew that she could never sell *Absent a Miracle*. She understood so little about how or why she had painted the canvas and the recurring dream it was based on, but she knew one thing for certain, she was not supposed to profit from the amazing work. It was a gift to the world that she had simply midwifed. She would bequeath it for exhibit some place where others could enjoy it. Then she would be free to get back to her old life that would never be her old life again, now that it had a Jake-sized hole in it. Who knows? she thought, I might find a new agent, one who likes my style and believes in me. She remembered what Jake always said. "Don't think about outcomes, just do the right thing." Claire was ambushed by a longing to hear her husband's voice again, not just its echo in her head that was growing fainter and harder to hold onto.

Not until she was contained in the empty, confined space of the elevator in her building did she slump under the pressure of her stressful day. Approaching the front door of her apartment, she sensed a figure in the shadows, leaning against the wall of the fourth-floor landing. Her adrenaline surged and spiked her heartbeat as she stopped in her tracks.

"Mrs. Lucas, I hope I didn't scare you." The man stepped forward and Claire recognized the tall, tentative figure of Richard Markson.

This visit, Markson seemed more relaxed, and ready to join Claire for a cup of green tea in her small, square kitchen that had open shelves lined with colorful fiesta ware. He'd lost his stern look, but his face was drawn. Claire bit her lip. Their talk this morning had probably upset him. "Let's go inside." She led the way into the living room, where her guest dropped into the beat-up club chair that had always been Jake's perch. "Mrs. Lucas, it's my turn to make an odd request," Markson said, as he looked down at the delicate China cup and saucer Claire liked to mix and match where they rested in his slender palm. "Just call me Claire, Richard," she said, at ease now, as she sank into the couch with her legs tucked under her.

Richard looked her in the eye. "Claire, I'd like you to come with me to Jerusalem." Her tired mind whirred, as she tried to pinpoint in which US state there was a town called Jerusalem. There was a Bethlehem, Pennsylvania, but she couldn't recall a Jerusalem. Did it have something to do with his sister? With Hilde? "Where's Jerusalem?" she asked him.

"Jerusalem is in Israel," Richard said.

"You want me to go with you to Israel?" Claire was taken aback.

Richard put down his cup and saucer and leaned in, suddenly all business. "Claire, for a few weeks now, I've been studying your painting at the Vetch Gallery. When you left the message about Hilde, I didn't realize that Mrs. Lucas would turn out to be *the* Claire Lucas, the artist, until I came here and saw your work." He gestured around the room at the canvases that covered the pale gray walls like a jewel-colored mosaic. Claire smiled at him, the first person ever to call her *the* Claire Lucas. "I thought I sent you running and screaming after our talk this morning," she said.

"I don't run, and I don't scream." He grinned, and Claire noticed how the smiled brightened his tired face, made his blue eyes crinkle, and showed off two rows of even white teeth, in a mouth that looked sensuous, now that he was relaxed. "No, your visions of Hilde just added another piece to a puzzle I'm trying to solve," he said.

Claire interrupted him. Hopefully, she now had a second chance to make a better first impression, and show Richard Markson that she was sensible and rational, and not some flaky, woo-woo type. "Richard, after we met this morning, I saw my doctor. He thinks that I have a problem with my retina or optic nerve or something—something medical. I've been under a lot of stress, not sleeping, and not thinking straight. What you said is probably right. I didn't have a vision of Hilde. I likely saw her face on the poster in the grocery store and my imagination got the best of me." There, she'd cleared it up. No matter what this funny stuff is with my eye, she thought, I have no right to turn this guy inside out with nutty claims.

Richard eyed her for a moment, then mentally brushed off her speech, and changed the subject. "Claire, as part of my work, I collect, study, and sell rare manuscripts and artifacts. Two of my associates are currently investigating a very important scroll found on the Jordanian side of the Dead Sea."

"Dead Sea as in the Dead Sea Scrolls?" Claire tried to recall an online article she'd read about the famous archaeological finds.

"Sort of, but this new parchment is called the Angel Scroll, and it was found in a different area of the Dead Sea," Richard explained. "It's different from the previous finds in some pretty amazing ways, and it's at the center of an intense effort to translate and decipher it." He paused, but Claire was too confused to say anything. "Claire, the parchment is giving us fascinating new insights into the early Christian community in Jerusalem. It also makes some startling predictions."

"About what?"

"The scroll predicts that early in the third millennium, three great works of art from three unknown artists will emerge. And these paintings will act as symbols or spiritual signposts."

Claire frowned. What is happening? she thought. An ancient scroll is predicting events in the art world? Now it was her turn to be perplexed. Did all my talk about visions this morning make this guy think he could come back and start rambling on about psychic stuff and weird ancient prophecy? She looked at him, but he gave no clue that he was strange or eccentric, as he sat on Jake's chair looking very self-possessed. "What does this have to do with me?" she said finally.

"Claire, we think that *Absent a Miracle* might be one of the three paintings predicted by the parchment." Richard paused to let his strange assertion sink in.

"Why do you think that?" Claire felt her cheeks flush, but she stayed even. Good, Richard thought, she's taking it better than I expected. "Because, you are an unknown artist," he said, "and your work displays two of three marks that might identify it as one of the three paintings. Mark one is that the canvas is warm to the touch. Your canvas feels warm. Mark two is that it appears to be healing. I have personally seen your work create a calming, healing, and restorative effect on those who view it."

"OK," Claire said, feeling nonplussed. Her canvas had stood in sunlight and next to radiators, so no doubt it often felt warm. And people did talk about it being healing, but she thought that was more to do with the growing hype surrounding it. "What's the third mark?"

"When displayed together as a triptych," Richard said, "the three paintings will act collectively as a new visual gospel of sorts, a vehicle of transformation for the New Age."

Claire tried to process the outlandish claims. He looks sane, she thought. Does he actually believe this stuff? Is he seriously asking me to believe it? Sensing her skepticism, Markson threw more details at her. "Whether what the parchment predicts is true or not," he said, "the Angel Scroll is a genuine, early Christian artifact. It's a mystical writing from an esoteric tradition that existed more than two thousand years ago, making it tough to know if its message is literal or metaphorical. We initially doubted that the paintings really existed. We thought the scroll might be describing a parable of some kind. Eventually, we decided the best course was to take the prophecy literally and go looking for the paintings." He stopped and grimaced. "So that's my job. I'm searching for the proverbial needle in a haystack, well three of them actually. I'm on the hunt for three allegedly miraculous paintings by three anonymous painters, with not the faintest clue about where to find them."

"And now you think *Absent a Miracle* is one of the three paintings? Claire let her skepticism seep into the question.

"Yes, Richard said. "It was amazing when we discovered your painting, and it displayed two of the three marks predicted by the scroll."

"Who's 'we'?" Claire asked.

"I'm working with two associates. Father Karl Brandt is from Bavaria. He's a Benedictine monk, translator, and brilliant linguist. Professor Myron Kushner, we call him Mike, is a scholar of Hebrew and Jewish mysticism at the Hebrew University in Jerusalem and New York. They're in Jerusalem right now, translating the text. I've been scouring galleries in Europe for weeks with no luck."

"No faith in the stuff made in the good old USA?" Claire teased and sipped her tea.

"I never imagined I'd find one of the paintings in my own back yard," Richard confessed. "I couldn't believe it when I got back from Europe, heard the buzz about your painting down in

Soho, witnessed it for myself, and realized it might actually be one of the three."

"You've no idea where the other paintings are?" Claire was curious despite herself.

"No. We were hoping you might help."

"How?"

"The more we know about you, the easier it might be to find the other two artists." Richard saw that she didn't know how to react. "Claire, you look tired. I don't mean to overwhelm you. We can speak again tomorrow if that's all right." He stood up, and to her surprise, Claire felt sorry to see him go. This talk with an interesting man, in the dying light of a fall afternoon, felt good after so much solitude. The thought snaked through her mind and made her feel guilty, like she was betraying Jake.

Richard had one more question. What inspired the painting? Claire explained that it was based on a recurring dream that she'd had many, many times. "The painting calms others, but it upsets me. In my dream, I see a young, Christlike figure in a bedroom in India." When she said "Christlike," she saw how Markson swayed slightly, like he'd been pushed by an unseen finger. "This Christ figure and the dying woman both seem at peace, but the husband is heartbroken, and I can feel his sorrow as he pleads for a miracle that he doesn't receive."

They were both quiet for a moment, and when he spoke, Richard cautioned her that if she agreed to go with him to Jerusalem, they would have to leave within a few days. He knew it was short notice and she'd probably have to talk it over with her husband.

"My husband is dead," Claire said, shocked at how evenly she was able to speak the awful words. She saw Richard's face fall and felt sorry for making him squirm—again. "I think that you and I both know what it is to live absent a miracle," she said. "Let me show you out. Call me in the morning."

For the second time that day, Claire led Richard Markson out through the hall. Midway, he gestured to a canvas he liked and Claire smiled. "Ah, that's called *Sunlight*, and it's one of my favorites too." He muttered something about her being talented, and she was surprised by how much his compliment pleased her. She sensed it wasn't easy for him to give praise.

"*Absent a Miracle* is far beyond what I usually produce, and it's not really typical of..." Claire began her disclaimer, ready to admit that these paintings couldn't hold a candle to the one in the Velch Gallery that had captured Richard's interest, but he interrupted her. "I'm talking about this work here. These are good." He gestured up and down the hallway filled with Claire's creative outpourings.

"Thank you," she said, holding the door open for him to leave. And as she closed it, she swallowed unexpected tears.

Chapter Two

Angel Scroll

The driver thrust his hand out of the cab window in a crude gesture, cursing in rapid-fire Hebrew at the idiot who had cut him off. In Jerusalem, like in New York, Claire realized, you risked it all when you climbed into the back of a taxicab. Beside her, Richard Markson shot her a look that said he wouldn't let any harm come to her. He needn't have worried, she was enjoying it all, even the hairy cab ride from the airport to the hotel. Evening was falling, and a warm, dry breeze rushed in through the speeding cab's open windows. She looked out, intent on absorbing the sights and sounds of Jerusalem, marveling at how the ancient and modern lived side by side.

It had been just three days since Richard had invited her to come along for a meeting in Jerusalem with his colleagues Kushner and Brandt. Life is what happens while you're making other plans, she thought. The last time that life had surprised her, with Jake's diagnosis, it had kicked off a nightmare. By contrast, this trip to Jerusalem was a delight and totally unexpected. Like turning the corner in New York City and finding a sunny meadow instead of the bustle and grime of a familiar city block.

"We're here." Richard reached into a back pocket for money to pay the driver. Each time she inspected the man, Claire found more to admire, like his long legs scrunched up in the tight space of the cab. Random musings, she told herself. No one could ever measure up to Jake.

Claire was impressed with the elegance of the Mount Zion Hotel, only a stone's throw from the Benedictine Dormition Abbey where, Richard said, Kushner and Brandt were hard at work translating the parchment scroll. He'd scheduled a meeting with the two scholars for the next morning. Inside the hotel lobby, Richard checked in and handed Claire her room key. "You go on up. We have adjacent rooms. I'll finish here and send up your bags. Let's meet in the bar over there for a drink in thirty minutes, okay?" Claire nodded and headed for the elevator.

Just thirty minutes later, she sat, showered, and changed, waiting for Richard in the beautifully appointed lobby bar. She flipped through a slim guide to the hotel and the city. The Mount Zion Hotel dated back to 1882, and for most of its history it had been the Hospital of St. John. Claire studied the lower floor, where it was easy to see the Turkish influence preserved in the distinctive window arches of the remodeled building. Oversized couches with overstuffed cushions in muted neutral tones sat on pale marbled floors, softened by the generous foliage in oversized planters.

She spied Richard's tall figure moving across the lobby. How old was he? Forty-five? A little younger? She was thirty-five, and she guessed he was no more than a decade older. He lowered himself into the chair facing her. His sandy blond hair looked darker now that it was wet and slicked back after a hurried shower. Dressed down in jeans and an open-necked, yellow polo shirt, his vibe seemed younger and more virile. And there it was again, that hint of subtle cologne. She breathed in to trap the delicious woody notes before they had a chance to escape and waft away.

Energized by unexpected adventure, Claire had dressed like a holidaymaker in a festive turquoise skirt and white cotton blouse. She licked her lips and tasted the first coat of lipstick— coral pink—to grace her full mouth in forever. Finding herself in a happy and excited mood, she'd pouted into the hotel mirror, lightly applying makeup to her long-ignored face, in a beauty ritual that like so many others she'd abandoned in her grief.

"Sorry to keep you waiting." Richard smiled. "I spoke to Brandt. They're expecting us after breakfast tomorrow, so I thought I'd take you for a little sightseeing beforehand. We don't have much time, I'm afraid, but the least I can do is to make sure you see something of the city."

He sounds all business. Claire thought. Does he feel obliged to act as tour guide? "You don't have to do that. I know how busy you are," she said.

"No trouble. My pleasure." He sounded brusque and looked up at the waitress who had arrived to take their order. "Coke, please."

Claire felt off balance. Reluctantly, she realized that she wanted Richard to be as excited about showing her the sights as she was about seeing them with him. He had treated her to first-class seating on the plane ride over, complete with champagne and an upgraded menu that gave the whole adventure a glamorous and slightly romantic feel. Seeing now that she secretly harbored unrealistic expectations alarmed her. Get a grip, she thought. This might be a pleasure trip of sorts for me, but it's all business for him. She smiled at the waitress to hide her unease. "White wine please."

Richard rubbed his hands together, relieved that the rush to deliver Claire to Jerusalem in record time had come off without a hitch. "So, Brandt is very excited to meet you. He asked me to brief you a little before tomorrow."

About time, Claire thought. Until now, every time she'd tried to ask about the trip, the parchment, or his colleagues, Richard had found a way to shut her down. He sensed her irritation. "I don't mean to be cryptic. It's just that this whole endeavor is very confidential. Let me fill you in a little, so you'll be ready for tomorrow."

She slipped off a strappy sandal and tucked a foot under her on the couch to signal she was all ears. Richard stressed yet again that the parchment was very sensitive material.

Brandt had negotiated to buy the text on the black market and purchased it with an enormous amount of Vatican money. Only a handful of high-level clergy in Rome knew that Brandt had the parchment and was at work translating it.

"Where was your Angel Scroll found?" Claire asked.

Richard waited until the waitress was done serving their drinks. "Two Bedouin boys found it in caves at Wadi al Mojab on the Jordanian side of the Dead Sea."

The original Dead Sea Scrolls, Richard explained, were found between 1947 and 1956. Thousands of fragments of biblical and early Jewish documents were discovered in eleven caves near the site of Khirbet Qumran, on the shores of the Dead Sea. These important texts revolutionized scholars' understanding of how the bible was transmitted. They shed light on the general cultural and religious background of ancient Palestine, from which both Rabbinic Judaism and Christianity arose. "The scrolls were controversial," Richard said. "Scholars believed that many of the documents were written by a radical Jewish sect called the Essenes. Certain scholars argued that Christ Himself was a member of the Essene sect."

"And was He?"

"Some say yes, some no. There were several Jewish sects in Christ's time. The differences between them hinged on the interpretation and observance of Jewish customs and laws, and beliefs about exactly when and how the Messiah would come to save the Jewish people."

Claire listened carefully to Richard's tutorial, as he explained that the Essenes had been radicals, separatists, who established a community outside Jerusalem near the Dead Sea. They observed a solar calendar and considered the Jewish Temple defiled, refusing to worship there, and they celebrated Passover two days before other Jews.

"The theory that Christ was an Essene has always been controversial," Richard explained. "If he were an Essene, it would completely change the timetable of His last recorded week on earth. Christ would not have gone to the Temple and celebrated His Last Supper or Passover meal when the Gospels say He did. And to most Jews of the time, whose religious life centered on the Temple, Christ, if he were an Essene, would not have been considered a 'good Jew.'"

"What's your opinion?" Claire asked.

"Got a week to spare?" he laughed.

"So that's the Dead Sea Scrolls, what about your scroll?" Claire asked and Richard hesitated. "Claire, the only man who really understands what the Angel Scroll says is Father Karl Brandt. I know a little, and Kushner is helping him with translation, so he knows more. Father Brandt needs your help, so he is the one to share what he thinks is important for you to know." He paused. "Claire, tell me what you know about Hilde." His question came out of left field, and she felt awkward. "You know, the flyer triggered the visualization, like you pointed out." Richard pinned her with a look. "That's not what you said at first."

"I was wrong, jumping to conclusions. My retina might be damaged. Oh, shoot!" she suddenly remembered the MRI scheduled for the next day. She should call and change it.

"Before you found out about a possible problem with your eye, what did you think you saw?" Richard wasn't backing off, and Claire tried to read the strain in his face. What would make him feel better, sharing honestly what she had seen or glossing over it? "Richard, for several weeks before I recall noticing the missing-person poster," she began tentatively, "I thought I saw the image of a woman in her mid-thirties, my age. She looked sad. Sometimes she was crying." She saw his expression darken. "When I noticed the flyer and recognized her, I didn't know what to do. I didn't know what any of it meant. I jotted down your number and called you on impulse. I didn't plan what I was going to say until you came to my apartment. It's not like I could even help you find her. I just saw her."

"How did you see her?"

"Not in my imagination," Claire insisted. "I really saw her. It's like looking through a small opening, a keyhole, and seeing a real person, not just a mental picture. Understand?" Richard nodded, but Claire doubted he could grasp what the strange experience was like.

He stood up. "We should turn in." Claire, still on New York time, where it was much earlier, was not remotely tired. "Okay," she said, trying to hide her disappointment. As they walked toward the elevator in silence, the atmosphere felt awkward for the first time that day.

"Are his real bones in there?" Claire whispered the next morning. She and Richard were standing before the tomb of King David, a huge stone coffin covered by purple cloth and adorned with what Richard told her were the crowns of Torah scrolls.

"I don't think so," Richard admitted. "Come on, I'll show you the Upper Room, location of the Last Supper."

They climbed the stone stairway into an upstairs chamber. Claire had expected a modest dwelling, but instead found herself in a large hall, with a ceiling supported by three pillars that divided the room into three naves. Richard pointed to the pillars, arches, windows, and other Gothic-style architecture. These were clear indications that the room had been built by Crusaders in the early fourteenth century, on top of a much older structure, possibly a church-synagogue of the early Christian community of Jerusalem.

"So this is where the Last Supper happened?" Claire said with a hint of wonder.

Richard looked sheepish. "Not exactly. The original room no longer exists, but it was probably on or near this spot."

"Where to next on this tour of alleged holy places?" Claire raised an eyebrow and Richard looked amused. "Our final stop for the morning will be Dormition Abbey."

Maybe showing me around is not such a chore, Claire thought. She'd slept well, and her mood this morning was light, despite last night's awkward ending, when they'd both stood in silence outside their adjacent rooms, fumbling with their key cards.

Back outside in the sunshine, Claire looked from where they stood at Zion Gate up to Dormition Abbey, which rose like a massive fortress from Mount Zion, topped by a high domed bell tower, a cone-shaped dome, and corner towers. She turned to her personal tour guide, who looked rested, relaxed, and very appealing. "It's called Dormition Abbey," he said, "because it's the place where the Virgin Mary is said to have lived after Christ's death, and where she died, or fell asleep for the last time before her assumption into heaven."

"For real or just another claim?" Claire teased, and Richard was forced to admit that once again the account was questionable, but Christ and His mother had almost certainly lived and died in or around Jerusalem. And even if these weren't the exact sites, they were close enough and very important to the faithful who made pilgrimages here.

Richard guided Claire through the abbey's courtyard. Originally, the basilica had been a Byzantine church. He pointed to the mosaic floor still preserved under glass. The Turkish sultan Abdul Hamid had granted the land to the German emperor Wilhelm II for the benefit of German Catholics. The present basilica was completed in 1900 and entrusted to German Benedictines in 1906.

Once inside, they made their way to the dark crypt at the basilica's center. Here, surrounded by six pillars, lay the wood and ivory statue of Mary, asleep. As she gazed at the ethereal image of the sleeping Virgin Mother, Claire heard the worshipful strains of a Gregorian chant.

"The brothers must be practicing," Richard said, as the cavernous space vibrated and echoed with the clear notes of the glorious chant.

"Just for me." Claire smiled.

"Just for you." Richard smiled back.

They proceeded to the circular apse, above the altar, where Claire studied the shining mosaics of Mary with the child Jesus. Richard translated the Latin words inscribed in the open book held by the boy savior: "I am the light of the world." Suddenly, in the egg-shaped, dark spot, near the corner of Claire's left eye, there was a flash of light, followed by another. A frisson of energy shot up from between her shoulders and radiated through her crown. She swayed a little as the light and music seemed to combine and absorb her.

"You okay?" Richard took her arm.

"Yes." Claire steadied herself.

"Let's sit for a moment."

"No, I'm okay, really." The spot was dark again. "Is it time for our meeting?" Richard checked his watch — 10:30. "Yes, it is."

At first look, Claire thought that Father Karl Brandt looked more like a jovial peasant than a serious scholar. The German Benedictine monk was sixty, Richard had said, but he looked older. Claire guessed that long hours translating religious texts, combined with the austere life he must lead in the abbey, had given the monk with the short, stocky frame his haggard appearance. The skin beneath his eyes was puffy, scored, and sagging. His strong chin jutted out. Thick white hair had been scissored into short spikes. His bright blue eyes, hooded but kind, looked out from under bushy brows deep into Claire as she was presented to him. But she found Brandt's penetrating gaze more reassuring than intrusive, like a promise that he could help a person get to the bottom of things, solve those niggling questions about life that sometimes conspired to make it feel meaningless. Claire tried to read the monk — intelligent, hardheaded, loving in a no-nonsense kind of way, and energetic.

"It is so kind of you to come, a very long way I know. We really appreciate it." The monk's German accent was engaging without being grating. And his strong, enthusiastic handshake left Claire feeling that with men like Father Karl Brandt around, the world was in safe hands.

"I'm Myron Kushner, but my friends call me Mike." So this must be the professor of Hebrew and Jewish mysticism, Claire thought. He ducked a little and smiled as he introduced himself. He was short like Brandt, balding slightly, and brown eyed. Richard led the introductions, like an all-American golden boy, towering over his associates.

"So sit, please." Brandt directed her to one of the four chairs set around a dark wood occasional table. They were in a library, in a section of the abbey off limits to tourists. "So we don't need small talk, eh?" Brandt began with refreshing directness.

"No, let's have at it." Claire had as many questions for the monk as he appeared to have for her.

"Claire. I'll call you Claire, yes?" Brandt lifted his caterpillar eyebrows, and Claire nodded. "Claire, tell me about your visions, your painting, and your dreams."

Wow! Straight to the point. Visions, painting, and dreams. Brandt, a complete stranger, had managed to sum up the curious combination of events that had marked her life in the last miserable months since Jake's death. "What would you like to know?" She inhaled, trying not to tense up in the face of the oncoming interrogation.

"Richard tells me that your painting is based on a dream," Brandt began.

"Yes, it is," she said, repeating what'd she'd told Richard in New York. "I've had the dream many times. A husband is pleading with what looks like a young Christ to perform a miracle that will save his wife's life, but the young holy man only leaves her to die."

"The work is in a small gallery but has quite a following. Many people are coming to see it. Richard has personally seen dozens stand in front of it for a long time and become very affected."

Claire saw Brandt was well briefed. "Yes, apparently people find the painting very soothing and uplifting."

"That surprises you?"

"Yes, it does, because the dream that the painting is based on is painful to me." Claire steadied her voice. "I feel the husband's heartbreak and despair, and how oppressive the sick room is."

Brandt saw her distress and averted his eyes when he asked her to say more. She forced her fingers through a tangle in her dark curls, determined to answer his questions. She'd come to Jerusalem, all expenses paid, to help these three intriguing characters, if she could. "My husband, Jake, died shortly before I began having this dream. He had a rare blood disorder. He was young, only thirty-eight. I suppose the painting expresses my grief, my anger at a careless God who wouldn't answer my prayers and allow my husband to live." She looked Brandt in the eye, unafraid to reveal that her faith in a benign creator had died when she lost Jake.

"But in your painting, it is the wife not the husband who is dying," Brandt pointed out. Claire nodded and it suddenly occurred to her how strange it was that having refused all offers of counseling after Jake's death, she now found herself in the back building of a Benedictine abbey in Jerusalem, analyzing her dreams with a linguist monk and his two sidekicks. "I suppose I felt that in some ways I was dying too," she explained. "The happy life I wanted to continue, that I thought would go on until we were old, just evaporated in the most painful way." Claire glanced up and caught the stricken look on Richard's face.

Why, Brandt asked, did she choose to paint a dream that was so upsetting? His tone, deliberately even and matter of fact, helped Claire hold onto herself as anxiety broke over her. "I didn't choose. I had no choice. I was driven to put the dream on canvas, compelled. The madness of grief, I suppose. It was my outlet, where I vented my pain. It took almost six weeks. I painted night and day, and when it was finished, I was exhausted."

"I have seen photographs, and the painting is very beautiful and very inspiring." Brandt meant his words to be soothing.

"Thank you. I can't really take the credit for that." Claire looked away.

"You painted it, didn't you?" Brandt tilted his head, not accusatory but curious. Claire said that in truth it had painted itself, and the skill level and style were beyond what she had ever demonstrated in her work before. It was a relief to finally voice her genuine bewilderment at her remarkable accomplishment.

"None of your upset shows in the work," Brandt remarked. "It is very healing in nature, very peaceful."

"Yes, but I don't know why." Claire pushed the cuticle of her left thumb.

"Claire, why is the scene set in India?" Brandt was still unhurried. "The Christ of your painting resembles an Indian holy man in some ways."

Claire nodded. "According to the logic of my dream, it just so happens that this Christlike figure is in Benares, visiting a wealthy man."

"Do you know that Benares is an ancient and very holy Indian city on the banks of the Ganges river? It's also known as Vanarsi," Brandt said.

Claire shook her head. "The first time I ever heard of Benares was in my dream, where this guru seems to have adopted the dress of the locals and goes about with three Indian followers." She noticed how Brandt squinted and adjusted his position in the chair, where he sat flanked by Richard and Mike. "There are no followers in the photographs of the painting that I saw," he said.

She hadn't painted them, she explained, even though they were always present in her dream. "They waited for their master in the hallway outside the bedroom. I think they expected him to heal the woman, but instead he is, how can I put it? He is in awe that the woman will die, like her death is meant to be, and it's a wonderful event." Claire looked around the table at the three faces staring back at her with curious expressions.

Tentative now, Brandt started to speak but paused and changed direction. What could Claire tell him about the problem with her vision? She caught Richard's eye and he looked away, embarrassed perhaps that he had given Brandt such a thorough briefing of her personal affairs. Of course, she told herself, the reason I'm here is to discuss my experiences and help with their project. But part of her had wanted to believe that her talks with Richard had been private conversations between new friends, between a man and a woman who liked each other.

Claire took a deep breath and thought about where to begin. Then she told them about the dark egg-shaped spot or keyhole opening near the corner of her left eye, and the strange light, distortions, and images that had appeared there. Was there any connection between her nighttime dreams and her daytime visions? Brandt wondered. Claire said she didn't know, and suddenly, she was at ease talking about the strange, unwanted experiences she had guarded for so many months. "The disturbances with my eye started right after I finished the painting," she said. "So did the bad headaches. My doctor thinks it's stress. I'm scheduled to have tests when I get back to New York."

Brandt stood, signaling an abrupt end to the meeting. "Claire, we thank you so much for your time this morning. It can't be easy discussing these matters with strangers."

"It's getting easier." Claire rose, feeling unburdened, lighter. It was her turn to quiz Brandt. "Richard says you think I can help profile the other two artists. I have a few questions."

"Yes, and I'd like to answer them, but at dinner. Take a break." Brandt put her off. "Richard will take you shopping in the old city. You'll come back later, and we'll break bread together, yes?" He took her hand with both of his and shook it warmly. The monk had brushed her off, but Claire let her momentary irritation go. She had spilled her guts, and before the day was out, she'd make sure she got the rundown on the parchment, its predictions, and what they might mean for her life, if anything.

The afternoon with Richard was fun and exciting. They lingered at an outdoor café over a lunch of humus, pita, and a traditional Israeli salad made with feta, cucumber, tomatoes, parsley, lemon, and mint. Next came a stroll through one of the many markets crowded with stalls and carts that were piled high with merchandise made of clay, metal, glass, and fabric. Clothes and souvenirs, decorative crafts, and brightly colored textiles caught Claire's eye in a never-ending parade of tempting goods. But she had no intention of buying any of the exotic cargo.

"Come on, you can't leave empty handed," Richard cajoled, and she was finally persuaded to buy a small painting on wood of the sleeping Virgin, a replica of the abbey sculpture he had shown her that morning. She went in her bag to pay the seller what he asked for the souvenir. No way! Richard scolded her. She was supposed to haggle. "Really, it's the way they do it here. Trust me he won't let you have it for less than he intends." Claire hesitated and Richard rolled his eyes. "You're a New Yorker for goodness sake!"

"But a very polite one," Claire winked at him and then made a feeble effort at haggling, finally settling on what she thought was a good price, and carrying off the painting that the satisfied seller had crudely wrapped in paper.

Richard put his arm around her shoulder to steer her through the crush of pedestrians on the narrow walkways. Leaning into his hold, she glanced up at his face and noticed how the color darkened at the outer edge of his lips, calling attention to how even more strikingly sensuous his mouth looked when viewed this close up.

Back at the hotel, her handsome escort led her through the welcome coolness of the air-conditioned lobby and into an elevator. When they were outside their rooms, she noticed him check his watch, always aware of the schedule and the reason for their trip. "Look, it's close to 5 p.m. now. Dinner with Brandt is at six. I'll meet you in the lobby at 5:45, okay?"

Claire unlocked the door, kicked off her shoes, and lay on the bed. For the first time in over a year, she had spent a perfectly enjoyable day with no sadness, grief, or depression threatening to capsize her. It felt so good to get away from the misery of her pared down existence in New York. She relaxed for a while, before picking up her phone to check voice mail, and dialing in made all the anxiety she'd thrown off come crowding back. Two new messages: the hospital confirming her rescheduled MRI. Fine, she'd be back in good time for the appointment. Next, an excited Deirdre Vetch. Hearing her agent's voice, Claire's stomach dropped like an elevator in free fall. "Claire, hi, it's Deirdre. Fantastic news! Lucien Gray went for the asking price — one point five million. He's coming in to sign the papers in an hour. You were right. You are a talented painter and a savage negotiator. Congratulations!"

Panicked, Claire hung up, calculating the time in New York where it was still morning. Surely Deirdre couldn't have concluded the deal so quickly. She called the gallery

"Good morning, Vetch Gallery."

"Danielle, it's Claire Lucas. I need to speak with Deirdre right away."

"Congratulations, Claire."

"Thank you."

"Amazing, eh?" Deirdre was triumphant.

"But I don't want you to sell." Claire sounded plaintive.

"I know, I know, seller's remorse, but believe me, the money will ease the pain."

"I'm serious, Deirdre, I forbid you to sell my painting," she said, her voice stony now.

In the icy silence that followed, Claire could feel Deirdre Vetch, thousands of miles away in Manhattan, steel herself. "Claire Lucas, I have no idea what your problem is, but I do know I am your legal proxy with power of attorney that you gave me, along with a verbal authorization to sell your painting for one point five million dollars. I accomplish this feat, and instead of jumping for joy, you perform another insane flip flop. I'm not blind to what's going on in your life and fueling your instability, so I'm willing to cut you some slack, but I do need you to stop screwing around." Deirdre paused for breath and to slow her roll a little. "Lucien Gray left thirty minutes ago with his copy of the bill of sale. He left behind a bank check for the full amount due. I was going to suggest that you send him a note and a gift, but right now I'd appreciate it if you would just get a grip."

"I want you to call him and tell him that you made a mistake and I want the painting back." Claire was trembling.

"Listen to me, you ingrate," a now well and truly out-of-patience Deirdre Vetch snarled, "I will not call him. We are, at this moment, packing up the painting for secure transport to Mr. Gray's New York apartment. He wants to take possession immediately. I'm about to go supervise the job myself. I suggest that in a couple of days you come down to the gallery, so we can talk about this piece of business and the future of our relationship."

"I'm out of town." Claire hoped Deirdre couldn't tell she was crying.

"Well, when you get back then. Goodbye, Claire."

"I want to call Gray."

"That's not possible. He's en route to London." Deirdre was unyielding.

"Where's he staying?"

"I wouldn't tell you even if I knew. I worked too hard to do this deal, Claire. Give it a few days. You'll get used to it." Deirdre paused and then delivered her parting shot. "It's a lot of money. Now you're free to paint whatever trivialities you like." Click.

Claire stood in the hallway, pounding on Richard's door. When it opened, she saw he was wrapped only in a towel and naked from the waist up. Seeing her panicked expression, he waived her in and gestured toward a chair where she could wait while he dressed. Minutes later, still barefoot but dressed in jeans and a tee, he gave her his full attention.

"Deirdre Vetch sold my painting." Claire watched Richard's face fall.

"Did you know she was negotiating a sale?"

"Not seriously. I knew there was an interested buyer called Lucien Gray. I was trying to stall, so I told Deirdre to quote him an exorbitant asking price, one million five. I never dreamt he'd pay it!"

"When did this happen?"

"This morning."

"So fast? Can't you stop it?"

"No, the guy's a total creep," Claire groaned. "He really wants the painting. I don't think there's any way they'll let me out of the deal. Deirdre is furious with me. She won't even let me contact Gray."

"But she can't sell without your consent." Richard paced while Claire explained the mess she was in. After Jake's death, she'd been upset and distracted, overwhelmed with managing their affairs, so she had given her agent power of attorney and the authority to sell her work. And by directing Deirdre to ask for one point five million dollars for *Absent a Miracle*, she had, in effect, agreed to its sale.

"But you changed your mind, and you had no intention of selling. Either way, you're entitled to get it back," Richard reasoned.

"I know, so what do I do?"

"I'm not sure, but don't worry, we'll figure it out. Go freshen up for the meeting with Kushner and Brandt. The more heads the better, right?" Richard mustered a smile and Claire felt a faint hope return.

Claire waited with Richard and Kushner for Brandt to join them in the small library where they had convened earlier. Kushner checked his watch. "Six ten. It's not like him to be late. Let me go hurry him up." Only seconds later, eyes flashing worry, Kushner was back and gesturing for Richard to follow him. The men hurried the short distance down the corridor to Brandt's study with Claire close behind. Standing in the doorway, her eyes went immediately to where Brandt lay on the floor, groaning, as Richard and Kushner crouched next to him. "Is he alright? Is he having a heart attack?"

"He's bleeding!" Richard said, and Claire saw where blood oozed from Brandt's head onto the dark wooden floor and was soaking into the fringe of a worn oriental rug. Pressing the back of his injured head, Brandt tried to sit up.

"Karl, what happened? Did you fall? Did you hit your head? For goodness sake, lie back down." Kushner tried to stop his friend from rising, but Brandt shoved him away. On unsteady legs, he inched across the floor before dropping into an armchair and covering one-half of his face with his palm. "Someone took the parchment," he groaned. Claire saw that the black circles around the monk's eyes were darker, his face even more haggard than this morning. Her disappointment about the sale of her painting vanished, pushed aside by worry for the missing parchment that a growing intuition told her might hold significance for her and her future.

A half hour later, the stressed-out quartet sat in Brandt's study, sipping brandy that Kushner had broken out to take the edge off their nerves. Injured but still firmly in control, Brandt refused to go to the abbey infirmary. Instead, he described the surprise attack to his friends, occasionally removing the ice pack Richard had given him to tame the swelling.

"For crying out loud, keep the ice on your head, or you'll have a lump the size of a bowling ball," Kushner groused, pointing out again that Brandt's lacerated scalp needed stiches, worried and annoyed that his stubborn friend kept refusing a trip to the infirmary.

"He was wearing a habit," Brandt recalled of his attacker. "I thought it was one of the brothers. He knocked on the door and said he had come to collect dirty dishes." Claire glanced at the tray on a small table beneath the window that held the remnants of a simple lunch — bread crusts, orange peel, a coffee cup. She guessed that lost in his work, Brandt often took meals in this small intimate space. The study was imbued with the spirit of its occupant, serious but welcoming, charming and cluttered, but a little austere. There were mountains of books, piled high in crooked, unsteady towers, as well as a few pieces of masculine furniture: a large oak desk and chair, wall-to-wall bookcases for even more volumes, and two easy chairs in front of a tiny blue and white tiled fireplace. Claire sat in one of the armchairs. Richard perched on its ample arm. Brandt was stationed in the other, while Kushner sat grumbling in the desk chair.

Brandt ignored Kushner's grousing and went on with his account. "The thief must have done reconnaissance because he knew exactly where the scroll was kept. I didn't pay any attention at first. I was working. I don't know what made me turn. Just a feeling, or maybe I heard papers rustling. I saw him holding the metal box containing the scroll. I knew then there was something wrong because the hood of the habit covered his face completely. He hit me from behind as I got up."

Brandt looked anguished, Claire thought, so different from how at ease and jovial he had been earlier. But his anguish soon turned to outrage, as he ranted about how the criminal had violated his space, attacked his person, and worst of all, had made off with the priceless Angel Scroll.

Watching him get worked up, despite Kushner's pleas to calm down and keep the damn ice on, Claire had no doubt that the monk would prove a formidable opponent for anyone trying to take him on. It was probably only by operating in stealth mode that his attacker had escaped a good kicking from Brandt, who was short but muscular and feisty as hell. She looked at the heavy bronze statue of an eagle with its wings spread that Brandt's assailant had used to knock him down. It was now back in its spot on the bookshelf. That thing must weigh a ton, she thought. He's lucky his skull didn't crack open. "Hard Bavarian head." Brandt said, grimacing, as though reading her thoughts.

"You kept the parchment in here?" Claire was surprised that the monk would house such an important document so carelessly. The way Richard described the scroll, she had expected it to be locked in a vault in the bowels of the earth. Brandt turned defensive. His office was the safest place for the parchment. "I study manuscripts. This is my work. Except for a handful of people in Rome, no one knows I keep the scroll here."

"Well, someone found out." Kushner stated a troubling fact, and Claire watched the wheels turning, as each of the three colleagues pondered who the thief could possibly be, and how he knew the scroll existed, let alone its whereabouts.

Richard faced Claire. "I hate to ask you this, but you didn't tell anyone about your trip? About the scroll?"

Claire shook her head. Her mother was dead, and her father had remarried and lived in Massachusetts. Since Jake's death, she'd withdrawn, so they rarely spoke these days. She pretty much ignored calls from friends and relatives, pressing nine on the keypad to delete most messages before even listening to them. "Claire, just ringing to see..." Delete. "Claire, I know you don't feel like talking, but..." Delete. "Claire, isn't it time that..." Delete. "Claire, I can only imagine..." Definitely delete. Delete, delete, delete. She'd never been much of a joiner. Her life had mostly comprised of painting and Jake. He was her best friend. Now he was gone, she preferred to be alone, too much so. Sitting in an abbey of all places, Claire saw how contracted and colorless her life had become, as she holed up in the apartment, painting when she could, taking long walks around the city, feeling lost, unmoored. "No one knows I'm here," she said, and the three men nodded sympathetically. She imagined they pitied her, a lost, lonely widow whose withdrawal from the world had gone all but unnoticed.

Richard volunteered more bad news. "It gets worse. Claire's painting has been sold."

"Mein Gott!" Reverting to his native tongue, Brandt slapped a hand to his forehead and then winced.

"I didn't want to sell." It was Claire's turn to be defensive. "There's a collector in New York called Lucien Gray who's been after the painting for a while." She explained again how she'd demanded one point five million dollars, an exorbitant sum, and double what Gray had initially offered. She was sure he'd never pay. Except he had. The sale had gone through that morning.

"No one is supposed to know about the scroll, or how the scroll and paintings are linked," Kushner said. "But word has obviously gotten out because the painting and the scroll are both gone in a single day. And that seems like a very strange coincidence."

"At least we know where the painting is," Claire offered. "In Gray's Fifth Avenue apartment. Deirdre is having it packed and delivered today, but I don't have the first clue about how to get it back. I doubt I have grounds to sue, and even if I do, it'll take forever to hash it out legally. I might not win, and I'm sure that Gray isn't going to hand over the canvas in the meantime."

"We have money. However much this Gray person wants," Brandt offered. "He's not impervious to profit, I'm sure."

"You mean buy it back for more than he paid?" Claire remembered what Richard had said about Brandt buying the scroll for a vast sum. Where did these people get their money? She thought monks took vows of poverty and lived with bare essentials, but here was Brandt tossing money around like a Saudi prince. Richard was skeptical. "If Gray knows about the scroll and the painting's significance, then he won't sell."

Twenty minutes later, Claire stood to leave Brandt's office, impressed that despite the trauma of the attack and the double whammy of losing both the parchment and the painting, the monk had managed to keep a cool head, figuratively and literally, since he was still holding the ice pack to his cut and bruised skull. The monk reassured his friends that they would take one step at a time, until they had sorted it all out. Claire and Richard should return to New York and try to buy back the painting. Brandt and Kushner would stay in Jerusalem to look for the stolen scroll. Her new friend gave Claire a warm embrace goodbye. "Don't worry, this is what I do. I decipher codes and solve mysteries. The answers are always there when you look closely."

The next morning, Claire found herself on flight headed for London instead of New York. It had been Richard's idea for her to call Gray's Manhattan apartment, act like the anxious artist who had created Mr. Gray's latest painting, and demand to speak to him about its proper care.

Yes, Gray's houseman confirmed, the painting was there, but no, Mr. Gray was not. Yes, he knew how valuable the painting was; a security firm was coming to install special alarms, but no, he could not tell Claire Mr. Gray's whereabouts in London.

Claire's reply was a lengthy tantrum. She ranted that she would sue Gray, have his houseman fired, and wrestle any number of security guards to retrieve her painting, if she couldn't this minute call Mr. Gray and discuss the proper maintenance of her masterpiece.

Claire hung up the phone and punched the air in triumph. "Gray is staying at Claridge's in London."

"I have no words." Richard shook his head, as he watched Claire revert from crazed prima donna back to sensitive artist, who had, he admitted to himself, an incredibly sexy voice.

Chapter Three

The Sienese Painter

"Luxury, absolute luxury," Claire whispered, as she gripped the brass banister and ascended the sweeping staircase with Richard, on their way to adjoining suites on the third floor of the Mayfair hotel Claridge's, watering hole for the world's elite. Talk about first class all the way. She had packed in more international travel and luxe living in the last two days than she had managed in the entire thirty-five years leading up to them.

In the bedroom off her private sitting room, the weary traveler collapsed onto the opulent four-poster bed hung with its blue and gold silk canopy. She was exhausted. I'll just close my eyes for a second, she thought, but the next thing she knew, it was morning, and she was lying fully clothed on top of the bed covers, where she'd passed out. Someone was banging on her door, as the gray light of a cloudy London day came through the windows, unobstructed by the curtains she had failed to close. Ouch. Her neck was stiff, and she had a headache. What time was it? 10 a.m.! Thump, thump, the loud knocking was bruising her brain. "Please stop," she croaked, as she dragged herself off the bed, overcome by nausea, no doubt from stress and fatigue. She opened her room door to find Richard, alert and smelling, like the first time they had met, of a subtle cologne and fresh air. He strode past her into the comfortable suite. "I followed Gray to the Burlington Arcade. He's shopping, but he did make reservations for an early lunch in the hotel dining room, so he'll be back soon, and we'll be ready for him."

"Aren't you tired?" Claire felt like she had been shot from a cannon and suspected she looked correspondingly disheveled.

"No, I was too wound up to sleep." Richard selected a grape of a perfect size, color, and shape, from the porcelain fruit basket set on a highly polished side table, and popped it in his mouth. "Look, freshen up and come get me when you're ready. And eat some breakfast so you're ready to take on Gray."

"But what am I going to say?"

"I have a plan. Take your time. I have some calls to make." Richard left, and the door closed behind him with an expensive click.

***

The painter watched the steady stream of people move in and out of the magnificent Gothic cathedral, the Duomo of St. Catherine in Siena. Its spires pushed toward heaven, while its elaborate façade, three massive entryways, and round central glass window reminded mere mortals of the grandeur of God's world and the relative puniness of their own. The light-colored structure was dedicated to the beloved St. Catherine, the fourteenth-century Dominican mystic, who longed to be a monk, but remained a simple woman. She was known to pray continuously and found the courage to chastise even popes and queens. Catherine survived the Black Death and could not write for most of her life, dictating her inspired letters and works to secretaries. Throughout her thirty-three years of life, she was moved by a burning love for God that brought her dreams and ecstatic visions.

The interior of the stone church was cool, perfumed with incense, and illuminated by flickering tapers and votives in crimson glass holders. Here and there, the faithful knelt and somehow managed to lose themselves in prayer, despite the buzz of sightseers, who pointed and exclaimed at the church's beauty in loud whispers.

The painter's pale blue work shirt and light cotton pants were splattered, smeared, even encrusted in places with oil paint from the vivid palette he favored: cobalt blue, cadmium yellow, madder lake red. He exited the dim, fragrant interior of the duomo and stepped into the bright sunshine, registering none of the scene before him, as visitors milled around the large piazza just off the church.

The atmosphere was festive as the modern paid homage to the ancient, but the painter didn't notice. He was not observing, not seeking inspiration. He suffered. He made a right turn and headed down one of the narrow, paved streets. They were lined with tiny shops and their typical outdoor displays of yellow and blue hand-painted pottery, distinctive to Tuscany: cheese bowls, plates, napkin holders, and kitchen jars.

All morning, the painter had worked frantically, putting the finishing touches to his canvas, the lines and gestures coming freely. As energy welled up inside, the artist discharged it through his brush. As he laid on the paint with a sure movement in one area, he eyed another place on the large canvas and knew what to put there. He made decisions quickly, brushing on color that was perfect. Unerringly, he knew the right shape, the proper hue. The blue leaned against orange here; violet rested on yellow there. As he worked, he stepped back to take in his canvas, and his eye rejoiced, while his heart clenched at what he saw on his easel. He struggled to quiet an anxious stream of thoughts and questions. How long can this effortless creativity last? When would the unseen intelligence that directed his work evaporate and take his happiness with it?

It hurt to paint this way, riding an urge, fighting off fear, wrestling with a power that acted through him. He had channeled an almost supernatural energy through the flesh and bone of his arms and fingers, directing it through wood and bristle, and onto canvas. He wasn't painting from life. The still life set on the table in his studio was old, the fruit shriveled and moldy. His favorite model, Luisa, had not come in weeks. The scene he painted was all in his head. His studio smelled like stale wine. For five nights he had fallen asleep on his couch, exhausted and afraid that come morning it would all have left him, the perfect vista he saw behind closed lids, the sureness with which he mixed color, the energy that coursed through him. At last, this morning, he had finished the painting, and now he felt wrung out. He had left his apartment for the first time in days to take a walk and break loose from the hyperactivity that brought intense pleasure but also depleted and overwhelmed him.

He arrived at Il Campo, the marketplace before the Palazzo Publico, City Hall, which was once segmented for use by different merchant classes. Still agitated, he circled the marketplace twice quickly, until slowly the squeezing in his stomach and the tightness in his chest eased. His head began to clear. He looked up and finally noticed the life all around him. It was almost the lunch hour. Tourists and the odd Sienese sat at the trattorias' outdoor tables. The painter watched a woman dig into a bowl of risotto con funghi, the rice light and milky, a regional dish and one of his favorites. I'm hungry, he realized. When did I last eat? Two or three days ago? He walked more slowly now, his restlessness abating. He sat in the shade of an awning and ordered a glass of wine and the risotto that had tempted him. Panic left him. No rush, he thought. Okay to slow it down. There was time. The canvas was finished, and, who knows? maybe there would be others.

The painter finished his food and studied the marketplace. Siena in September was glorious. The buildings surrounding Il Campo, built in the fourteenth century, were some of the most beautiful in the world. He thought about the craziness of June and August when Il Campo was the site of Il Palio, the world's oldest horse race. After hours of flag waving and pomp, teams from the city's seventeen districts rode bareback, risking death or serious injury, in a ninety-second, three-lap race around the circular Campo. The winner carried off "Palio," a banner adorned with the face of the Virgin Mary that would decorate the altar of the victor's local church. For six centuries, deadly competition had characterized the biannual race that was the high point of the Sienese year, when Il Campo was crowded with onlookers who were almost hysterical with excitement.

The painter loved the city's beauty and mysticism. Seekers of all kinds, not just Christians, came here to feel the mystery and intrigue that suffused the duomo, the medieval structures, stone walls, and narrow pathways. There was power in Siena. It throbbed on every street corner of this busy metropolis that had prospered until the Black Plague halted progress and left the splendor of the medieval city unchanged. The painter closed his eyes. He could feel the power. When he opened them, he was not alone. Standing over him was a handsome, middle-aged man, immaculately dressed and reeking of wealth.

"May I sit?" The man's voice was polished, a northern accent, almost certainly Milanese, but maybe a hint of a southern dialect still in there somewhere. The painter didn't know the stranger, but he gestured for him to sit anyway. They made an interesting pair, the painter in his work clothes, his artist's costume, and the businessman wearing his money and success so stylishly, so nonchalantly.

Once seated, the man wasted no time on pleasantries. "I went by your apartment and your neighbor told me I might find you here. A friend of yours was in Milan not too along ago, Gio Monte?" The painter nodded. He knew Gio. "His parents are friends of mine," the stranger continued. "Gio showed me this." He flashed his cell phone and the image of the very painting that, as they spoke, sat completed on an easel in the painter's studio. The photo was a little blurred, and of an unfinished canvas, but it was still easy to detect the power of the work and its unique vibrancy. "I quite like this painting," the man said casually.

"I think you must like it a lot to come all this way based on a half-assed photo of an unfinished canvas." The painter was equally cool.

"I'm traveling in the area for business, and it makes it more interesting for me to mix a little business with pleasure. But you are right, I like the painting very much. And I'm sure that since you painted it, you want money as well as praise for your work." The man smiled.

"I do." The painter smiled also.

"I'm interested in seeing the painting."

"I'm very busy." The painter shifted in his seat. Even without the tell-tale move that gave away his nervousness, the man knew that the painter lied and was not busy, was in fact a little lost, unsure of his talent. Puzzling. The work in the photo promised to be very special. He expected more confidence from the man who had hauled it from his unconscious and flooded a canvas with its power.

The businessman said none of this and just smiled again. "Of course you are busy, and that is why I would like to pay you for your time." He pulled out an exquisite leather wallet, supple and paper thin, took out a stack of large bills, folded them, leaned forward, and tucked the money under the painter's discarded plate. "I am sure this is not enough," he said disingenuously, "but it's just to show you that I really want to see this painting of yours. Maybe later this afternoon since I must leave Siena by early evening. Perhaps I could come to your studio, say around six?"

The painter cringed at the thought of bringing this pristine man to his wreck of a studio. He'd call Luisa to help tidy up the place. "Yes, that sounds fine. Do you have a business card?" The man pressed a hand lightly to the breast pocket of his suit jacket, which he had not removed despite the afternoon heat. "Excuse me, but today, I find myself without."

The painter knew the man was lying. No matter, he could get his name and address from Gio Monte. This guy was a serious player, and someone he should have in his network. The man stood to leave. He picked up a thin attaché case, which the painter noticed matched the wallet. Immaculate. The guy was groomed to within an inch of his life. "This was delightful." The man lied so easily. "I look forward to later." The painter nodded and watched as his anonymous but intriguing visitor turned and strolled away.

Buoyed by not just one but two gratifying events, a completed canvas, and a potential buyer, the painter ordered another glass of wine. Retrieving the money that the man had stashed under his plate, he whistled at the extravagant amount. The painter was quite shrewd and knew what the buyer was insinuating. In signaling his wealth, Mr. Anonymous was inviting the painter to ask a high price for his work. But by indulging the painter with such a large sum just to view the work, he was also flexing. I am wealthy. I am powerful. I throw money around because I have so much. I am not a man you can play with. A subtle intimation, but one the painter liked.

***

Claire shivered, despite the well-heated dining room. The light summer skirts and skimpy tops she had packed for sunny Israel were woefully inadequate for a chilly, drizzly day in London. As she eyed the door to the dining room, her shiver expanded to a shudder when she spotted Lucien Gray and a companion being escorted to their table. They seemed to be yammering a mile a minute, and from the odd syllable Claire could catch, it sounded like they were speaking Italian. Both men were immaculate in dark suits and crisp shirts. They looked like they'd stepped out of one of the fashion ads in the stack of magazines she had flicked through, while she and Richard waited for the pair to arrive.

Hidden at a table for two, behind a well-placed potted palm, Claire and Richard watched unseen as Gray and his companion conversed with gusto over their pricey lunch of Dover sole with asparagus and potatoes au gratin. Too nervous to eat, Claire sipped hot tea and waited until it was time to make her move. After less than hour, Gray's guest stood, excused himself, and left Gray to sip his coffee and settle the not insubstantial bill.

"Go now!" Richard cupped Claire's elbow and propelled her out of her seat. She ignored the uncomfortable pounding of her heart and shortness of breath as she snaked through the room full of diners and arrived at Gray's table. Uninvited, she dropped into the chair next to his. Gray was startled but managed a sly smile. "Ms. Lucas, lovely to see you again, but I notice you are still agitated. My houseman told me how upset and unreasonable you were on the phone."

"Not really." Claire stared straight into Gray's sneer, and under the table, she made loose fists, like she was getting ready to square off with a schoolyard bully. Instead of looking at her, Gray concentrated on elaborately folding his fine linen napkin, while he addressed her in a mocking tone. "You are so worried about your painting, which has hung with minimum security in Deirdre Vetch's shabby gallery, with grubby tourists gaping at it day in and day out, that you have flown all the way to London to lecture me about its maintenance. Right?"

"Not exactly." Claire was nervous but ready to deliver the offer she had spent the last hour rehearsing with Richard. "Mr. Gray, there is another buyer for my painting, and he's willing to give you substantially more than what you paid for it."

"No deal." Gray tossed the napkin aside. Then, as an afterthought, he asked, "What do you care about another buyer? He's giving you a cut?"

"That's right."

"What does Deirdre think?"

"We haven't discussed it yet. The buyer approached me personally through an intermediary."

"No deal." Gray signed the credit card slip with a flourish.

"Don't you even want to know what he's willing to pay?"

"How much?" Gray was standing over her now.

"Two million."

"Really?"

"Yes."

"Not bad for a rookie like you. Well, if he'll pay that now, who knows what he'll pay six months or a year from now?"

"The offer's got a fuse on it. Sell within twenty-four hours or it's off the table." Claire was impressed with her nerve.

"No thanks." Gray's sneer became a fake smile stretched over bleached teeth. "I am devoted to your work, Ms. Lucas. It's not a commodity that I'm willing to sell to the highest bidder. So, you see, there's no need for you to chase me around, badgering me about how to look after it. I hope I've proved that to you. Or was that just a ploy to find out where I was so you could hustle me and resell it for more money?" Claire stared at him as he spat his parting insult. "You and Deirdre are like two money-grubbing peas in a pod."

Only when her nemesis had pivoted and headed toward the door did Claire allow herself a look at Richard, who was watching from their table. She squished her mouth to one side and rolled her eyes, with her palms up, to let him know no deal. Their plan hadn't worked. He winked and she felt better.

Holed up in Richard's room, sipping her fifth cup of Earl Grey, Claire was starting to feel tea logged. "I'm sorry," she said for the umpteenth time.

"Not your fault. Don't worry." Richard was checking his phone. "We knew it was a long shot."

Claire looked down and admired the lavender cashmere sweater she wore. Realizing his companion had packed no warm clothes, Richard had bought it for her on his trip to the Burlington Arcade where he'd followed Gray.

"Claire?"

"Yes."

"When you describe your visions, you say they appear in an egg-shaped spot near the corner of your left eye, right?" Claire nodded and squinted to look down at the spot which was black. No picture show today. She'd been too distracted to even think about it, which just showed that she could ignore her strange eye problem if she lived at breakneck speed.

"Good. Go get your things, there's someone I want you to meet."

"Who?"

"Hurry, we're short on time. I'll tell you on the ride down."

"Ride?"

"Yes, I rented a car. We're going for a jaunt in the English countryside."

***

Luisa climbed the three flights of stairs to the painter's apartment. She was nineteen, young and strong, but today she didn't feel well. She rested on the landing, put down the straw bag filled with groceries and placed the back of her hand to her forehead, hot. To her cheeks, hot too. She licked her lips. Luisa was beautiful in a ripe way, a strong way, domed forehead, high cheekbones, and a nose that was slightly hooked and a little large, but a perfect accompaniment to her full mouth, dark brown eyes, and cascade of thick, black hair. How many times had the painter sketched her? Painted her? She didn't like his drawings. He made her look distorted and unattractive. He called it abstract. She called it ugly. Today, he didn't even want her to pose, but to shop for food and clean. He had said she was an inspiration, a muse, and now he wanted her to wash his floors. He'd called earlier and told her to come to his place right away. Lucky for him she had the day off work. She headed up the last flight and knocked on the door. "Ciao, ciao," she called. No answer.

Marone! What a pigsty! Paints everywhere, tubes, tablets, powder, soiled brushes all over the floor. Nope, she was not going to organize this mess. She'd just heap what she could on the large table he used for supplies. What about the rest of it? Dishes piled up, dirty clothes strewn around, old food everywhere. Disgusting! She carried the groceries to the kitchen and unpacked them: cheese, bread, fruit, tomatoes, spaghetti, olives, mozzarella — the usual stuff he lived on.

For two hours she cleaned, usually not a problem for her. Her mother had grown up on a farm, and the women in her family knew how to work, but today the exertion tired her. She was hot and starting to ache. Maybe the flu. Please no, she couldn't afford more time off from her job as a receptionist at a dentist's office. She sat on the beat-up couch. She'd washed and polished the brown leather, but it was impossible to get the paint stains out. She looked around the studio, a typical artist's digs. Light streamed through skylights in the sloping roof, canvases leaned against the walls, and paint, paint was splattered everywhere, dripped and smeared and baked onto floors and the few odds and ends of beat-up furniture. But she'd really picked the place up. He'd better pay her well and she wanted the money today.

Luisa eyed the easel. Of course she would never tell the painter that she didn't like his work, the crazy angles, the sharp edges, the way he distorted objects till they were unrecognizable. He'd shrouded the canvas he was working on with a sheet. What's he up to now? On impulse, she stood and pulled away the sheet, unprepared for what she found underneath. This is not something he could create. She backed away from the canvas, edged toward the couch, and plopped down. She gazed at a luxurious garden that was drenched in light, made of light. Each flower, each blade of grass was alive and growing. Luisa was transfixed. It's so beautiful, she thought. How is it possible that he painted this? The way light seemed to come from all directions, bathing the garden and splitting its colors into so many exquisite hues.

She stared for a long time and realized that looking at the gorgeous work relaxed her. She swallowed. Her throat didn't feel so scratchy now, and she wasn't so hot, but she was tired. She wanted to gaze forever at the mesmerizing garden, but she just had to rest her eyes. She closed them and fell sleep.

An hour later, the painter came home. Surprised to find his model and housekeeper asleep on the couch, he shook her awake gently. "Time to go, bella." Luisa struggled to wake up, squinting up at him and trying to remember where she was. He smiled. "The cleaning wore you out, eh?"

He's in an unusually good mood, she thought. "You are a pig!" she said, fully awake now. She pulled herself up and adjusted her rumpled tee shirt and pants. "I want my money. Now!" She knew he would try to wheedle and whine and put off her pay day for as long as he could. She held out hands that were older than the rest of her and looked rough, chapped, and red from years of doing all kinds of menial tasks and daily chores, scrubbing and cleaning, fetching and carrying. The painter smirked and pulled out his money. Luisa had never seen him with such a stash. He didn't count it off, just grabbed a few bills, folded them in half, and stuck the generous wages in the pocket of her tee shirt, mimicking the largesse of the nonchalant businessman, who had tucked a thick wad under the painter's lunch plate.

"Grazie." She felt revived. The sleep had definitely done her good. "I was fighting a cold I think, but the nap made me feel better."

"Great!" The painter sat on the arm of the couch and gave her a grin and a wave as she headed for the door. He was not particularly handsome, the girl thought. He was what, thirty-five? Far too old for her, but tonight she found him strangely attractive. He looked boyish, and charming, as he perched on the couch with an excited look that seemed shaped by good news. "I like your painting." She glanced over at the canvas. "I think it's really great."

"Thank you." He smiled again and seemed genuinely delighted with her praise.

"I mean I really like it. I think it's the best thing you've ever done."

"Me too." He sent her off with one last wave as she closed the door behind her.

He walked to the easel and loosely draped the sheet over the canvas, careful not to touch where it was still a little tacky in places. It would be weeks before the oils were completely dry. And then the painter set to waiting. It was almost 6 p.m., and his guest was due any minute. He picked up charcoal and paper, scrawled a few preliminary lines, and then tossed down the implements, too edgy to work. Mr. Anonymous was wealthy, and he definitely wanted the painting, but the painter suddenly felt reluctant to let it go and was gripped with the certainty that he wouldn't part with it. He had other paintings, good ones. Not as accomplished as this latest work, but good enough.

He approached the easel to remove the sheet and then changed his mind. Looking at the canvas would only create more turmoil. Even though he had painted it, he found the work astonishing. He'd spent hours staring at it, trying to understand its origins, marveling at how it had come through him, painted itself really, although he would never say that to anyone. Or maybe he should. Isn't that the way it is with works of great genius? Inspired works? Aren't they all really a gift from the universe? Some unknown source? A Mozart sonata, a Beethoven symphony, a Picasso abstract, Michelangelo's David, all acts of unfathomable inspiration.

He was getting ahead of himself and feeling jumpy. Mr. Anonymous would pay big money, and the painter needed money. He had cooked up a batch of half-baked but ambitious plans, and money was the oil that would grease the engine of the success he craved. But still, the painting was like a great love, a beautiful woman that you just can't leave behind when life calls you to move on. Maybe he could keep the painting and get the money. He'd talk the buyer into a commission, a new painting like this one only better. Bubbling with anxiety, he dropped onto the couch and took a deep breath, throwing up his hands, unsure of what to do next. He heard the footfall of his visitor climbing the stairs to his studio, and he wanted to shout at the man to take his money and go away. Hearing a firm knock, he got up to answer the door and found the buyer unruffled, not in the least bit out of breath from the climb. Clearly, he kept himself in good shape. The painter opened the door wide by way of invitation, despite the competing urge to slam it shut on his smug guest and the temptation of big money he was about to dangle. The man stepped inside and beheld the scruffy interior. Of course, he thought, it was such a cliché, the shabby setting of the struggling artist, who cares nothing for his surroundings, and is so absorbed in an interior world that he is oblivious to his exterior setting. The well-groomed connoisseur despised this idea. He loved beauty, needed it. He had grown up in Naples, poor, the son of a fisherman, but not ignorant. Even as a child, he had understood beauty, and the power of beautiful objects that, as an adult, he would crave, pursue, and ultimately attain. He could remember in detail every important acquisition he'd ever made, every first: his first good suit, first fine linens, first important painting, exclusive home. The first bottle of wine he had bought at auction, and the perfect crystal he had drunk it from. He savored it all, took none of it for granted. He enjoyed wealth and status, of course, but status was not the point. The point was that beautiful possessions were as essential to him as air. They helped define him, express his purpose in the world, justify his existence, and erase the ugliness that had marked his early life.

"Nice place," the buyer lied again, as he stood in the middle of the large paint-stained floor and took in the dump he would have to endure, until he acquired the latest treasure he'd set his greedy sights on. "Is this the painting?" He nodded toward the easel and its shrouded canvas.

"There are some other things that I want to show you." The painter signaled his jumpiness, darting forward to intercept his visitor, who was making a beeline for the easel.

"Why not, since I'm here?" Mr. Anonymous agreed. The painter nodded toward canvases lined up on the floor, indicating with a sweep of his arm that this was where he wanted the buyer to look. The visitor paced up and down, surveying the higgledy-piggledy parade of canvases that leant against the dirty wall. He said nothing, and only nodded, careful to hide his impatience and contempt. This is worse than mediocre, he thought, as he cast a resentful glance at each canvas. What dreck. For the first time, he began to doubt what was beneath the sheet on the easel across the floor. He worried that this no-talent bore could produce anything worth a second glance from him. If Gio Monte had conned him, he would hear about it. But all the while, he stayed quiet, just waiting for a respectable amount of time to go by, so he could turn away from the detritus propped against the wall, and finally view what he had come for. Discover if it was what he hoped it would be.

The painter could tell the buyer detested his work, even though he made no comment and just looked at the paintings, cool and collected, too much so. His bruised ego was inflamed. Well, screw you. What do you create? You only know how to consume. You know jack shit about producing, about the talent and struggle it takes.

"These are interesting," the buyer said after a minute, and it occurred to him that to date, his entire social relationship with the jittery moron across from him had been built on lies. "If I could see the painting in the photograph, we can talk later about my buying some of your other work." What the hell? he told himself. He could chisel a little off what he planned to offer for the main purchase and use it on a couple of the small garbage works, just to placate the baby.

The painter was tense. He approached the easel and, almost in slow motion, he pulled away the sheet. The feeling was indescribable. Only in the presence of the greatest works of art is there a moment when the beholder becomes aware that all thoughts have halted. At this moment, a shudder runs up the spine, perhaps as the energy within seeks to connect with the energy without, to unite the body with the universe at large, in the same way that electricity runs to ground. The buyer felt the energy course up his spine once and then once again. The painter didn't look at his canvas, only at his visitor, riveted by his reaction. That shut you up, didn't it? he thought, still angry at the silent contempt he had seen in the elitist jerk. The same jerk who now stood speechless before his masterpiece.

"This is beautiful." The buyer had no interest in dissembling or playing games. He saw the worried look on the painter's face, and knew he had to act quickly if he were to carry off the painting that he absolutely had to have. The thought that he might lose his chance to own it sickened him. Regaining his composure, he took a checkbook from his inside breast pocket. The checks were untraceable and carried no identifying information, for moments like this when discretion and anonymity were needed. He thought about a sum and then doubled it. He folded the check and handed it to the painter. "This money is yours on two conditions. I take the painting right now, and you promise never to contact me."

The painter unfolded and looked at the check, then looked again to make sure the stupefying amount written there was real. He nodded and didn't dare look at the painting, couldn't subject his heart to seeing and then releasing it. Instead, he slumped on the couch. His earlier excitement and anticipation were replaced by defeat and inexplicable dread, despite the small fortune written on the check that he now let flutter to the floor.

The excited buyer picked up the paint spattered sheet and fashioned it into a makeshift wrapper for the large canvas. It was still a little sticky in places and felt strangely warm. Of course, it had been sitting in the sunlight that streamed through the studio's skylight. A driver was waiting downstairs. Together they'd devise a way to get the newly hatched painting, easily four by six feet, back to his hotel. He maneuvered his purchase as far as the door.

"I quite like this." Feeling uncharacteristically sympathetic to the plight of the dejected soul sitting on the beat-up couch, the buyer pointed his foot toward a nude, the smallest canvas, nearest the door.

"Take it." The painter didn't look up.

"Ciao." Mr. Anonymous tucked the small painting under his arm and, leaving the studio door wide open, he wrangled the large canvas down three flights of stairs. When he reached the sidewalk, he gently leant it against the luxury SUV idling there. Walking to a garbage can in an adjacent alley, he lifted the lid and crammed the painting of the poorly executed nude inside, before replacing the lid. He took a deep breath. He'd lied about having to leave tonight. He was in town until the morning. He planned to eat a light supper in his room, order a fine bottle of wine, play his favorite music, and contemplate the extraordinarily beautiful object he now possessed.

Chapter Four

Vesica Piscis

As they parked the rental car in the late-afternoon light and got out, Claire took a long look at Richard's friend, Josie McLean, the middle-aged American professor they'd stopped off to pick up. Cryptic as usual, Richard had not really explained much on their rushed journey down to Somerset, only that Josie was a good friend from academia, a gifted historian and anthropologist. She was currently on sabbatical in England to study early goddess worship, and had agreed to give them a tour of a historic English landmark that Claire might find interesting.

"But why do you want me to meet her? Does she know about the Angel Scroll?"

"No she doesn't, and it's best if you don't mention it," Richard cautioned. "I just think Josie might have some useful insights into your experiences."

"How? Why?" Claire pressed him.

"Wait until you meet her. You'll see. Now let me concentrate on this whacky, English, opposite-side-of-the-road driving madness, so I can get us there in one piece."

Claire knew that Richard had curtailed any further chat, leaving her to nap and give in to the jet lag she couldn't seem to shake.

Josie was now pointing to the hill before them. The pleasant-looking professor was in her early fifties, fit and trim in slacks, a sweater, windbreaker, and sensible walking shoes. "This," she announced, "is Glastonbury Tor, and the stone tower you can see is all that remains of St. Michael's Church built in 1360. Beneath us is a labyrinth of limestone caves. Many of the early Celts who lived here were Druids, who bleached their hair with lime and combed it back. With their bleached hair, pale skins, crude leggings, and checked blankets fastened at the shoulder with primitive clasps or broaches, these early Celts were a daunting spectacle to their Roman adversaries."

Claire turned all around to take in the view of the flat farmland known as the Somerset Levels or "the summer country." Over the last two thousand years, first the Romans, and then British monks, had built an intricate system of sea walls and canals to connect what was an inland sea and rich marshland prone to frequent tidal floods. Of the four hills that rose from the landscape, Glastonbury Tor was the highest, sticking up some five hundred feet from the lowlands. Josie pointed out a labyrinth of terraces built on the hillside once used in ancient goddess worship. If they looked carefully, they could pick out the goddess's form in the landscape. The tor was her head, the Chalice Hill was her belly, and the ruined abbey marked her womb. A spur of land stretched out to form her left leg. Another strip of land represented a right leg bent at the knee and tucked into her body.

The professor's passion for the ancient and hallowed landscape was on show as she spoke. "No one is sure when the Glastonbury area was first occupied, but historians guess it was about 1360 BCE — before the Christian era."

Claire whistled. "Old!"

Josie nodded. "Yes, that's almost fourteen hundred years before Christ. We do know that the first occupants were Celtic Druids. Glastonbury is famously the location of one of three Druidic perpetual choirs. These eternal choirs made music twenty-four hours a day, every day of the year, literally 'enchanting' the land."

Climbing further up the base of the tor, they came upon the ruins of Glastonbury Abbey, and Josie explained its long, storied history. "Tradition says that in 37 AD, Joseph of Arimathea, an Essene who gave Christ his tomb and protected Him during

His ministry, came here after Christ's crucifixion. He came as a refugee sent by the disciple Philip to evangelize England."

Claire shot Richard a look, trying to remember what he had said in Jerusalem about Christ being an Essene, but he was listening closely to Josie's lecture. "This place is where Joseph of Arimathea and twelve acolytes built a wattled church," Josie continued. "At that time, the Celts in the region worshipped a deity named Easus, who had died and was supposed to come back to life. So when the Druids heard about Jesus from Joseph of Arimathea, they saw in him the return of their Easus, and they gave this spot, known as Ynys Witrin, as the site of the first above-ground Christian church. After its construction, Jesus was said to have appeared to Joseph and his followers and blessed Britain's first church, dedicating it to his mother, Mary."

Josie made a sweeping gesture across the landscape. "So, this is the birthplace of Celtic Christianity. The abbey that was eventually built here became a powerful site of pilgrimage for Christians, until it was ransacked during the Tudor period. King Arthur and Gwynevere are buried here."

"King Arthur and Gwynevere aren't just characters in books and movies? They really existed?" Claire asked.

"Oh yes, they existed." Josie smiled. "Arthur was a king in this region, but certainly not as glamorous as Hollywood portrays him."

"Let's go to the Chalice Well, Josie," Richard suggested, and Claire sensed from his tone that something significant awaited them there.

Josie led them toward the revered Chalice Well, also known as the Blood Spring, which for two thousand years had pumped 25,000 gallons of water daily into underground, man-made chambers. "They call it the Blood Spring because the water is stained crimson," Josie explained. "Non-believers say it's due to a high iron content. The faithful claim the color is a sign that the blood of Christ once flowed here. Legend says that Joseph of Arimathea and his eleven followers brought the chalice used at the Last Supper, in which drops of blood from the wounded Christ had been collected. Before he died, Joseph supposedly buried the chalice, which became known as the Holy Grail, here in Glastonbury's landscape. The legend of the Grail merged with the Celtic myth that a life-renewing cauldron was hidden in the region. This fueled the great Grail Quest by the Knights of the Round Table. They searched for the Holy Grail, believing it to be a source of eternal life. And over the centuries, generations of pilgrims have journeyed here to drink from the red-tinted waters."

"How incredibly magical and mysterious," Claire said, fascinated by Josie's account. She smiled appreciatively at the brainy professor, who was now pointing very deliberately at the ornate cover of the Chalice Well. Examining the cover closely, Claire saw it was adorned with a familiar egg-shaped symbol, exactly the shape of the mysterious spot at the corner of her own left eye. "What is that?" Claire pointed, as Josie outlined the shape with the tip of a long slim finger. "This ancient symbol is known as the vesica piscis, or fish vessel. Notice it's made from two circles of the same radius that are intertwined. Where the circles interconnect, you can see the famous almond shape known as the vesica piscis, or by its Latin name for almond, mandorla."

Claire studied the symbol, and like in Dormition Abbey, she experienced what felt like a surge of electricity run the length of her spine, radiating through her crown, as light flashed across her left eye. Once again, Richard took her arm to steady her. Claire turned to Josie, who was eying her thoughtfully. "Do you recognize this symbol?" the professor asked and Claire nodded. "Why don't you tell me about it."

"The vesica piscis is the basis of much of sacred geometry," Josie explained. "It symbolizes many sacred and nonsacred things. Its elliptical shape echoes the shape of the human eye, the mirror of the soul. The shape also symbolizes the womb. Christ and Christianity were birthed from Mary's womb, the gateway through which the immaterial Christ entered the material world. It's one of the reasons why Renaissance painters often placed Christ and Mary within almond-shaped flames. The almond-shaped Jesus fish was also the secret symbol that early Christians used to recognize each other. And the Greek word for fish is ichthys, which is an acronym for 'Jesus Christ who rose from the dead.' The arched windows of Gothic churches echo this shape, which was a common design used throughout Christian architecture. Today's churchgoers might be shocked to know that two spires on each side of many churches were often intended to represent the primordial goddess with her legs in the air, revealing her vulva, the church itself, where the mysteries took place."

Josie McLean had spent much of her academic life as a professor, lecturing extensively on goddess worship, and how the presence and power of the vesica piscis were to be found in most cultures. Today, she offered her tutorial exclusively to the attractive American artist, who had come for this hastily arranged tour with her good friend and respected colleague, Richard Markson. Claire was only the second woman Richard had ever brought to visit, in all the years Josie had known him.

"To worshippers of the great primordial goddess," she continued, "the vesica piscis represents the womb of nature, the source of life. As Celtic Druids adopted Christianity, they combined their deep reverence of the goddess by carving her on the cornerstone of their Celtic churches, where she can be seen holding open her oversized vulva that stretches from her chin to her groin."

"Wow, that's some visual!" Claire's quip interrupted the seriousness of the lecture and made them all laugh.

"Yes, it's a good one, isn't it?" Josie chuckled, and then she described how the shamans and alchemical healers of Siberia, ancient Egypt, Israel, the First Nations of North America, and the Polynesian Islands all held the vesica piscis as a powerful symbol of fertility, creation, and healing. It was a portal where the upper and lower worlds intersect, the great womb of space from which all things emerge.

"Once you become aware of the vesica piscis," Josie told Claire, "you'll see it everywhere. Would you like a taste?" She gestured to the Lion's Head Spring, where visitors were permitted to drink.

"Why not?" Claire followed her guide over to the spring to sample the mythical waters.

"I'm going down. I'll meet you both at the bottom," Richard announced to Claire's surprise, leaving the two women alone. Boy, he's really engineered this whole visit, she thought as she turned to Josie. "I'm sure Richard told you about the egg-shaped spot in my vision where I see things. Have you any idea what it is? What it means?"

"I don't know, Claire. It could be a medical anomaly, a fascinating coincidence, a trick of the mind, or even an optical illusion."

Claire frowned. "Suppose it's none of those things?"

Josie tented her fingers and rubbed them together, sliding one palm across the other, the way she always did when working out a tricky next move, as though the friction would produce the answer she was looking for. "Claire, I can tell you what I really think, but I don't want to confuse you any more than you already are."

"Not sure I could be any more confused."

Josie's entire career had been dedicated to keeping alive the lessons that the rich history of places like Glastonbury taught. She honored what it revealed about human development, about ancient ways of knowing, spiritual technologies, and psychic phenomena. She revered the long-forgotten practices that had helped ancient man decipher the most confounding aspects of life and miracles of existence. And she knew that her discoveries were not always embraced by a world that had moved on from a time when enchantment was once an authentic spiritual practice, and not just some product from Disney.

Claire interrupted the professor's musing. "Josie, Richard obviously brought me here because he wants me to hear what you have to say. Because he thinks you can help me make sense of why I am either hallucinating, or witnessing bizarre occurrences through my very own mandorla or vesica piscis, or whatever the Druids, or shamans, or medicine men call it. So come on, let me have it."

Josie studied Claire for a moment and decided on candor. "History is filled with mystics and visionaries from all cultures and religions," she said. "From our own Christian tradition come St. Catherine of Siena; St. Theresa of Avila; St. Theresa, the Carmelite nun of the Little Flowers; Bernadette of Lourdes, and Joan of Arc. All female, all possessed with spiritual foresight to see and understand symbolically."

"All hysterical, perhaps," Claire suggested.

"Maybe not. Hysteria is often the sign of the medial or psychic woman, not grounded in the rational, but totally intuitive, able to sense the unseeable and work from an inner knowing."

Claire looked out across the tor, suddenly homesick for her apartment in New York, for Jake, and her old life that was familiar and normal.

"Richard told me about your painting," Josie said. "Didn't you dream of a holy man, a Christ, and work day and night to capture the dream, painting in a style that was totally different from your own?"

Claire kept her gaze on the landscape that held so many secrets and myths. "That was just a dream."

"Isn't day-to-day life just a vision of sorts, a persistent or habitual waking dream?" Josie asked.

Claire felt confused. Since Jake died, she didn't think that she even believed in God anymore. She had been raised a Catholic, but that was just a convention that no longer meant anything to her. "I'm not a religious person. Not spiritual even," she reasoned out loud. "I haven't looked for mystical experiences."

"Our indoctrination by the mainstream teaches us to adopt a concrete set of beliefs that are handed to us, and to ignore inner knowing," Josie said. "But at night, in dreams, and in meditations, we explore the deepest aspects of our own unfathomable minds. Sometimes we even encounter powerful images there, like the Great Goddess, the Virgin Mary, even our enlightened self or Christ consciousness. Aren't these just powerful archetypes that live in our psyche and become animated when we detect their symbols in the world around us? We experience them as being out there in the world, when really they live in here." Josie pointed first to her heart and then to her head. "Claire, don't frustrate yourself looking for tidy, reasonable explanations. Maybe because of your bereavement combined with your artist's temperament, the gates of perception have opened to you, and you've been awakened to new states. You're discovering aspects of your psyche that you never knew were there. Don't fear it. Don't try to label it. Be patient and perhaps you'll learn to understand this spiritual emergency you're going through."

"I had visions of Hilde and I didn't know her," Claire muttered.

Josie nodded. "So I hear."

Claire looked right at the older woman. "How could I see or visualize someone I didn't know?"

"The eyes, especially the third eye, see all. While the conscious memory retains only a fraction, the unconscious mind, like a computer, stores every experience and memory.

"But I never met Hilde," Claire argued.

"It's not uncommon for the properly initiated to be familiar with people and events that exist outside of their conscious awareness," Josie claimed. "To most early cultures, foresight, vision, and premonition were so common as to be mundane."

Claire frowned. "And my eye?"

"It makes perfect sense to me," Josie said, "that you would experience visions through a mandorla, an almond-shaped opening or space that symbolizes the intersection of upper and lower worlds, conscious and unconscious. The question really is why are you having these visions and dreams now?" Josie let her words sink in. "Keep in touch, dear. I want to know how you are doing. And I want you to begin seeing all this as normal."

"Normal!?" Claire gave a sarcastic laugh.

"Yes, normal," Josie insisted, and then she became serious. "I'm so glad Richard came and brought you here. I've been worried about him since Hilde died."

Claire saw a chance to learn more about Richard's past. "Was Hilde Richard's only sister?"

"Sister?" Josie halted. "Hilde was Richard's wife." Seeing the confusion on Claire's face, the professor realized she'd let slip a fact that Richard, for some reason, didn't want his new companion to know.

A streak of questions tore through Claire's mind, but she placed a reassuring hand on the older woman's shoulder. "I suspected Hilde was Richard's wife," she lied. "I'm sure he didn't know what to expect when he first came to see me, under such strange circumstances. And right now, he's still raw. He'll explain in his own good time, so please don't mention that you said anything to me."

"I won't," Josie said, swiping at the cool air on Glastonbury Tor. "I'm such an idiot,"

Claire smiled. "It's not your fault. You've taken me and my crazy story in stride."

Josie wagged her finger. "You're not crazy. You just need to understand things from the proper perspective. Now, shall we go for some tea?"

"Please, no more tea!" Claire pleaded, as the two women linked arms and headed down the hill.

At the bottom, Richard was waiting for them, leant against the compact rental car and talking on his cell. Claire felt her guard go up. Here was this compelling new figure in her life, so handsome, so intelligent, and thoughtful. There was no denying his appeal, but he had lied to her.

It was dark when they dropped Josie off at the white stone cottage with its postage stamp lawn that she rented. Lit by a streetlamp, the professor waved them off from behind her quaint garden gate. On the ride back to London, through the dark English countryside and narrow winding lanes, Claire feigned sleep. She didn't trust herself to speak to Richard, alternating as she was between hopeful attraction and growing mistrust. Maybe what she'd told Josie was true. Maybe Richard had lied about Hilde to protect himself. But he knows better now, she thought. He knows me better and could come clean if he wanted. We're both widowed. I don't talk about Jake unless pushed, but I've tried very hard to be open and helpful, even when it hurt. I've thrown myself into this whole bewildering situation, while he plays it close to the vest. He's generous in many ways, but so stingy about sharing himself and what he knows. Maybe I should be just as reserved.

Back at the hotel, Claire declined Richard's invitation to share a nightcap and said a cool goodnight. She slept fitfully, beset with strange dreams. She was Joan of Arc, riding a white horse and carrying a pennant decorated with the image of the Virgin Mary. When she woke up, she felt tired and depressed, despite her luxurious surroundings.

Chapter Five

The Dealer

Karl Brandt stood in the lobby of the small hotel in a neighborhood built on one of the seven jabals or hills that make up the Jordanian capital of Amman. Out of his monk's habit and in street clothes, he was ready to set out for a meeting with an antiquities dealer he knew as Ansari Al Halou. It had been six months since he had stood in the same hotel lobby with Kushner, ready to meet with Halou for the first time to verify the dealer's claim that he possessed an authentic ancient parchment, found on the Jordanian side of the Dead Sea, and known as the Angel Scroll.

Several weeks before that first meeting with Halou, Kushner had briefed Brandt about the dealer and the new scroll's existence. "His name is Ansari Al Halou, an antiquities dealer in Amman with connections throughout the region. He's a touch ruthless but legitimate. Word is that some weeks ago a man brought Halou the parchment. Supposedly, that guy bought it from a man, who bought it from a man, who bought it from some Bedouins around Wadi al-Mojab."

"What's the asking price?" Brandt asked.

"He wants eight million US dollars," Kushner replied. Brandt gave a mirthless laugh. "I wonder what the guy paid the Bedouins for it."

"Probably a few bags of camel dung," Kushner deadpanned, and Brandt let out a real laugh.

Brandt's initial meeting with Halou had, like the one set for today, taken place in a discreet location, a house belonging to friends of the dealer. Kushner and Brandt had set out from the hotel lobby, anxious to get matters under way. The parchment they were about to investigate could be the culmination of years of searching by Brandt, for an undiscovered, authentic, and first-hand account of the early Christian community in Jerusalem.

Dressed in casual European clothes, the two friends made their way through the bustling markets or souqs. They passed an endless succession of cafés and kebab stands, until Kushner led them into a less congested, residential neighborhood, and through an archway into a well-tended garden. As they approached the low, two-story white house, the front door opened, and a man in traditional Arab dress, a white long-sleeved cotton thobe, greeted them by touching his forehead.

Halou was waiting for them in a sitting room that was elegant and understated. Worn but costly rugs covered tiled floors inlaid with brightly colored mosaics. Low sedans upholstered in pale fabric were dressed with brightly colored silk pillows.

"Mr. Halou, I would like you to meet my associate, Matheus Koch." Kushner used the alias they had concocted to shield Brandt's identity, and after a few minutes of small talk, the three men got down to business. Halou spoke first. "I hear that the Benedictines are very interested in this spectacular parchment."

He's figured out who I am Brandt thought, but he said nothing.

"And I expect to be hearing soon from Frederick Paltz in Jerusalem. He'd love to get his hands on this material," Halou continued.

"You're sitting down with interested buyers, so why talk about others?" Kushner sounded sharp.

"It's important that these buyers know there are plenty of others who are interested in the merchandise," Halou snapped.

"The price you're asking, I very much doubt it," Kushner scoffed. Brandt interrupted the tense exchange. "Mr. Halou. I don't doubt that you have other prospective buyers, and we appreciate you entertaining our interest, but to decide if what you're selling is something we really want, I must authenticate it first. I need to see a sample of the parchment as well as photographs of actual text."

Halou scowled. "I will show no one the parchment until they come with the money to buy. If I gave every interested party a little piece of parchment as proof, there'd soon be nothing left of it, right?" He pursed his lips and sniffed. "I do have photographs, however. You'll take them and study them. If they show what you like, then I'll sell you a fragment of parchment for two hundred and fifty thousand dollars, which you can subtract from the cost of the scroll if you buy it." Halou reached into his briefcase and pulled out a large envelope containing several eight by ten photographs that he passed to Brandt. "Mr. Halou, Kushner has told me how you came across the parchment. You certainly have a great deal of expertise. What more can you tell me? What's your opinion on its authenticity?"

The parchment, Halou explained, had been preserved in a large clay jar but was in pieces when it was found. It was about six feet in length, maybe a thousand lines. "In my opinion, it is genuine," he declared.

When Kushner and Brandt left the meeting, they had agreed to take and study photographs of the scroll's text. If satisfied, they would return the next day to buy a 100-millimeter square fragment of parchment for analysis, under Halou's terms. In return, Halou would take the scroll off the black market and deny its existence to anyone who inquired about it. This would give Brandt the time he needed to rustle up Vatican money to buy the parchment. Then would come the problem of spiriting the scroll across the Jordanian border into Jerusalem, without damaging the delicate manuscript more than it already was, and without the authorities detecting the illicit purchase of a priceless artifact. They would worry about that later.

Following that first meeting with Ansari Al Halou, Brandt and Kushner had locked themselves in their small, shared hotel room. They rolled up their shirtsleeves and sat at a table under an overhead fan, anxious to examine the photographs Halou had given them.

Looking back on the day, Brandt remembered their excitement, and how, through the open window, street noise had come in; the incessant honking of horns as cars tried to push through the crowded streets and souqs. Brandt had opened the envelope and spread four black and white photographs on the table before them. They revealed fragments of an ancient parchment, so blackened in places that it was difficult to make out many of its characters. Looks similar in appearance to the scrolls found in the caves at Qumran outside Jerusalem, in 1947, Brandt decided. But he dearly hoped that this latest scroll might contain evidence that it was written during the actual period of Christ's ministry.

Kushner spoke Hebrew fluently, but Brandt was far more adept at translation. He scanned the photographs, looking for clues, or a place to begin deciphering the scroll's message. At first glance, the language appeared to be mixed, post biblical Hebrew, a little Greek, and Aramaic. For three long hours, the two men worked with intense concentration, occasionally pointing to a word, asking a question, taking notes, making observations.

Eventually Brandt stood up and stretched, almost ready to take a break, when his eyes fell on a series of words that rendered him speechless. He picked up the photograph and brought it close to his face, scrutinizing it with bloodshot eyes. Kushner stopped working and stared up at him. The hand holding the photograph fell to the monk's side, as he gazed out of the window and across the street to the market that brimmed with life. Then he spoke the words slowly and very carefully, quoting from the line of text he had translated. "In a vision shown to the author Yeshua the priest." The name was unmistakable to both men. "Yeshua" was Hebrew for Jesus. Brandt was filled with urgency. His mind raced to form a plan that would convince the Vatican, with no notice, to shell out eight million dollars for a disintegrating black-market parchment. He had to buy the scroll and unlock its profound messages, before it was snatched up by bad faith operators, or lost to posterity altogether.

On this, his second visit to Halou, alone this time, Brandt again approached the house that was the designated meeting place. The same houseman showed him to the familiar sitting room where Halou greeted him. "Koch, how are you?" He emphasized the name they both knew was an alias. Brandt got straight to the point. "I paid you an enormous amount of money for the parchment."

"And I turned over a priceless antiquity."

"The deal," Brandt stressed between gritted teeth, "was that I bought not only the scroll but also your silence about its sale."

"I didn't tell anyone that I sold it to you," Halou shot back.

Brandt heard a note of genuine defensiveness in the dealer's voice. "The scroll has been stolen," he said.

Halou smirked. "I'm so sorry. I will let you know if it turns up here."

"And miss the opportunity to sell it again? I doubt that."

"So little faith for a man of faith," Halou scoffed.

"I place my faith where it belongs," Brandt countered. "I think you know who stole it."

"I assure you," Halou said, "I do not know who stole the scroll, and as yet, I have not heard that it is back on the market."

"I want to know the names of anyone who inquired after the parchment." Brandt sounded firm. "Even if you didn't tell anyone, an interested party knows you sold it to me."

Halou was rattled. "I can't give you a list. You're not the only one who demands discretion."

Brandt dropped into a silk upholstered chair. "Trading undeclared antiquities that are national treasures is illegal."

"So is buying them," Halou hissed.

"I am, as you well know, a Benedictine monk and would never break the law." Brandt flashed his most pious expression. "Just give me a list and I'll go away. With or without you, I will find out who stole the scroll, and if that person is an associate of yours, and you've withheld their name from me, I will report you to the authorities, so I do expect full disclosure from you."

After a moment, an aggrieved Halou took a Mont Blanc fountain pen from his top pocket, thought for a moment, and quickly scribbled nine names on a paper he handed to Brandt. "Don't tell anyone that I gave you this." Brandt took the list, stood up, and nodded. "Agreed."

Back on the street, Brandt studied the names, but didn't recognize any of them, a few Israelis, three Arabs, a couple of French, an Italian, and a German. Quite an exclusive and international club of would-be buyers, all after the same rare find that Brandt had managed to win and somehow lose. The monk's gut told him that Halou was not directly involved in the robbery, but it was likely that someone he knew might be. He walked at a clip back to the hotel, relieved that he had a place to start, and sure that someone on the list would bring him closer to the scroll.

***

Claire was back at Lenox Hill Hospital, on Manhattan's Upper East Side, where she'd had an MRI only days before. Today, she had an early morning rendezvous with Dr. Bentley. He greeted her, and cupped her small hand, holding it prisoner in his two that were mottled with age spots. His simple touch made Claire's knotted insides unravel, like a ball of string tossed down a staircase. She tried to tug her hand free from the small nest that the kind doctor had trapped it in, but he held on tight. "We need more tests, okay, dear? And then I am going to admit you for observation."

"Yes to tests, no to being admitted."

"Claire, if we confirm what we suspect, it means that you're walking around with an aneurysm, a bulging blood vessel in your brain that might rupture. The result could be a serious stroke or death."

"Will you operate?" Claire focused on practicalities to stop her growing panic from spinning out of control.

"Maybe, depending on its size."

"So, I'll come in when you're ready to operate, not before."

"We want to keep you quiet and monitor you," Bentley said.

"Is this aneurysm what's creating the problems with my vision?"

"Possibly," Bentley replied. "These things can cause visual disturbances."

"OK, let's get after it." Claire took off her jacket. "Let's get the tests over with so I can get out of here."

In between having blood collected and an EEG, her cell rang. "Claire, where are you?" It was Richard, and he sounded harried.

"At Lenox Hill, having a few more tests done." She tried to sound unperturbed.

"Everything all right?"

"Yep."

"When will you be through?"

"Not sure. Why?"

"We have to go to Vermont, right away."

"What's in Vermont?"

"Brandt is. He wants to see us. I'll pick you up at your apartment. Can you be ready at 1:00 p.m.?

"I think so."

"Good. Pack an overnight bag. See you then." He hung up.

With the battery of tests done, Claire paced the small examination room, waiting for Bentley. Finally, he came in, looking at her chart. "Good news. The MRA confirms that it is

77

an aneurysm, but quite small, so the likelihood of it rupturing is low."

"So?"

"So, I'm going to let you go home, but I want you to take it easy. Manage your stress. Plenty of rest. We're going to keep an eye on this thing. If your symptoms get worse, headaches, neck pain, blurred vision, you call me straight away, okay?"

"Okay." She felt her fear begin to subside.

"I mean it, Claire, keep it down. No pressure. No stress. This is serious stuff."

"Got it." Claire snatched up her bag and headed for the door. Filled with relief, she turned to peck Bentley on the cheek and caught a comforting whiff of peppermints.

Chapter Six

Prophecy

By the time Richard texted to say he was outside her apartment at 1p.m., Claire had packed an overnight bag and was ready to go. She stared at the cold gray waters of the Hudson River, as they crossed the bridge out of Manhattan and headed upstate. Once clear of the city, she settled in to enjoy the journey and the stunning displays of fall colors. Leaves of scarlet, burgundy, gold, and bronze were poised to fall and enshroud the damp earth with a deep cover that Claire could imagine rustling and disintegrating underfoot. The artist in her broke down each vista into simple shapes and colors. What wouldn't she give to set up her easel and working with her oils, turn a canvas into a blaze of color, as she lost herself in her efforts to capture the show that nature put on so effortlessly?

Richard glanced her way from time to time. She felt the distance between them but decided there was no point trying to close it. It seemed ridiculous to her now that she had wanted to ignore the invisible no-trespassing sign he held up and penetrate his cool exterior. She had been lonely, starved for contact, and for a moment she'd warmed and blossomed under the attention he'd shown her. I read him wrong, she told herself, as she focused on the countryside beyond her window. I mistook his interest for attraction. He's a man on a mission, and he's only invited me to go with him today because I have a role to play in his work, not his life.

She let Bentley's diagnosis sink in. It was serious but hopefully not fatal. Just more bad news in a year that had produced a bumper crop of traumas. Right now, she needed to be quiet and absorb her latest disappointment, her ill-conceived notion of romance with Richard that had fizzled before it could flare.

She took the familiar action of going inward. That's how she had survived after Jake's death, by recoiling emotionally and curling up very small inside herself, so she could contain the painful feelings that had accelerated from her core and threatened to blow her apart. She had flung herself on top of terrifying emotions, muffled them, until she was no longer vibrating from the crazy rhythms of grief. That's how she had stifled the impulse to writhe from loss, from the amputation of the best, most precious part of her life — her relationship with Jake. And after a time, it was as if her insides had hollowed out into a deep, deep well. If she strayed and tumbled into its depths, she knew that she'd sink and be lost. So each day, she moved slowly, careful not to stir up the uproar it had taken so long to calm.

Claire pressed herself against the car's tan leather upholstery and took deep breaths, inhaling and exhaling slowly. Beside her, Richard stayed quiet, as if he also recognized the need for silence. He was inscrutable, hard to read, even harder to get to know. The young widow thought about Jake, and how from day one, he had been an open book.

"Hello, beautiful. Where have you been all my life?" Claire recalled Jake's first words to her, as she stood behind the hostess station where she worked on random evenings. She was painting during the day and making the rent by waiting tables or hostessing at a popular restaurant across from Lincoln center. "Did you really just say that?" she asked the tall, wide-shouldered guy, with slightly long, curling hair, who was next in line for a table. "I did just say that." He smiled shamelessly.

"And do you get all your pick-up lines from reruns of Miami Vice?" She lifted an eyebrow, trying not to laugh because he was laughing.

"Who do the ladies love more than my man Don Johnson?" he asked, feigning a serious tone.

"Well come back when you have his looks and his bank account from circa 1985." Claire watched him laugh again, and his good looks struck her, as she examined his friendly, open face. There was something about his strong physique and his height, combined with his playful approach, that made the banter with him fun. Guys were always hitting on her in the restaurant, even the married or taken ones. They low-key flirted , as they checked on a reservation, while their wives and girlfriends hung back, intent on looking pretty and aloof. Claire knew unwanted attention from creeps was an occupational hazard that came with working in the hospitality trade, and she took it in stride. "Are you dining alone or expecting friends?" she asked the jokester.

"I'd like to have dinner with you, please." The guy was incorrigible. Claire just put her head to one side and gave him the look, as in, really!? "Table for four. My friends will be here soon," he said, chastened but still smiling. Claire led him to a four top. Over the next hour, she periodically looked over at him and his friends, a group of schoolteachers from what she could tell, as they ate their burgers and fries and chugged beers. Invariably, he was laughing, or in the middle of telling some story to get the others laughing. Sometimes he glanced her way and caught her watching him.

As his party was leaving, the handsome flirt handed her a scratched-out business card and pointed to the back, where he had carefully written his name and number. "Here's my phone number, please ring me." He sounded so earnest and sincere, not at all flippant and jokey, that Claire was moved to be generous. "Maybe I will, Mr..." she read the name, "Mr. Jake Lucas."

Their first date was at a Cuban restaurant in the West 90s, not far from Columbia University, and near where Jake had managed to snag a rent-controlled apartment. The best part, Claire realized, when she played the evening over in her head afterwards, was how little time they'd spent on courtship games.

She hadn't acted all vampy, well maybe she had a little, but mostly they had talked seriously about their lives and career goals. Jake didn't just ask a few polite questions, he wanted to know everything in forensic detail. Where had she gone to school? Why did she come to New York? What was her painting style? Who were her influences? Had she sold anything? When could he see her work? The guy meant business. What you saw was what you got, and what Claire saw immediately was that Jake Lucas was ride-or-die. He was strong, kind, secure in himself. He didn't need to play games, put her on her back foot, keep her wondering if he liked her as much as she could already tell that she liked him. "Are you really this nice?" she asked him as they ordered their third beer of the evening.

"Man for others," Jake said with an authoritative nod of his head, as he brought the long-necked beer bottle up to his lips.

"What does that mean?'

"I went to a Jesuit high school where the ethos and motto was to raise boys to be 'men for others.'"

In the annals of women who had been cursed with crummy boyfriends, Claire could not claim that she was anyway near close to the top of the registry. But she'd had enough subpar suitors to recognize that in meeting Jake Lucas, she had pulled a winning ticket in the dating lottery.

Claire looked out of the car window, not seeing the countryside now, but replaying memories and watching herself on that first magical date with Jake, as he made her spray beer with a joke intended to crack her up, right as she was taking a swig. That was the night I found my best friend, she thought, my husband, my lover, my favorite person in the whole world.

The travel companions drove all afternoon, mostly in silence, eating up daylight and the highway. They sped through small Vermont towns, and villages that thinned out, until finally all that remained were roads hemmed in by open fields and woodlands in full autumnal regalia.

It was late afternoon when Claire heard the car's turn signal, as Richard swerved into a long gravel driveway that led to a series of farm buildings. Grazing cows, their noses buried in the low-lying mist, impervious to chill, weren't tempted to look up as the gravel crunched beneath the wheels of the car. Richard parked outside a long, two-story, rambling farmhouse, the main structure in a complex of outbuildings, smaller dwellings, and barns.

"We're here." He turned off the engine, got out of the car, and stretched. Claire followed him as he began walking toward the main entrance. "We'll get the bags later," he called to her. As Richard approached the double front doors of rough-hewn oak, Claire saw him collide with a tall figure who was exiting.

"Richard." The man, dressed in stylish outdoor gear, held out his hand.

"Trevor." Richard stiffened, nodded, and entered the building, ignoring the outstretched hand. Claire walked through the door that the polite stranger now held open for her, nodding her thanks. He flashed a dazzling smile, eyes in shadow beneath a tweed peaked cap, and then headed toward a cluster of parked cars.

Inside, Richard, always the consummate gentleman, who seemed never to forget his manners, was nowhere to be seen. But at the end of the long passageway to the right, she could hear him, his voice raised. "Karl, what the hell is he doing here?"

"Trevor was kind enough to come up from Boston to help us." Claire recognized Brandt's deep, unmistakable voice and accented English. "My apologies, Richard. You made better time than we expected. He intended to be long gone before you arrived."

Claire entered the kitchen in time to see Richard glaring at Brandt. He turned his back to her and faced the large red AGA stove that heated the spacious room.

"Claire, my dear. Always you travel so far to see me. Danka. Thank you." Brandt opened his arms and Claire walked into his embrace, grateful for the older man's warm welcome.

"Come with me. I want you to meet a good friend." With an arm around her shoulder, Brandt tactfully led her from the kitchen through a set of French doors, as she turned for another look at Richard, whose back was still turned to hide his upset.

"Claire, this is my good friend, Bodhipaksa," Brandt said. Claire could not tell if he was Chinese or Vietnamese, but the Asian man, dressed in the simple wine-colored robes of a Buddhist monk, was slight like a child, no more than five feet four inches tall. He took Claire's hand and looked into her eyes with a gentle curiosity, holding her gaze for so long that after a while she had to look away.

"Bodhipaksa has been kind enough to offer us a base of operations here," Brandt explained.

"What is this place?" Claire risked peeking at her host again.

"This is Apple Valley. It's a working sangha, where Buddhists and members of the larger community come on retreat, to work, meditate, and study the dharma, the teachings of Lord Buddha." Bodhipaksa's gaze lasted longer than his answer.

"It's the last place they'd look for a Benedictine," Brandt said and both monks laughed. "I can give you a tour later," Bodhipaksa offered. His English was good, but his accent was quite strong.

Claire nodded. "Yes, thank you, I'd like that." Again, she was met with a long look and a smile from the small, cheery monk. This guy doesn't shrink from eye contact, and his smile is infectious, Claire thought, feeling more upbeat after the long, heavy day. Bodhipaksa noticed her mood shift, and he laughed like a child, free and full of delight — an invitation to lighten up. Relax, it's not so bad, his look said.

In the kitchen, Richard had regained his composure and was setting out coffee cups. Claire caught his smile as she came in and knew it was an apology for forgetting her earlier when he saw Trevor. "I made a pot of coffee," he said.

Brandt gestured for them all to sit at the oversized plank table, inside the large, cheerful kitchen with its oak beams, ladder-back chairs, and comfy settle. Blackened pots and pans hung from hooks above their heads. On whiteboards fixed to the plaster walls were printed schedules for study groups, general chores, and kitchen duty.

"So where are we?" Richard got straight down to business.

"The only person outside our group who knew I had the scroll was Halou," Brandt said. "I went to see him. I don't think he knows who stole it."

"Are you sure?" Richard asked.

Brandt shrugged. "Just a feeling. He seemed genuinely surprised when I told him about the robbery."

"Gentlemen, hold up!" Claire interrupted the two men who turned to look at her. "The time has come to fill Claire in—from the top," she demanded with more firmness than she intended. "I know that I'm not part of the inner circle of this top-secret mission, but I think you owe me some explanation instead of continually fobbing me off."

"Fobbing?" Brandt asked, his grasp of idiom failing him.

"You keep ignoring me," Claire told the monk. "Pushing me off, and refusing to give me a full explanation. I don't mean to be rude, but if you want me to cooperate, I think I'm entitled to know more about what's going on, since I'm obviously along for the ride."

Brandt nodded. "Of course. You're right. I'm sorry. Let me try and boil it down for you," he said, expanding on what Richard had already shared. The Dead Sea Scrolls, found in 1947, were a collection of documents dating back to the time of Christ, and the three centuries preceding His ministry. Both before and during the time of Christ, the area around the Dead Sea was home to various Jewish communities, including the Essenes, and the early Christian community that formed after Christ's crucifixion. It was always hoped that, aside from the discovery in 1947, the caves might hold other abandoned documents. Brandt had personally led expeditions in hopes of finding texts dating back to the time of Christ, and the beginnings of His Church in Jerusalem, that could shed more light on the man and His ministry. And then, a while back, two Bedouin boys on the Jordanian side of the Dead Sea had been playing in caves, when they found a clay jar. It contained a parchment called the Angel Scroll, approximately 1,000 lines of ancient text, authored by a man named Yeshua the priest.

"Claire," Brandt said, "you should know that Yeshua is Hebrew for Jesus."

Claire set down her mug, sloshing coffee on the table. "Jesus wrote the scroll?! The Jesus?!"

"We can't be sure that the author is *the* Jesus of Nazareth," Brandt clarified, "but we know for certain that a man named Jesus the priest wrote the Angel Scroll."

Richard chimed in. "Remember I told you how some scholars believe that Jesus may have been part of the Essene community that lived around the Dead Sea? If true, it's easy to conclude that as a rabbi, He would teach and write documents that His early followers kept after His death and stored in caves. It's a compelling coincidence that the author of the Angel Scroll is called Yeshua or Jesus the priest."

Claire was beginning to understand what all the fuss was about. "Why is it called Angel Scroll? What does it say?"

Brandt explained that the scroll was loaded with mystical Hebrew imagery and descriptions of angels. In Latin, the word angelus meant messenger, and the scroll appeared to be an important message from the early Christian Church to later Christian communities. Translation was slow and difficult. The scroll's mixture of ancient languages — Greek, Aramaic, and Hebrew — often bore little connection to the modern tongue.

And even harder was knowing if certain passages should be interpreted literally or symbolically.

"We're not sure if we're dealing with parables whose meaning we have to interpret, or with literal prophecy that predicts future events," Brandt said. "The parchment is damaged, so there are breaks in the text, making it hard to link one section to another. And remember, the author lived over two thousand years ago and didn't share our modern outlook, so we're translating writings that are often oblique and hard to understand."

"What have you learned?" Claire asked.

"Jesus the priest anticipated that over time, the meaning or the spirit of Christian teachings might be lost in translation," Brandt explained. "In each era, it would become necessary to deliver the teachings in fresh ways, using diverse methods. The good news of the gospel should come through clearly and directly to every generation without being misrepresented and misunderstood. For this reason, he prophesizes that in the third millennium, a new gospel will emerge that bypasses language. Instead of words, it will convey its message through the power of symbolic images contained in three divinely inspired paintings."

Richard expanded on why this notion was both believable and intriguing. The Renaissance period represented Christianity in art that the masses could embrace. Few could read, but most could understand pictorial representations of the scriptures. This was one reason why Catholic churches were adorned with art and iconography to inspire and tell the story of Christ, His saints, and His Church. The Reformation, aided by the advent of the printing press, attempted to strip away this visual splendor and return focus to written scripture that would lead followers to cultivate a more personal relationship with God. Protestant reformers saw the Catholic Church's vast display of iconography as idolatrous and corrupting. They wanted to declutter Christianity and emphasize the written word in the bibles that, for the first time, were being printed in greater numbers.

Claire looked at Brandt. "So this is about pictures versus words?"

"What this is about," the monk replied, "is an ancient document, which prophesizes that a new gospel will emerge right about now. Christ's message of love, forgiveness, and redemption will remain unchanged, but the medium will be different. Three paintings will combine to create a pictorial gospel as a direct form of inspiration to guide the hearts of modern man."

"And what does this gospel painting teach?" Claire asked.

"Jesus Christ taught many things, but ultimately, He left us with two key commandments: to love God and to love our neighbors as ourselves." Brandt's eyes were soft with the promise of Christ's simple exhortation to humanity that was seemingly impossible to achieve.

Claire touched her forehead. A slow throb was starting at her left temple and her vision blurred slightly. She knew now the cause of these upsetting physical sensations. Nothing mystical. Nothing linked to ancient prophecy, just a bulge in a vein in her brain. Or was it an artery? She couldn't remember.

"Are you okay?" Brandt looked into her face with a concerned expression.

"Yes, I'm all right." Claire was in no rush to share her diagnosis, which was troubling but not urgent. She was more interested in Brandt's revelations. "Go on, please."

"So that's it," Brandt concluded. "Translation is not complete, but we believe we have deciphered the most important passages."

"So, two thousand years ago near Jerusalem," Claire tried to summarize what she'd heard, "an Essene called Jesus the priest foresaw that we would need a twenty-first century gospel, and somehow predicted that a trio of amateur artists would create it with three inspired paintings? Seems like a mighty long time ago. Should we really be accepting messages so ancient and unreliable as, forgive the pun, gospel?"

Brandt smiled. "There is no time with God, Claire."

Claire shook her head. "I cannot even begin to understand what that means."

"I mean that God is omniscient and omnipresent. Space and time are man-made concepts. God penetrates all space and time and exists in the eternal now. His word is outside of time."

Claire laughed. "Sorry, I'm still not getting it, and I have a question. What I do know about the New Testament is that it's filled with accounts of Christ's miracles. Don't you think it's a little strange that my painting depicts the absence of a miracle?"

Brandt's voice became quiet, as though he was sharing his innermost hope. "Claire, if the prophecy is true, what I expect is that together the three paintings will work in a way that I cannot fathom to soften hearts, increase our capacity for love and forgiveness, and diminish our tendency for hatred and fear."

Claire pushed back. "But you can't be sure that the prophecy is literal and not metaphorical. And there's no guarantee that the paintings really exist."

Brandt was insistent in his belief. "I have faith that the three paintings do exist and will display the three marks predicted by the scroll: warm to the touch, healing, with each canvas representing one-third of a miraculous triptych. Your painting bears the first two marks and probably the third. We'll see when we put it with the others."

Claire remained stubborn in her skepticism. "Yes, my painting is warm to the touch. That could be an unusual chemical reaction. Yes, it affects people, but good art is supposed to be affecting."

"Nothing wrong with finding all three paintings," Brandt said undeterred.

"And then what?" Claire asked.

"The proof of the pudding is in the eating."

"Meaning?"

"Meaning that the paintings collectively will have a transformative effect, or they won't. I have nothing to lose by collecting them to find out." Brandt concluded his case for the defense and the prosecution relented. "Seems reasonable," Claire allowed.

"Well, if you don't have faith, you must at least use reason." Brandt winked and turned to face Richard. "I've been summoned to Rome," he said, his tone suddenly more serious. "I suspect they think I had something to do with the Angel Scroll's disappearance."

Richard frowned. "How so?"

"As you know, only a limited panel was convened to study the original Dead Sea Scrolls. Such tight control created disagreements and conflict, and it hurt the effort. Because I used Vatican funds to purchase the scroll, church higher-ups demand strict secrecy. They've authorized only a few scholars to translate it. Both Kushner and I strenuously disagree. I'm demanding that the work be opened up to include more experts and diverse minds."

Richard nodded along. "I agree."

"My critics in Rome suspect I engineered the scroll's disappearance so I can leak it and get my way," Brandt growled. "I have allies at the Vatican, but I have plenty of enemies, too, and a couple of them are questioning my honesty and loyalty. They think I'd stoop to stealing."

Claire touched the monk's sleeve. "I'm sure you can explain."

"I'm sure I can when the time is right, but not now."

"Aren't you making it worse by not going straight to Rome to clear things up?" she asked. Maybe so, Brandt allowed, but he had written to the Vatican, stating his position and his innocence. "I've no doubt that my superiors want to interrogate me in person, but showing up for a third-degree grilling is less important to me than finding the scroll and the paintings. And anyway," he argued, "I suspect that once I'm in their clutches, they'll try to sideline and separate me from the project. Then the church will work to recover the scroll and assign someone else to translate it, and I won't accept that. We must retrieve it first."

Claire saw the monk's intensity. The scroll was an obsession. "If you do find it first, will you tell others about it?"

"That's something I have to work out with my maker. And my superiors."

Claire noticed Bodhipaksa coming in through the French doors, grinning. She smiled too. He sure was a feel-good character.

Chapter Seven

The Healer of Saint Michel

Janine clapped the young man's back. Cupping her hands and rhythmically striking between his shoulder blades, she made a hollow, thumping sound. Soon it started to work. The thick mucus in the patient's lungs loosened and dislodged, so that Sebastian was able to spit it up into the tissues that he pulled like pale magician's scarves from the box next to the water jug, medications, and inhalers that littered his nightstand. The clapping hurt, but it eased the build-up of mucus that filled his lungs and set off violent coughing and choking spells so bad he feared he'd drown in his own secretions.

He gave Janine a wan smile, and she gave him a firm nod. The good thumping she'd administered had done the trick and eased his torment, at least for now. His frail body had turned against him and was running wildly out of sync, like a machine gone haywire. He could already feel it producing more of the frothy, blood-specked sputum, and all that other gunk, as Janine called it. "Come on, Sebastian time to get the gunk up." That's what she said whenever she set to clapping his back.

Janine was his best friend, a dedicated nurse, and a no-nonsense straight shooter, who'd picked up the habit of caring for other years ago. Sebastian leaned back on his pillows, clammy and a bit shaky from the exertion. "Thank you. What would I do without you?"

"It's just what I do." She shrugged off his thanks. She's so unsentimental, the sick man thought. Kindness is second nature to her, and not just a fond idea. Not a bumper sticker slogan. Kindness was a gritty commitment written into Janine's DNA, and she cared for others whether they deserved it or not. "My mom always said that kindness is treating people better than they deserve," she had told him once. "And let's face it, that includes just about everybody."

She adjusted his pillows, easing him into a comfortable position. To say he was so sick, he looked boyish for his thirty-six years, she thought, and his face seemed somehow luminous, despite the advanced cancer that ravaged his lungs. Every day, it was getting harder for him to manage the one act essential to his survival — breathing. As he lay on his bed now, fragile and wrung out from months of savage illness, Janine knew what was in store for him. Keeping his diseased lungs clear was getting harder, as bacteria continually colonized there. Despite her and his doctors' best efforts, a chronic pneumonia, like the one plaguing him now, would soon, in a biological coup de grace, overwhelm his system, until his poor, exhausted body surrendered to death. Heavy hearted, she sat in a chair in the corner of the small bedroom, placed her stocking feet on a worn ottoman, and picked up her book.

"You can take off," Sebastian said.

"Nah, I'll hang out for a bit. I don't have to be at the hospital until six and..." she eyed her phone, "it's only five."

"Thought you might need some time away from sick people?" Sebastian raised eyebrows that looked especially dark against his pale face.

"You're not my patient, you're my friend," Janine corrected him, because technically, she wasn't Sebastian's nurse. She just cared for him during the downtime between her shifts in the cardiac unit of the local hospital, a few miles west of Saint Michel, where she and Sebastian had gone to school and grown up together.

In the lull of the afternoon, the two friends rested in a companionable silence, until inevitably their attention strayed to the large canvas, perched on an easel, next to the bedroom window. Sebastian, its creator, had entitled the work *Farewell on the Road*. In the background, a sunset of gold and pink hints at a paradise just beyond the sky's splendor. In the foreground, three men in simple robes stand on a dusty road and wave to a fourth, their master, who has traveled some distance from them. He's leaving them behind to journey ahead, deep into the painting, toward the magnificence of the evening sky, the brilliance of the sunset, and what lies beyond.

Janine looked over at Sebastian and saw his eyes were wet. The painting always evoked such longing in him. She felt it too. How it took a tremendous act of will for the three men to resist following their friend on his journey. The setting sun was about to drop behind the horizon, and a light in the three men's lives was about to be extinguished as they said goodbye.

"Sebastian, come on now." Janine coaxed him with a small laugh. He blinked, releasing large tears that rolled down his pale face, streaking his sunken cheeks. "Please don't upset yourself. It's just a painting."

Sebastian nodded and turned his face to the wall. Just a painting. That's what the local priest had been telling parishioners for weeks, but every day, the sick arrived, along with the curious, convinced that the canvas could cure them. Over the last six weeks, Sebastian had hosted an endless stream of visitors, until last week, Janine had stationed herself at the front door to halt the foolishness. She chastised a posse of five who'd come by with the familiar demand that they be let in to touch Sebastian's canvas and be healed. "You cannot come in. Sebastian is very sick, and you are exposing him to germs and infection that could kill him."

"Then let us put the painting in the church," a young woman, who Janine knew was in the early stages of multiple sclerosis, shouted. Janine stared her down. "You know that Father Bertrand doesn't want the painting in the church. And he doesn't want you coming here to harass Sebastian. He's made it clear he believes that it's just a painting. It is not a religious artifact. It is not a miracle worker."

"Three cured of diabetes, another better from arthritis, one child cured of autism, and dozens more restored and energized."

Janine recognized the speaker as her father's old pal, Louis Bourreau. "Louis, that's a lot of hype. People get better under their doctor's care."

"Sebastian is a mechanic, not a painter," Helen spoke up. She worked in radiology at the hospital. "How could he create such an accomplished painting? He doesn't have the talent to paint something like that. And the painting is warm. Why is it warm? It's got healing properties, and people just want a chance to let it help them."

Janine held up a hand to quiet the noisy speculation. "Sebastian has always sketched and doodled."

"Yeah, but nothing like this," Helen argued. "If he won't let us come in to see the painting, then he should let us take it to the town hall or the community center, since Father Bertrand doesn't want it in church."

"Sebastian loves that painting," Janine said. "He won't let it out of his sight. Stop pestering him. It's not fair. And tell me, if the painting is supposed to heal people, why hasn't it cured Sebastian?" Janine swallowed the emotion that was tightening her throat and strangling her words. Her deepest wish was that her good friend, who had helped to pull her through so many tough times, an unhappy childhood, disastrous romances, and the trials of nursing school, would receive a miracle, but she knew that was impossible.

"Maybe it will heal him," Louis ventured.

Janine was out of patience. "Sebastian smoked two packs a day from the time he was a kid, and now he has stage four lung cancer, and no relic, holy water, mountain of novenas, or crazy superstition can save him. Go away, all of you."

She closed the door and leant against the banister, crying out her frustration. Only when she was composed again did she rejoin Sebastian and make light of the fiasco that was occurring daily on his doorstep. "They think you have the painting next to the window and St. Bernadette under the bed," she told him.

"I don't mind them looking at the painting if it makes them feel better. I like to look at it." Sebastian's voice trailed off as he gazed at his masterpiece that was now the talk of the town.

This afternoon, as the patient once again studied the canvas, Janine tried to coax him out of his obsessive need to ponder his work. "Sebastian, it's very beautiful, but it makes you sad. Why don't you let me put it away?"

"No, no! Please leave it where it is. I need to look at it, Janine. That's where I'm going." Sebastian's eyes, set deep in his bony face and wide with emotion, looked enormous and almost translucent.

"Where are you going, Sebastian?"

He pointed to the long, dusty road he had painted. "I'm off home, down that road."

Janine tried to say something, but her throat was burning from the effort to hold back tears.

"Janine, I want to go home." His plea was heartbreaking and Janine felt undone. "You are home, Sebastian."

"Well, this here only feels like home," he said. "We run around, going here, going there; this dream, that distraction, but always, somewhere deep inside, is the voice calling you back to your real home. It's like going to the fairground. Remember when we were kids, how we loved the lights, the roller coaster, the rides, and the games? But night falls, and it's time to leave the lights and set off down the dark lanes, following the moon. Remember how we used to come home from the fair across the fields by moonlight?"

Janine took his hand. "I remember."

"Maybe it is just a painting," Sebastian sighed, seeming to change his mind. He didn't know what the painting meant. Didn't know how he had managed to produce it even. Hadn't a clue what he was doing half the time. When Doc had told him he was sick, that he was dying, the panic had paralyzed him. He bought the oil paints and brushes just to take his mind off things. He wanted to escape the incessant terror that accompanied thoughts of his death that he couldn't wrestle into acceptance or resignation.

The mechanic had always wanted to try his hand at being an artist, and he figured that with a terminal cancer diagnosis, he was running out of time. The answer to the question of what he should paint had come to Sebastian in a dream. He dreamt of a long road that he instinctively knew was leading homeward. On it were four men, but only one, who looked to be a master of sorts, was traveling on and leaving his three followers behind. Sebastian worked on the painting at a frantic pace, with more energy and expertise than he realized he had. Putting paint to canvas brought unexpected feelings. As he painted *Farewell on the Road*, the sick man began to see his death as a return to where he had begun, to a home that he longed to see again. Finally, relief and resignation were upon him, and the more he painted, the more these comforting feelings grew. Within only weeks, he had finished the work, and his fear of a fast-approaching death had turned into acceptance, anticipation even.

"As much as we enjoy life," he told Janine now, "there is a part in all of us that understands that to be here, in this world, means we have forgotten an essential truth, and eventually it calls us back. See the three friends?" He pointed at the canvas. "They long to go with their master. They know it's beautiful where he's headed, but they can't follow, not yet. They must fulfill their purpose first."

"I understand," Janine said, although she didn't really. She stroked his bony hand, tracing a blue vein in his wrist down to the knuckle of a long, frail finger. "It is hard to say goodbye, Sebastian, but you know you can go home whenever you like. It's okay."

Sebastian smiled, his eyes still shining from the wetness of spilled tears and a secret knowing.

***

Claire found a place in the dining room at Apple Valley, along with about thirty other students and visitors. They sat on benches, on either side of four long refectory tables. Most were in casual American dress. Others wore monk's robes and had shaved heads like Bodhipaksa. Claire sampled the brown rice and vegetarian chili she had stood in line for. Not bad. She looked up. Across the table, Richard was chatting with a pretty young blond, in her early twenties, who was twirling a twist of long honeyed hair around a single flirtatious finger. She looked like she'd be more comfortable in a bar than in a meditation hall.

"Dharma bunny," Claire heard a woman say close to her ear.

"Excuse me?" Claire turned to the woman who had set down her plate and was claiming the seat beside her on the bench. She was in her late thirties, dressed in sweats, and reasonably attractive, despite her sour expression.

"Chicks like that," the woman pointed her fork at the blond, who was showcasing for Richard her high cheek bones, flawless complexion, and seductive smile, "are called dharma bunnies. Pretty young things looking for a guru. Groupies to the rock stars of the spiritual world."

Claire was confused. "I didn't know there were rock stars here."

"No, not actual rock stars," the woman explained. "Some of the Western Buddhist teachers sometimes act a little like rock stars. They enjoy having their female followers, an entourage, or harem. You know."

Claire didn't know. "What about you? Why are you here?" she asked.

"Me? Not so young and I don't need a guru. I'm in search of some peace of mind. I've been divorced for two years and I'm still mad at my ex."

Claire looked up and saw Richard trying to catch her eye. He smiled at her, and her chatty neighbor caught the look. "That your boyfriend?" Claire thought the woman seemed overly forward for a Buddhist, or a meditator, or whatever she was. "No, he's a..." Claire looked for the right word, "colleague. We're here visiting a friend."

"Really! Who?" the woman mumbled through a mouth full of lentils.

Boy, this one's nosey! Claire thought, as she explained that they were at Apple Valley to visit Bodhipaksa. She was pretty sure her dinner mate wouldn't know Brandt, but she didn't want to talk about him and risk breaking the rules of the secret brotherhood.

The woman looked impressed. "Bodhipaksa is amazing, so famous, but authentic, the real deal. Have you read all his books?"

"Not all," Claire hedged. She had no idea that the little man of the eternal grin was a prolific author and famous to boot. She looked at Richard again. He was staring at her with an amused look of desperation that screamed rescue me from the dharma bunny! Claire picked up her plate, excused herself, and walked from the dining room into the hall. Richard followed, and they sat on the staircase, eating with plates balanced on their knees.

"Bodhipaksa is leading a meditation right after dinner. You should sit in," Richard said. Claire remembered her unsuccessful attempts at transcendental meditation in college. She always seemed to fall asleep. "I might nod off."

"Bodhipaksa won't mind."

"Are he and Brandt good friends?" she asked.

"Very good friends."

"Surprising, given their different callings."

"Their callings are identical. It's only how they express them that's different," Richard corrected her.

"What about you?" Claire asked.

"What about me?"

"What are you? A Buddhist? A Catholic? A Southern Baptist?"

Richard set his plate beside him on the step. "None of those labels fit."

"Then what do you believe in?"

"I believe in love." He said it without hesitation, and Claire saw that as soon as he had made this charming utterance, he looked embarrassed and wanted to take it back. She came to his rescue. "And I believe that your blond dinner companion, the dharma bunny, is looking for love in all the wrong places, and if she spots you, you're toast. Here, give me your plate. I'll take it to the kitchen, while you make your getaway."

He handed her his plate. "What's a dharma bunny?"

"Pretty young thing looking for a personal guru."

He grinned. "She has her own business making scented candles. She wanted to know my favorite scent."

"And what is it?" If I can't know his big secrets, maybe I can score a few small ones, Claire thought.

"Vanilla," he said and then nodded. "Definitely vanilla."

"Good. Now I know what to buy you for Christmas."

A bell sounded. "Your invitation to meditation," Richard declared. "Here, let me take those. I ain't scared of no dharma bunny." He took the dirty dishes and headed for the kitchen.

***

Aside from a small chip on its rim, the pot was as perfect as the day that a skillful potter in an Etruscan village had molded it from clay, over two thousand years ago. The reddish pot rested on a plinth in the Office of Antiquities, just one among the sprawling warren of offices within Rome's Vatican City.

The Office of Antiquities contained an unusual treasure trove of ancient artifacts. Its occupant, Father Vincent Malveau, loved the objects that it was his job to acquire and study on behalf of the Holy See. The Catholic Church was one of the world's single largest collectors of antiquities, and it was Father Vincent's job to help locate and acquire art and artifacts that held religious and historical significance.

Vincent looked up from a Celtic manuscript he had recently acquired to ponder the collections that graced his office. Nothing too important, of course, statuary, manuscripts, Etruscan pottery, and bronze work, ancient coins, a medieval tapestry, and a lesser-known relic or two. The church either displayed or kept under lock and key, in untold warehouses, the innumerable priceless objects it owned.

Vincent recalled the first artifact he had ever found. As a nine-year-old boy in France, digging in the woods, he had uncovered the remains of an Iron Age ax. Antiquities had intrigued him ever since. They lay under the ground for centuries or millennia even, waiting to be found. The last person to touch them, a primitive man or woman going about the everyday work of survival. They never knew that one day there might be no trace of their human existence, but the simple pot that they carried water in, or the weapon they used for hunting, would be admired, under glass in a museum, or on a shelf, in the office of a devoted religious servant.

Vincent answered the knock at his door. "Come." His visitor was right on time. Father Bertrand shuffled in, looking every inch what he was, a typical parish priest, plodding, kind, and wise to the ways of managing a wayward flock. A couple of weeks back, Vincent had called Bertrand to discuss the so-called Healer of Saint Michel and his allegedly miraculous painting. Saint Michel's auto mechanic, Sebastian Bartres, had apparently picked up a paintbrush, after being diagnosed with cancer, and created a masterpiece that was supposedly healing villagers.

Vincent allowed a few minutes of chitchat to put his guest at ease. He reminisced about his own humble beginnings in the north of France, not too far from Bertrand, actually. The pair really did have so much in common. Of course, Vincent worked these days amid the prestige of the Vatican, while Bertrand toiled in a parish, with a stiff weekly schedule of masses, confessionals, and matters related to the spiritual upkeep of the dwindling number of locals who still considered themselves practicing Catholics. Finally, Vincent turned the conversation toward his real interest, Sebastian Bartres, and his unusual painting. "Will Sebastian agree to let us bring the painting to Rome for investigation?" he asked Bertrand.

"Oh, no, no. The young man is very attached to the painting and keeps it in his bedroom." The priest wheezed a little. The excitement of the trip had stirred up his asthma.

"It's not uncommon for the Church to examine such claims. Parishioners are usually ecstatic to be at the center of such things," Vincent suggested.

"Well, I've played it down," Bertrand said. "Some of the towns people are all worked up as it is. I didn't want to encourage them, not until I had consulted with Rome."

Malveau feigned approval. "Very smart. How long has the young man got?"

"I don't know. Not long, days, weeks at the most."

"Any family?"

"Just a sister in the South. He's close to a childhood friend, Janine Mercier. He'll probably bequeath the painting to her if that's what you're getting at."

"Not the Church?"

"He hasn't been to mass in years." Bertrand sighed liked he'd lost one for the home team.

"Maybe he could be persuaded to donate the work in light of the goings on, the claims of healing," Vincent suggested, but Bertrand shook his head. "I don't think so."

"Okay, leave it for now." Vincent's manner turned chilly. "Keep your eye on the painting but continue to downplay the situation. Thank you for coming in. We'll talk later, after..." he hesitated. "When a change in ownership is imminent."

Vincent stood, and Bertrand understood that their meeting was concluded. He'd been a priest for thirty years. He knew the pecking order and how to read the cues. He shook Vincent's hand and turned to leave. Bertrand had originally written to his local bishop about Sebastian's painting but had heard nothing back. He'd been surprised to receive a call directly from Malveau at the Vatican, who claimed that the letter had been passed to him for follow up.

"Remember I asked you when we spoke on the phone to feel the canvas to see if it was warm to the touch?" Vincent asked now.

"Sebastian keeps the canvas by a window in the sun all day, so yes, it feels warm." Bertrand said goodbye and left Vincent's office. He made his way along the corridor, trekking down what seemed like a mile of red carpet. Later, he planned to find a small trattoria and indulge in a simple dinner and glass of red wine.

Inside his office, Vincent picked up his phone to call someone he knew was extremely eager to hear all about the extraordinary painting in Saint Michel.

***

"Our true nature, our Buddha nature, lies beyond the monkey mind, the discursive thought, the chatter that distracts us all day long." Bodhipaksa sat, legs crossed, back straight, in the lotus position, facing his students.

He stopped talking and smiled, looking gently from one eager student to another, as though nothing pleased him more than to behold these faces of earnest concentration. He continued. "In meditation, we focus our attention on a single object, something that is simple, natural, and constant — our breath. We follow the breath out, and as we do this, we notice there is a natural pause or gap before we breathe in again. It is in this gap that we find the peace, the quiet of our true nature, beyond thoughts, grasping and desire." He smiled again, sure that he was sharing the most unbelievable good news. Claire looked around the meditation hall and saw his students grinning as wide as Bodhipaksa. Wow, what a love fest!

"As we follow our breath, thoughts will arise," the teacher went on. "Gently acknowledge each thought, let it go, and return your awareness to the breath. Rest your mind in the natural gap between the out-breath and in-breath. Rest your mind in the openness of space."

Oh to rest my mind, Claire thought, as she settled down to meditate. She fixed her eyes on the mat of the student in front of her, but she could not focus on her breath for more than a few seconds at a time. Thoughts crowded her mind, and for thirty minutes, she wrestled with agitation, boredom, frustration, sleepiness, until finally, she began to feel her body relax, and it became easier to follow her breathing and slow her thoughts.

After forty-five minutes, a bell chimed, a high, reverberating note, and Claire looked up to see Bodhipaksa's perpetual smile resting on her. She smiled back. He is so gentle, she thought, the least aggressive person I think I've ever met. Able to focus so completely on another, until you feel you are the only person in the world who matters to him in the moment. After a long, lonely year with no one around to care about how she was, or where she was, Claire enjoyed being reflected in Bodhipaksa's gentle smile.

After meditation, she found Richard waiting for her outside the hall. He'd come to take her to Brandt's room, which was a good deal larger and better furnished than her own tiny cell with its narrow bed and chipped porcelain sink.

"It's possible that another painting has been found," Brandt said as they came in. "In northern France. The painter is dying. I got the call earlier."

"A call from whom?" Richard asked.

"I'm not sure." Brandt frowned. "The caller didn't give a name, only that he was a friend in Rome. Maybe it's a message from my Vatican colleague, Monsignor Robert Fitzpatrick. At any rate, the Vatican knows about the painting, so we need to get to France soon."

The news hit Claire like a gut punch. "The painter is dying?"

"Lung cancer. Very sad. He's only thirty-six." Brandt shook his head.

Unbidden and unexplained, rage and pain swept through Claire, triggered by news of the imminent death of a stranger, thousands of miles away, a young man like Jake, a painter like her. She let out a wail, then dropped sobbing onto Brandt's bed. And despite her mortification, the heartache that she had only dared graze, in the loneliness of the long nights after Jake's death, erupted in the reassuring presence of her two new friends. She felt Richard's arms enfold her, as he tried to soothe her upset and contain his own.

"I'll come back later," Brandt said, and Claire heard the clatter of the old metal latch, as the monk closed the door behind him. For ten minutes, she cried until sobs softened to periodic whimpers, and she was finally resting, encircled by Richard's arms. Her wet face was pressed against the fine cotton of his expensive shirt that she had drenched with a deluge of tears. "I'm sorry..." she began to apologize, but he shook his head, as if giving way to such wrenching hurt was an act he understood completely, even if it was one he didn't dare risk.

At breakfast the next morning, Claire reached out to Brandt as he sat eating oatmeal laced with homemade maple syrup at the kitchen table. "I'm sorry for my embarrassing display."

"No, no, no," Brandt whispered, and he squeezed her outstretched hand. As she was washing her bowl, Bodhipaksa came in from his outdoor chores, cold air and mist emanating from his gamine frame. "A small tour before you leave?" he asked, his eyes bright, despite the early morning hour. Claire's bag was packed and loaded in Richard's car, along with that of Brandt, who would be traveling with them to New York. She had a few minutes before they set out. "Let's go."

She stepped into the chill of early morning with her diminutive host. His only concession to the cold was a cable-knit sweater over his wine-colored robes, and a pair of green rubber boots. Bodhipaksa pointed out the orchard, the study hall, and various outbuildings used for producing the farm's apple crops. Claire shared how much she had enjoyed meditation the night before.

"It is good to do this practice every day. If you find it difficult, try little sittings instead of long ones, but just do it," the monk urged.

"I'm sorry," Claire said, "I don't know much about Buddhism. Is Buddha your Jesus?"

Bodhipaksa smiled. "Buddha was a man, just a man, but he was bodhi, that is awake to his true nature. He taught one thing, suffering and freedom from suffering. You know suffering?" He tilted his head, looked straight at her, and didn't turn away from the grief his question brought to her face. "My husband died almost a year ago. There is no place to run from suffering like that."

"Of course," Bodhipaksa said gently. "But even so, when we understand how things really are, it is possible to suffer less."

"That's a neat trick. How do you do it?" Claire was flippant to avoid another crying jag.

"By remembering that our true nature is separate but not separate." Bodhipaksa spoke deliberately, feeling for the best explanation. "We are like both water and wave," he said. "The wave looks separate. It can be small or large, fast or slow, but the wave is also water, and not separate from the rest of the water. We think ourselves separate, a wave that is different from all the others, and this is true, but in meditation we try to experience how we are also water, not separate at all. What was your husband's name?"

"Jake."

"If you want to find Jake, leave the world of thoughts. Escape even thoughts of Jake. Rest your mind in the reality of the present moment. Let go of sad thoughts, and happy thoughts. Rest in the moment just as it is, uncluttered by your thinking. Feel yourself connected to space that is the ground of your being. Feel how you are part of all that surrounds you." The monk gestured to the fields and barren orchards. "This is where Jake is, in the leaves, the trees, the ground underfoot, the sky, and the sun. He is indivisible from the space within which you yourself arise. With every breath, Claire, come home to the present moment. Come home to Jake. Be the water."

"But I want the waves, Jake and Claire together." She let out a laugh that was already turning into a sob.

"Of course." Bodhipaksa smiled. "This is what a wave does. It desires, suffers, forgets its ultimate nature. But the way to freedom is to remember that at the same time we are the wave, we are also the water where there is no suffering." Claire took his hand. "Thank you." Bodhipaksa laughed and led her back to the house.

Lucien Gray's townhouse on East 64th Street, off Park Avenue, was gorgeous. Claire had often strolled past the three- and four-story homes in this neighborhood, trying to peer into the lower windows that kept intruders out with their decorative wrought iron bars. But she had never made it inside one of these show homes until today.

Gray's Puerto Rican houseman, Nelson, led them into the expansive foyer where their footsteps echoed on large black and white marble tiles arranged in a bold geometric pattern. Claire was afraid to speak in case Nelson recognized her voice from the phone call when she had pummeled him for Gray's whereabouts in London. She let Richard do the talking.

"Stuart Adair from Mason, Dickerson, and Straight." Richard handed the houseman the business card he had dummied up on his office printer. "This is my associate, Mary. She will be taking a few photographs of the painting for our files."

"The insurance company has already been." Nelson sounded annoyed.

"Yes, I know, so much red tape, but we're insuring an asset worth a good deal of money."

"I'll show you where it is. We have to take the stairs to the third-floor library because the elevator is out of commission."

"That's okay." Richard smiled, and they began the ascent up the wide carpeted stairs, through the core of the opulent townhouse. Paintings by Hockney, Lichtenstein, Warhol, and Max hung on the walls and airy stairway. Lush arrangements of flowers escaped their outsized urns and vases that were set on antique tables and pedestals. Big money, Claire thought. I bet Gray's annual florist bill is more than Jake made in a year as a teacher. Her heart was drumming. It had been Richard's idea to pose as an insurance agent to get in and eyeball the painting and security system at Gray's place. With a few calls to his contacts, he'd been able to zero in on which firm was insuring Gray's new acquisition.

The master of the house was out for the day, they had learned, when Richard called for an appointment to view the painting. He had spoken with Nelson, whose job it was to coordinate an endless round of services and appointments relating to the smooth running of his boss's costly residence. They wouldn't need Mr. Gray, Richard had reassured the houseman. The major paperwork was complete. Just some last-minute follow-up, that was all.

"Let me know when you're done." Keen to tackle other chores, Nelson left the two visitors in the library with the newly secured painting. Claire knew immediately it was a reproduction. "That is NOT my painting," she proclaimed.

"You sure?" Richard approached the canvas and touched it. It was not warm, and the paint was tacky in places. Claire snapped a few photos with her phone. "I know every centimeter of my canvas, and this is not it. It's an amazing repro though." Where on earth was the real painting then? Claire mentally reviewed a series of possibilities. Had Deirdre knowingly sold Gray a fake? Or unknowingly sold him a fake? Had the original been resold by Gray or stolen without him realizing? Maybe Gray had stored the original and was displaying a reproduction. It was not uncommon for collectors to do this. From outside the library, Claire heard the bellow of a vaguely familiar voice. "For crying out loud, Nelson, why is the damn elevator broken again?" She froze, realizing Gray was back. Richard darted to the library door and, peeking out, spotted Gray, who was headed down a long corridor toward a master suite. He waited until the homeowner had disappeared into the bedroom, then beckoned Claire to follow him. The pair never noticed the security camera, no larger than a cigarette packet, on the far corner of the library ceiling, as it finished recording their visit. Seeing the coast was clear, they trotted down three flights, through the foyer and out onto the street.

Nelson climbed to the third floor to see what Gray, home early, was shouting about, probably the busted elevator again. He found his boss in the library, but the agents were gone. "Did they leave?" he asked.

"Did who leave?" Gray was snappish.

"The two insurance agents who came to photograph the new painting." Nelson took Richard's card from his pocket and handed it to Gray, who eyed it closely. Something was amiss with the card. Gray had been dealing with Mason, Dickerson, and Straight for as long as he had been collecting, and this didn't look or feel like one of their business cards. He picked up the phone, dialed the firm's main number, and asked to speak to his personal agent. "Sandy, did you send over a Stuart Adair to photograph my new painting today?"

"No, the file is complete on that, and I don't know any Stuart Adair."

Gray hung up and looked up at the blinking green light of the security camera. "Nelson, get me their pictures."

***

The two trespassers rejoined Brandt back at Richard's apartment. Claire was anxious. It had been bad enough knowing that Gray had her painting, but at least she knew where it was. Now, Gray had a reproduction, and the original could be anywhere. Brandt was reviewing the photos she had taken in the townhouse. Richard was pacing. "We should go back and talk to Gray," he said. "Make him tell us where the original is, assuming he knows."

"Karl, what do you think?" Claire turned for answers to the monk, who was dressed like a regular guy in jeans and a sweater. Brandt looked up from the photos. "I think that the scroll was stolen, and now the painting is stolen or missing. Two thefts, one thief."

Richard stopped pacing. "You think whoever has the scroll has Claire's painting?"

"To verify the scroll's prophecy," Brandt said, "it's essential to have the paintings, and if you know how to steal, then why buy? Maybe Gray is an accomplice, maybe not. Either way, it's unlikely that he still has Claire's painting in his possession. Whoever the thief is, he's clever. He used us to find first the scroll and now the paintings, and he's taking them from us, like candy from a baby. If we are not careful, this same thief will track us to France and the second painting."

Richard pondered Brandt's theory. "Or maybe he's ahead of us, and he already knows where both the second and the third paintings are."

The doorbell rang and Richard went to answer it. When he returned, two officers from the NYPD accompanied him. They had come about complaints of trespassing made by a Mr. Lucien Gray. Claire marveled at how Richard was able to think on his feet and concoct a story for the officers. He and Mrs. Lucas had not planned to trespass in Mr. Gray's home, Richard told the two cops. It was just that Mrs. Lucas was recently bereaved and not herself. She didn't regret selling her painting to Gray, she just wanted to make sure it was cared for, and to photograph it one last time. Maybe Nelson the houseman had mentioned that she'd been ringing the house, because she was worried about the painting's maintenance? "I agreed to go with her," Richard told them in a stage whisper everyone could hear. "Help her slip in the place and check on the painting. Get her to calm down. You know how it is." He smirked.

The two officers listened and looked unconvinced, occasionally glancing over at Claire, who feigned strange looks and manic smiles. "We'll talk to him, but Mr. Gray may want us to charge you formally," the shorter of the two cops said. He scowled at Richard. "You'd better get your friend in order, or you'll be going down to the precinct, and she'll be in the psych ward. And don't leave town. Depending on what Gray decides, we might be back."

"Whatever you can do to help us out, guys," Richard said. "Please tell Mr. Gray she won't be bothering him again. Fingers crossed." Richard nodded, smiled, and led the two jaded street cops to the door. They glanced around the apartment, eyeing his collections of fertility fetishes, and overtly sexual sculptures of large-breasted primitives. Richard let them out and came back. "I don't think they liked my art," he said with faux disappointment.

***

Not until their SUV had reached the outskirts of the small burg of Saint Michel, in northern France, did Claire relax. Despite two police officers instructing them not to leave Manhattan, the three friends had driven to Boston's Logan airport, executing a series of maneuvers and detours to throw off anyone who might be following them. There, they had boarded a flight to Paris. Once in the French capital, they had rented a car to drive the final leg of their journey to Saint Michel, home to Sebastian, auto mechanic turned painter, and his healing work of art.

As evening fell, the three friends drove up to a small stucco house and Claire's newly restored calm began to ebb. On first hearing about the sick man who lived inside, her emotions had been so intense that now she didn't trust herself to meet him in person. A young woman with cropped hair, wearing nurse's scrubs, answered the door. She looked plain, no nonsense, and pleasant until she registered the three strangers huddled in the light rain on the doorstep. "I'm sorry, you can't come in. Sebastian is too sick for visitors, so you can't view the painting."

"Mademoiselle, if I might have a word." Brandt stepped into the house and gently but firmly guided the young woman down the hallway, so he could speak without his friends overhearing. Moments later, the nurse returned with a sullen look and opened the door wide to let Claire and Richard enter.

The small bedroom was bathed by a lamp's soft, welcoming light. The instant Claire entered, she saw Sebastian on the bed, propped up by pillows, and their eyes met. Again, a flash of light moved across her left eye, and she felt the familiar rush of cold air run up her spine to the crown of her head. Guided by a powerful but inexplicable feeling of recognition, she approached the sick bed, sat on its edge, and took Sebastian's hand. The patient smiled and greeted her in French. Janine stepped forward to translate. "He said thank you for coming. If you speak English slowly, he will understand."

Claire spoke slowly and softly. "Do you know who I am?"

"No," Sebastian beamed, "but I think you come to take me home."

"Yes, I think so." Claire was disoriented, her thoughts and feelings running in strange new directions. The pitifully sick young man whose hand she held was a stranger, yet he felt as dear to her as anyone could be. As dear as Jake had been as she held him close in his final days.

"I make the painting." Sebastian pointed to where a drafting light shone on a canvas near the foot of his bed. His guests turned to look at it. As Claire examined the work, the tightness in her body and knot in her solar plexus relaxed, and tension gave way to a sensation of lightness and ease.

"I remember now." Sebastian's eyes lit up, as though recalling a crucial memory that had slipped his mind long ago and remained forgotten until now. "First, we make the painting, and then we go home. Remember?" He looked at Claire to confirm his eureka, but she was unsure what he meant, so she simply replied, "I made a painting too."

"You ready to go home?" he asked.

"Maybe." Claire thought about the bulging vessel in her head, supposedly too small to end her life, but no doubt dangerous enough to be a serious threat. Unlike Sebastian, she was not ready to go give up the ghost.

"Sebastian, we need to take your painting. Is that okay?" Claire wasn't sure what prompted her to ask a dying stranger to turn over his artwork.

"D'accord! Of course!" He seemed delighted by her suggestion.

"You can't take his painting, he needs it."

Janine flashed Claire a look that said back off, but Sebastian put his hand on his friend's arm. "No, no, it's good. Let them take it. This way, I'm free to go home."

Janine's expression softened. "You sure?"

"I'm sure."

While the others loaded the painting into the SUV, Claire stroked Sebastian's hand. Without understanding it, she realized that they both recognized the fullness of the moment, and a sense of completion. Claire's mind was quiet. There were no questions, no confusion about the circumstances that brought her to these unfamiliar surroundings, to sit and caress the hand of a dying stranger. With unfathomable certainty, Sebastian felt like he was, in this moment, the dearest thing to her heart. His eyes were closed now, and his hand, bearing faint traces of far-off grime from his days as a mechanic, was still. Claire could not feel where the flesh of her own hand that held Sebastian's ended and his began. No waves, she thought, just water.

"Claire, we have to go." Richard was waiting for her by the door. Sebastian looked asleep as she kissed his forehead goodbye. Descending the stairs, she heard Brandt question Janine in a whisper. "How long?"

"He could be dead come dawn," the young woman sighed, echoing Claire's dream, and the words of an enigmatic Christ outside the sick room of a dying woman.

The small stone-built, whitewashed cottage, just north of Paris, was a summer residence belonging to one of Bodhipaksa's students. The monk's followers, Claire had learned, came from all over the world to study with him at Apple Valley. The place was rustic, damp, and chilly, clearly unused for some time. As she sat on a slip-covered couch, Claire was subdued, in mourning for Sebastian, though she didn't fully understand why. Smoke drifted from the fireplace, as Richard tried to coax damp logs into a fire that would dry out the cottage and warm its cold, exhausted visitors. Brandt was arranging a makeshift supper of bread, cheese, fruit, and wine, on the table in the open-plan room that combined living, dining, and kitchen space.

Claire stared at Sebastian's canvas that was roughly the same size as her own and propped against a wall. She had touched the painting repeatedly, and it had felt warm every time, even here in the chill of the cottage. Was it healing? Hard to say. Since they left Saint Michel, she had felt mostly numb.

With the fire finally lit, Richard wandered off to explore the bedrooms and returned with pillows and blankets that he placed by the fire to air out. "The sleeping quarters are a bit chilly. Why don't you bunk on the couch by the fire in here, Claire?" He tossed her a blanket and pillow. She caught them and nodded. Chilled to the bone, she was huddled close to the heat that the now roaring fire threw off.

The three ate in silence. Sensing that Claire was on overload, Richard and Brandt remained quiet, each man silently reviewing their situation and gaming out next moves. After the simple dinner, Claire changed into sweats and lay on the couch. Richard covered her with an Afghan. A lock of sandy hair slipped over his eye as he leaned down to adjust the blanket. She wanted to reach up, brush the lock aside and touch his cheek. She could smell his cologne and its undernote of vanilla that he had confessed at Apple Valley was his favorite scent. It mixed with smoke from the fire and clung to his cashmere sweater to create an irresistible odor. She wanted to bury her face in the firmness of his chest and the softness of his sweater, and breathe in his comforting smell, until all felt right with the world again.

"Good night." He leaned closer, like he might kiss her, but he straightened up instead. "Brandt and I will be just through here. Call if you need anything." He headed for one of the two downstairs bedrooms, just off the main living area.

Heart heavy and muscles aching, Claire settled down to sleep, but the exhaustion that had gripped her earlier evaporated. She stared into the embers of Richard's fire and threw on another log, watching the flames spring up through the blackened grate to lick the wood. She studied Sebastian's painting in the firelight. How skillful, the way light emanated from the sunset to drench the traveler but stopped short of lighting his three companions, who remained almost in shadow in the foreground. She scrutinized the light and found it alive with color—blue, violet, pink, and yellow. Not a bright white, but a throbbing spectrum of color that could combine to manifest any form.

The traveler waved goodbye. Untouched by the sadness that overcame his friends, he rested bravely in the poignancy of the moment, in the tension that only farewell can bring. You are, Claire thought, never closer to someone you love than when you tell them goodbye. She analyzed the figures in the painting, a master and his three disciples. They were dressed in robes and looked a little like the master and followers from her own dreams. After staring for a long while, she eventually abandoned all analysis, and allowed herself to relax in the space that the remarkable work created. It was restful, comforting, and brought her calm and at ease. Maybe this is what people mean when they claim my work soothes and heals them, she thought.

She drifted off to sleep. Influenced perhaps by the evocative tableau that was lit in the warm glow of the fire's flickering flames, she dreamed again that she was in India. This time she was in the courtyard of the house in Benares, eating a picnic with the three followers, but with no master in sight. Then, in a non-sequitur produced by the unpredictable logic of dreams, Claire was holding a brush and painting the rhododendron bushes that bordered the courtyard. As she painted their blooms into existence, she realized that she had the power to draw and color her world however she chose. The tallest of the Indian friends approached her, his face somehow changing as he neared, his features shifting. She stared and squinted. "Jake is that you?"

"They're beautiful," he said, and she recognized the warm, reassuring voice and comforting presence of her beloved husband, who appeared now, not as a hazy memory, but as a distinct and alive presence. He looked happy, delighting in the flowers she'd created with a few easy brush strokes. She faced him to soak up his praise, her eyes shining with tears of joy instead of grief. When she turned again to the bushes, they were gone. Only the void stretched out before her, a glistening darkness, trembling with the promise of a light that could coalesce to make any object. She looked for Jake, but he was gone too. He had slipped into her dream, inspiring her to paint with light and summon phenomenal beauty from the plenum of space. She was euphoric.

She awoke to a different darkness, and for a second she had no idea where she was. She scanned the blackness of the room. The fire in the grate had died, and only the faintest glow remained among the gray ashes of burned-out logs. Richard had made the fire, she remembered, in the cottage in France. She heard a rustling sound and knew a stranger was in the room, but immobilized by fear, she couldn't call out. The barest of light from a partial moon shone through the kitchen window and across the floor. It fell on the intruder as he took hold of Sebastian's canvas where it leant against the wall.

"Richard, help!" Her words came out in a hoarse whisper that made the intruder swing around to locate her on the couch. She registered his hesitation, watched him deliberate—should he take off with the painting or move to shut her up?

"Richard!" This time she produced a full-throated scream. Her cry galvanized the thief, who dragged the canvas across the floor to the front door. Adrenaline pumping, Claire jumped up, but immediately realized she couldn't catch the intruder, who was already angling the canvas through the open doorway. On the table by the couch, an object shimmered in the moonlight. She picked it up and felt the metallic coolness of a copper bowl.

She hurled it full force at the thief, hearing a thud then a cry as the bowl hit the man and clanged to the floor. Dodging furniture, she stumbled to the door, only to see him disappear into the darkness with his spoils. A light went on, and Claire spun around to see a bewildered Richard and Brandt half asleep in their pajamas.

"He took the painting," she cried, furious that the burglar had got the best of her.

***

As the gray dawn came on, the fire was relit. The three friends wrapped themselves in blankets and huddled over the rough plank table, drinking bitter black coffee, made from stale grounds they'd found abandoned in the kitchen cupboard. The thief had entered by cutting a glass pane in the back door and flipping the latch. To escape, he'd simply turned the deadbolt on the front door that Richard assumed would keep any unwelcome visitors out.

"So you saw him grab the painting and head for the door?" Richard asked again.

"Yes." Claire felt like a failure, though she recognized that there wasn't much she could have done. The thief had caught her by surprise, fast asleep, in the middle of the night.

"He didn't fumble with the locks?" Richard asked. Claire shook her head. He'd likely unlocked and opened the door, before grabbing the painting, to speed his getaway. "I'm sorry," she said again.

"Don't be sorry. I should have hidden the canvas. Stupid to leave it in plain view when we knew someone was after it."

"You think he's been following us?" Claire asked and Richard nodded. "Looks like it. Only Bodhipaksa knows we're here."

Claire saw that even Brandt looked discouraged. "What now?" she asked. The monk tried to put a good face on it. "The thief has taken all our candy. Maybe he has put it all — the parchment and the paintings — in one place. Perhaps, if we are lucky," he smiled ruefully, "we can find that place and get our candy back."

After breakfast, Claire took a walk in the rain-soaked lanes and fields out back to clear her head. She analyzed the tumble of events that had changed her life in a matter of only weeks, and how the wisdom of Josie McLean and Bodhipaksa had comforted and intrigued her, as she tried to make sense of events that baffled her.

The egg- or almond-shaped dark spot that Josie called a mandorla was still there, next to her left eye, but it seemed likely that the aneurysm was causing it. Aside from the play of light across it at Dormition Abbey, on Glastonbury Tor, and again when she met Sebastian, the strange opening that allowed her glimpses into another space or realm was quiet, no images or visions. She was having plenty of strange dreams, though. In London, she had dreamt that she was Joan of Arc, carrying a pennant adorned with an image of the Virgin Mary, almost like it foretold her coming to France. Or maybe it was just a coincidence. And last night, she had dreamed of India again. Ever since Jake had died, she'd longed for him to come to her in dreams. And at last, he'd snuck into her dream as one of the three Indian followers. The dream was so vivid, his presence so comforting and real that she could still feel him. "Come back to me," she cried, as warm tears mixed with the cold raindrops that blew against her face.

Her thoughts turned to the four travelers on the road in Sebastian's painting. Had she and Sebastian painted the same characters in different places? Why were her dreams set in India? The historical Jesus and his disciples had lived in Jerusalem. So what? Wasn't that typical of dream logic? People, places, and events became scrambled, distorted, and implausible, but the dream somehow still makes sense to the dreamer.

Poor Sebastian was gravely ill, his time running out. As she headed back to the cottage, Claire made up her mind to call him and ask about his painting. Who were the four men? Where was the place he depicted? Was it India? Why was one of them leaving and where was he going? Had Sebastian visited the same dream world she had, and painted what he saw there? Her meeting last night with the sick painter had been marked with a strange intimacy and dreamlike quality. The rain was starting to come down harder, but Claire slowed her pace. Inevitably, her thoughts were turning now to another sick bed. Painful memories of Jake's final days, long pushed off, were beginning to rise like noxious fumes, as her thoughts returned to the agony of her husband's sudden illness and death.

Jake was losing weight. Claire wrapped her arms around him, as they showered together one Saturday after a long bike ride. His torso and middle were noticeably thinner. "Hey, big guy, are you going too hard at the gym? Don't be turning into a light weight."

Since she'd known him, Jake had always been a big man, six foot two, and close to two hundred pounds with a strong build. He would have been at home on an oil rig, or commercial fishing trawler, or building site. Anywhere large, powerful men are needed to perform physically demanding work and do the heavy lifting. He was an avid gym goer, and a passionate outdoors man too. Fishing, hiking, biking, boating, he embraced anything that put nature in his sights and the sun on his back.

As he toweled dry, Jake laughed off his wife's jab. "Thought I'd try out as one of those chiseled pretty boys who look fine as hell in an Armani suite."

Claire kissed him. "I like my man with a wide chest and big strong arms. All the better to hold me with."

Within a few weeks, the weight loss was stark. Jake's cheekbones were too noticeable. He was pale with dark shadows under his eyes, and he was tiring easily. One Sunday, they had to abandon a gentle hike in the Palisades because he'd run out of steam. Claire was starting to worry. "You should see a doctor," she urged him for the umpteenth time. "If I don't feel better in a few days, I will." He waived her off, from where he lay on the couch, watching football. He'd been promising her "in a few days" for over a month.

The following week, Claire noticed a rash on Jake's back. She held up the mirror so he could see. "It's probably poison ivy from the hike," he said, straining to look over his shoulder and see the red bumps that were fanning out across his back. "Put some chamomile lotion on for me, darlin.'"

Yet more days passed. Jake was so exhausted he couldn't get out of bed and had to call in sick at work, a first as far as Claire could tell. His rash was spreading, his appetite was gone, and the weight loss was no joke. The worry was rising in her, sometimes spiking into panic. She looked down at her pale, exhausted husband in their bed. "That's it, Jake, I'm calling Bentley. Enough with the macho stuff." He nodded, and it frightened her that he'd stopped putting up a fight and joined her now in her worry.

"AML," Bentley said, "Acute Myeloid Leukemia. It responds well to chemotherapy if it's caught in time. Why didn't you come to see me sooner, Jake?"

Claire's blood ran cold at the silent warning in Bentley's question, which implied that they'd left it too late and should prepare for the worst, even as they hoped for the best. She pushed fear away, telling herself that Jake was in his thirties, strong, and resilient. Treatment began right away and Claire lived in a fog of worry, as they were caught up in a cycle of hospital rooms, bloodwork, treatment, and tests, while the now familiar sight of her weak, thin, and sick husband replaced the picture of health and strength he had always been. Where life had been predictable and comfortable, with a future that seemed clear and bright, now it took on a hazy, nightmarish quality. Somewhere, far off in the haze, warning lights were flashing, telegraphing the threat of disaster, like the lights of a runaway locomotive they couldn't see that was headed straight for them.

Jake was failing. The white blood cells needed to fight off infection were depleted, so was the hemoglobin he needed to oxygenate his body. He got a respiratory infection that turned into pneumonia. Claire couldn't sleep. She laid in bed at night, willing Jake to live, willing death to keep its distance. The lights in the mist were racing closer and closer, the disaster train bearing down on them. Panic reached into her abdomen to twist her guts and strangle her breathing. She began to pray. The Lord's prayer. A prayer for the sick. The rosary. She recited them repeatedly, mindlessly, not even thinking about the words, like a mantra to ward off evil spirits. How was it possible to bear this pain and tormenting anticipation? An all-encompassing feeling of dread haunted the present. Abject terror took hold when she contemplated the future.

"He only has days, Claire," Bentley told her one wintery afternoon in December. She fought the good doctor. "You don't know that. You can't be sure." But she could see the lights coming faster, closer, brighter than ever, as disaster raced toward them. She held Jake's hand almost ceaselessly for two days. Pain was pin balling through her insides, setting fire to her nerves and emotions. But her hand was perfectly still as it held his until the last moment came. And in that moment, an invisible dividing line, like crime scene tape, separated the two sides of her life. On one side, she was a young, optimistic wife, married to the person she loved beyond measure. On the other side, separated only by a single tick of the clock, she was a widow with no discernible future, alone in her agony, and brutalized by tragedy that had closed all the distance and barreled into them. That night, alone in bed, Claire uttered not a single word of prayer.

***

Back inside the cottage, she found Richard and Brandt at the table discussing their dilemma over more undrinkable coffee. "I need Sebastian's number," she called, as she stripped off her wet jacket, shaking the rain out of her wet curls. Brandt shook his head. "I'm sorry, Claire. We called while you were out, and Janine told us that Sebastian passed away early this morning."

Claire pictured Sebastian propped up in bed, huge eyes in his ghostly but expectant face. "I'm going home," he had said. I lost my chance to get the answers I need, she thought. The one person who could understand what is happening to me is gone. Stupid! Why didn't I ask while I had the chance? Brandt seemed to read her thoughts. "I hoped that Sebastian could tell us more about himself and his painting, but it wasn't possible." He turned his hands palm up, as if to say that they'd both come away empty handed.

Claire nodded and slid into a chair beside him. "What are you doing?" she asked.

Trevor Dunne had called, Brandt said. He'd been busy checking out the people on Halou's list. Claire noticed how Richard tensed when he heard Trevor's name. This was the guy they had run into in Vermont, whose presence had so upset Richard that it caused the heated exchange with Brandt. "Who's Trevor Dunne?" she asked and saw Brandt waiting, like her, to hear what their friend would say. Richard rubbed an antique nail head embedded in the table. "Trevor is a former colleague of mine, an excellent antiquarian." Now he ran his finger over a knot in the table's worn wood. "But we had words, and we're no longer on speaking terms. Even so, I recognize his expertise, and appreciate the help he's giving us."

What kind of "words" did Richard have with Trevor? Claire wanted to ask, but she decided not to pry. As usual, Richard was playing it close to the vest, and there was no point keeping him in the hot seat. She focused on the matter at hand. "So what did Trevor learn?"

Richard looked relieved to move on from a touchy subject. "He learned that one of the men on Halou's list is an Italian named Antonio Baggio, who was on a recent business trip to London. Remember how Gray met with an Italian in Claridge's?" Claire nodded. "Well, there's a good chance that was Biaggio. Trevor is looking for confirmation."

Claire was restless and as she paced the confines of the small cottage, she caught sight of the parchment on Brandt's laptop. She studied the stained and discolored text that was covered with ancient black characters, even, exotic, and incomprehensible. Could these black marks, set down over two thousand years ago, really foretell her life, predict her actions, and describe how she would paint a canvas that could cause so much interest, speculation, and frenzied activity?

She perused the house's well-stocked bookshelves and walked her fingers along the spines of oversized coffee table books: *The French Impressionists; French Country Cooking,* and *A Guide to the Great Cities of Europe.* Ah, good one. Claire pulled out the flashy travel book, flipping through glossy, full-page photos of Paris, Venice, and Rome, cities renowned for their museums, galleries, and spectacular works of art. How great it would be to take time off from this strange caravan she found herself in to explore these storied cities. They were all within striking distance but not listed on their erratic itinerary.

She let the pages of the book slowly slip and cascade between her fingers. What was that? A photo inset in the top right of a page caught her eye. She riffled back to find it again. There it was, small but unmistakable, on a page extolling the glories of the medieval city of Siena, a photograph of a triangular-shaped pennant adorned with the image of the Virgin Mary. It was like the one she had dreamt about in London. She read the caption. "Il Palio is the pennant awarded to the winner of the historic horse race, known by the same name, that is held biannually in Siena's historic Il Campo marketplace." Claire carried the open book over to Richard and Brandt and set it before them on the table. "We have to go to Italy," she announced.

***

Vincent Malveau's phone rang. It was Father Bertrand from Saint Michel. No, Malveau told the priest, the Vatican had not sent anyone to collect the painting from Sebastian before he died. He listened as Bertrand recounted the recent happenings in Saint Michel, and then the Vatican bureaucrat asked if the girl, Janine, had described the monk who took the painting away. He jotted down notes as Bertrand relayed a full description of Sebastian's final three visitors, a German monk out of habit in street clothes, and an attractive American couple. Malveau thanked Bertrand. He would discuss this unforeseen development with superiors and call the parish priest back when he knew more.

After he hung up, Malveau made a call. "I assume that Father Brandt has been relieved of his latest artistic find?" Malveau smirked when the party on the other end replied that Brandt no longer had the painting from Saint Michel. The priest hung up and called another number. "Monsignor Fitzpatrick, this is Vincent Malveau in the Office of Antiquities. I have some troubling information about Father Karl Brandt and the theft of a very special painting. May I come and see you?"

125

Chapter Eight

Anselmo

The three friends took turns driving through the night. Claire was knee deep in second thoughts. She was hauling her two friends on a grueling road trip across France into Italy based only on a dream, a photograph in a travel guide, and an intuition so strong that it completely overwhelmed her powers of reason. "I'm sorry. I can't believe I'm dragging you both all this way. I've no idea what I'm looking for when we get to Siena. I must be loco."

"When there is no clear reason, why not act on a hunch?" Brandt reassured Claire, who leaned forward from the back seat of the car and squeezed his surprisingly muscular shoulder.

By late morning, the trio reached Siena's city center, where they checked into a modest but cheery hotel that featured a small informal dining room off its lobby. Cut off from Vatican funds and managing on a leaner budget, the first-class travel Claire had been treated to initially was now firmly in the past.

The three exhausted travelers freshened up and reconvened to take stock of their situation. The Palio, the banner of the Virgin Mary that Claire had dreamed about and then discovered in the book at the cottage, had created an irresistible pull that brought them to Siena. But why? Who or what was here? A painter and the third painting, Brandt hoped, and he had another compelling reason to come to the ancient city. The parchment gave few clues about the location of the paintings it prophesied, but in a broken line of text, Brandt had translated the words "city of horses." He, Kushner, and Richard had racked their brains, trying to guess where this "city of horses" could be. Siena made perfect sense. Il Palio referred both to the pennant adorned with the Virgin Mary, and to Siena's dangerous, frantic, and thrilling horse race.

The friends looked at a map of the city and outlined their search. The good news was that the city center was quite small and manageable for the three explorers. And with the Duomo of St. Catherine and Siena's medieval architecture drawing tourists from all over the world, there was bound to be a thriving artists' community. This was where the trio would focus their hunt for an elusive painter and an exceptional work.

They split into two. Brandt went off alone, while Richard and Claire set out together. The two friends walked in silence, soaking up the sunshine that warmed the cobblestone walkways, glad to escape the chill that had set in farther north. Richard had noticed Claire taking medication at breakfast. "You never told me about your tests," he inquired carefully.

"Nothing to tell really," Claire hedged. "Migraine headaches. They make me sensitive to light and sound, and are probably what's causing the visual distortions."

Richard understood that Claire's strange visions were one of the reasons they had met. Knowing now how she fit into Brandt's work, he was sure these fascinating occurrences weren't simply the result of a medical problem. It was likely they were related to the types of visionary experiences that he, like Josie, had studied in cultures throughout the world.

He looked at the beautiful young woman who strolled beside him, the sun picking up copper highlights in her rich dark curls and catching golden flecks in her green eyes. She had been through a lot. He wanted to put his arm around her shoulder and draw her close, hold, and protect her. Instead, he pressed his hand for a moment on the small of her back, allowing himself to feel her warm skin through her white cotton artist's blouse, before he let his hand drop.

His touch caught her by surprise. The gentle pressure on her back felt so intimate and filled her with unanticipated pleasure that stirred sensations in her groin. She felt an aching need to lean into him. Tired, with her defenses down, she longed to tell him about Dr. Bentley's unsettling diagnosis. Today, she could sense Richard was drawn to her, open and attempting to get close, but she knew how abruptly that openness could snap shut. It's probably just friendly concern, she thought. What if he just feels responsible for me, protective because he's pulled me into a venture that's becoming something of an ordeal? How humiliating if I act on my feelings for him and then find out I've misread his affection. She wandered away from his side to regain her balance. Looking in a shop window, she let herself be distracted by the display of distinctive, hand-painted pottery.

Richard felt chastened. She was so light and free with me on that amazing afternoon we spent together in Jerusalem, he thought. She seemed to love exploring the old city and markets, but since London, she's been cool. Whenever I get close, she tenses up. I should keep some distance and not crowd her. It's a bad idea to push unwanted affection on her when she's obviously still grieving for Jake. It's too soon for her to think about being with another man. And then there's the lie I told her about Hilde.

Hilde. Simply to think of her was to feel her presence, vibrant, beautiful, inviting. She had brought color, excitement, and warmth to his somber life of rigid routines and serious study. No matter how hard he tried, he couldn't stop the memory of Hilde's beautiful face and perfect body from moving through his memory a hundred times a day. He saw her blond hair, cut in a shimmering, sophisticated bob. He pictured how she pushed the hair on one side behind her ears and stroked her neck, as if to remind him how exciting her touch was. He remembered how she would arouse him by absentmindedly caressing him throughout the day. She gave him lingering kisses hello in the morning, and trailed her fingers in a light touch across his back when he was lost in study. She sometimes ran her palm down his arm with an exciting pressure as they talked. And at night, her hands felt for him hungrily beneath the sheets, as he wrapped himself around the beautiful body he had craved all day and finally took his pleasure.

Richard had memorized every inch of his wife's lithe, petite frame that radiated so much sex appeal. She was vivacious, the center of attention in any group, but languid and seductive when they were alone. Mostly it was her laugh, throaty and full of easy warmth, that haunted him. Her cornflower blue eyes would brighten, and her lovely face would soften and transform itself with an even lovelier smile to accompany that unforgettable laugh. How could he speak of Hilde when it hurt so much just to think about her?

He watched Claire as she peered into a shop window. He didn't know how to explain to her his bafflement that she could arouse in him the same powerful and singular feelings that only one other woman had. But where Hilde had often made him feel off balance and unsure, Claire's presence helped to bring clarity that centered him. Hilde had been compelling but dangerous. Claire excited him, but somehow made him feel safe at the same time. He wanted to tell this remarkable and talented woman the truth about his past and close the distance between them. He wanted to explore and hold onto the intimacy he had glimpsed with her. Beautiful, mysterious Claire, he whispered to himself, I think about you all the time. I'm trying to put the past in order, to quiet old memories and ghosts, and to make sense of my desire for you that frightens and overwhelms me. And when I do, nothing will keep me from you.

***

The Sienese painter lay on grimy sheets in the chaos of his bed. Late September sun radiated from the skylight above. He imagined that the gold-tinted light invigorated others, like it had once energized him. It had called him to each brand-new day and a pristine canvas, white and ready for painting. But now the brightness just exposed him and the shattered state his life was in.

A malaise and distress had gripped him in the days after he'd sold his painting. And soon a crippling depression immobilized his body but churned his mind into a windmill of anxious thoughts. He fell into a deep hole that was filled with hopelessness and self-hatred. Never again, he imagined, would he experience anything other than this emotional torment that turned all his thoughts dark, his hopes into regret, and his faith into an utter mistrust of the world and himself. He'd never pick up a paintbrush again, he was sure, lost as he was in a subterranean maze of dead ends, with no energy to wash, eat, or go outside, let alone paint. Sapped of his life force, he sprawled on the bed or couch in his studio, rising only to brew pot after pot of coffee that jangled his nerves.

In the shambles of his apartment, the painter catnapped most of the day, drifting in the shallowest of slumbers, avoiding deep sleep. But at night, exhausted by his inertia, he fell into an unconscious state and was plagued by a vivid dream. In an unfolding dreamscape, he wandered through dusty, primitive streets, headed toward a fateful destination. Soon the low mud and plaster dwellings he passed were replaced by trees, bushes, and exotic plants, until he stood in the matchless and abundant garden he had painted. In a clearing, he spied an other-worldly figure, upright and ablaze with light. Did the energy radiate from the man, or was he drawing ambient light to him, sucking it from the landscape until it was concentrated around and within his being? The artist moved toward the man, but in an instant, the light from the radiant being was extinguished, the garden was cast into darkness, and the painter was alone, crouching in the blackness.

***

There was only a first name on the door, "Anselmo." Claire watched Brandt press the buzzer, and when there was no answer, press it again and again. They stood outside the small apartment, on the third floor of the building that the girl Luisa had directed them to. The Algerian who owned the local tobacco shop had sent them to Luisa. He said that she modeled for a local artist and had been bragging about some masterpiece the guy had just painted.

When they found her at the front desk of a dentist's office, Luisa had volunteered that a painter called Anselmo might be the person they were looking for. He wasn't much of an artist, except for a canvas he had just finished, a beautiful painting of a garden. She'd cleaned for him a few days back, and he'd been in the best of moods, but when she came by the next day, he'd yelled at her and told her to go away. She had let herself in with the spare key she kept and found Anselmo looking distraught, like someone had died. "He snatched the key, shoved me out, and told me to get lost," she complained to her three visitors. "I went back again the next day, but he wouldn't let me in. He's definitely in his studio. He might not answer the door. Just keep buzzing."

Brandt held his finger on the buzzer, and they could hear the loud, incessant electronic hum on the other side of the door. "We're not going away, friend," Brandt muttered as he administered yet another blast of buzzer torture. Claire heard the thud and shuffle of a body rising, hitting the floor, and moving toward the door. The apartment's occupant sounded raspy and infuriated as he shouted some garbled threat in Italian that she couldn't quite make out.

"Anselmo, we've come to talk about your painting," Brandt shouted through the door. "We have some information for you." Several seconds elapsed before Claire heard a snap and a click as the latch turned and the door opened. The young man Luisa had described as about thirty-five and handsome in his own way stood before them, bare-chested, in stained and greasy sweatpants. He looked degenerate. He had shoulder-length, greasy hair, heavy stubble, and his face was furrowed and collapsed, like the heroin addicts Claire sometimes spied on those New York City blocks that were rife with druggies. If this guy wasn't a junkie, he was finding other ways to ride life hard enough to wreck his health and gallop toward destruction.

"What do you know about my painting?" Anselmo said in accented English. His voice was shaking with emotion that Claire sensed originated at the center of a raw wound. We've got our man, she thought as she, Richard, and Brandt followed him into what looked like the dirty, depressing studio of a struggling artist, but emanated the sickening vibration she imagined might exist within the outer regions of a hell.

***

Monsignor Robert Fitzpatrick sat behind his massive antique desk in his Vatican office and eyed Vincent Malveau. He didn't like the man who seemed, for want of a better word, sinister. Maybe it was an aura of decay that rubbed off from all the musty artifacts that Malveau was continually ferreting out, cataloging, displaying, or squirreling away in warehouses. Preserving the Church's heritage was worthwhile, but the Vatican's chief cataloger seemed more at ease with objects than with people, captivated by the material rather than the spiritual. By contrast, Fitzpatrick saw his own spiritual calling as an invitation to work among the living. To help himself and others possessed of flesh and bone to dance with the dual energies of good and evil and, over the course of a lifetime, circle closer to the light.

"Exactly how did you come to find out about the painting in Saint Michel?" The senior ecclesiast could hear his own impatience as he questioned the tall, lanky, string bean, misfit of a priest who sat across from him. Fitzpatrick was glad that the desk separated him from his visitor.

"I've been keeping my eye on the files where reports of alleged miracles or healings are recorded," Malveau said. "I thought we might hear about one of the three paintings there."

"I see," said Fitzpatrick. In other words, the monsignor thought, you were snooping.

"I contacted the parish priest in Saint Michel directly," Malveau continued. "He had made a report to his local bishop that included claims of healing linked to an unusual painting in the town. The bishop filed a standard report with the Vatican office. I found it and thought I should check it out."

"Wasn't that overstepping your bounds?" Fitzpatrick couldn't resist spearing his visitor.

"I didn't mean to overstep. I was just using some initiative to check out a claim that seemed relevant to the scroll project. If it turned out to be nothing, nothing lost." Malveau's tone was casual and a little wheedling.

"Ah yes, the scroll project," Fitzpatrick sounded icy. From the get-go, he had been against this creepy, irrelevant bureaucrat's involvement in Brandt's assignment. He didn't see why a Vatican cataloger should be included in what was a sensitive, high-stakes enterprise to track down a priceless artifact. And look, he was right. The man had already gone rogue, running off unasked to investigate what was none of his business. "What happened next?" Fitzpatrick was deliberately brusque.

Malveau explained that yesterday, Bertrand, the parish priest who had reported the painting, had called him. He asked if the Vatican had requisitioned the canvas, because a monk and two associates had come by the artist's house, right before he died, and talked him into letting them take his painting. In a sin of omission, Malveau didn't mention that he'd recently summoned Bertrand to Rome for a private meeting. "I know Brandt is suspected of stealing the Angel Scroll. It looks now like he's taken a painting that should have come through proper channels to the Vatican." Malveau tried not to sound too smug.

Fitzpatrick drummed his fingers on the desk. First off, he pointed out, there was no proof that Brandt had anything to do with the scroll's theft. The monk had asserted his innocence and hadn't had the chance yet to defend himself in person. Second, they didn't know why Brandt took the painting in Saint Michel or even that he had. "Karl Brandt has been a loyal servant for more than forty years," Fitzpatrick announced to his slimy subordinate. "He has a track record of always acting in the church's best interests."

Malveau nodded like he agreed. Fitzpatrick was Brandt's friend and a strong supporter of the bull-headed Bavarian, but the senior ecclesiast was no idiot. He wouldn't back the Benedictine if it meant his own political destruction. Brandt had always been a maverick, skirting protocol to do things his own way, but now senior clerics saw him as a renegade, a thief even. Brandt's insistence that the scroll be exposed to broad study had alienated Church officials. It had been easy for a couple of them to suspect Brandt when the scroll went missing. The longer Brandt stayed away from Rome, the more even his friends grew suspicious. And now, behold, the unpredictable monk had taken off with a painting that was arguably church property. No one will guess, Malveau mused, that I was the anonymous "helper" who alerted Brandt to the painting in Saint Michel. The monk had been so keen to jump on the tip about the painting's whereabouts that he hadn't pressed the mystery caller for his identity.

"I'm sure Father Brandt has his reasons for taking the painting from Saint Michel, if he did," Malveau weaseled. "I just thought it was important, Monsignor, that you are aware that he has it—allegedly." Checkmate. Malveau had put Fitzpatrick in a difficult position by telling him that Brandt had swiped the painting. Even better, Fitzpatrick had no idea that, thanks to

Malveau, a party altogether unfriendly to the Vatican had stolen the painting from Brandt.

"Thank you. You may go." Fitzpatrick turned his attention to the papers on his desk. The interview was over. Malveau stood to leave, and Fitzpatrick had an afterthought. "Malveau, your involvement in the scroll project is suspended until further notice, so there will be no need for you to take any further initiatives."

"Yes, Monsignor." Malveau left the office. By all means, push me off the project, he thought. I got what I wanted. The less involved I am from here on out, the less anyone will suspect that I know why a priceless parchment, and the irreplaceable paintings it predicts, are about to vanish into thin air.

***

Claire relaxed with Anselmo outdoors at a trattoria in Il Campo. She took in the beauty of its sloping stone floor, and the ancient red and white buildings that encircled the marketplace. The clock tower of the brick town hall rose like a tall, square chimney stack. Each of its windows were framed with the familiar flame-shaped archways that Claire seemed to notice everywhere now, just as Josie had predicted she would. The scene was an everyday backdrop for Anselmo, but for Claire it was a fascinating new vista. She studied the young Sienese painter as they drank cappuccino. The color was back in his face, and he'd thrown off the despondency that had overtaken him before their arrival.

Once he was inside Anselmo's apartment, Brandt had skillfully broached the topic of the Italian's painting, without revealing too much about his real interest in the work. He explained that his small, handpicked team were studying modern examples of inspirational art. They wanted to understand how mystical or religious experiences influence uplifting works. Anselmo's name had come up as a local painter whose inspiration might lay within the realm of the spiritual or mystical. Anselmo said he wished he could help but couldn't. He'd made a mistake that had lost him his painting and sent him into an emotional tailspin. He'd sold his work to a wealthy, anonymous businessman from Milan. "In that case," Brandt had told the despondent artist, "maybe I can help track down the businessman and buy back the painting. I have funds to pay for artwork that we need for our study."

This idea had revived Anselmo. Selling his painting to the man he called Mr. Anonymous wasn't just a thoughtless mistake, he said, it was a sin. "I'd feel a lot better if you could help me get it back," he told Brandt. "The canvas really is inspired. It started as a dream about a garden, and then the dream transformed into a waking vision of sorts. Just by closing my eyes, I could envision this incredible paradise and then painstakingly recreate it on canvas. Here, take a look." Anselmo pulled out his phone and slowly clicked through a series of images that revealed the successive stages of the paradise he had painted in just a few short weeks. Initial sketches outlined the dimensions of the garden. Later images showed the canvas filling with lush foliage, awakened blooms, quivering leaves, and the gentle curling of delicate tendrils around branches. The painter had mastered color, form, and texture in the lushness of the vegetation, the silkiness of petals dusted with pollen, even the granularity of dust, and moist beads of earth.

Claire saw that Anselmo had crafted each section of the canvas with precision. There was no sign of error, of overpainting to correct a poorly executed shape or proportion. No wrong directions or reworking of the material. Instead, the painter had laid down every stroke perfectly, building up the composition slowly, surely, methodically. Almost like a computer program had whirred in his head, directing the brush in his hand to lay paint on the canvas. But the artist hadn't produced the automated output of a digital printer that delivers an image pixel by pixel. Instead, stroke by stroke, gesture by gesture, point by point, the color had been placed and trailed and dabbed upon the canvas with the bristles of a brush in the hand of a man.

Claire had looked around the studio for signs of an artist's usual aids and props, but she found none. No still life, photographs, or flowers to act as guide or inspiration. No open art books to suggest Anselmo has been cribbing from great works. He'd done it all from memory, Claire realized, because this was how she had painted *Absent a Miracle*. She had closed her eyes and transferred the scene in her mind's eye onto the canvas. The experience had been uncomfortable, sometimes painful, and always other worldly. An intense concentration, whose source she didn't recognize or understand, had focused her on the work. And an unseen master had directed her hands to select the colors, mix the oils, sketch the figures, and apply the paint.

In high school, she had mastered typing at high speed to snag jobs and make extra money typing dissertations or transcribing long lectures or recordings. With so much practice, typing fast and accurately had become automatic and second nature to her. Her fingers danced over the keys. No need to look at the screen. Every word, sentence, and paragraph was executed rapidly and perfectly. The whole time she had been creating *Absent a Miracle*, she had experienced a similar effect. Call it muscle memory or the brain on automatic. Call it channeling or an unseen hand painting through her. Whatever it was, Claire knew that crafting *Absent a Miracle* had been an extraordinary process and nothing like how she typically painted.

As Anselmo shared images of his artwork, Claire noticed a self-consciousness play across his face, with a look she recognized all too well. It said I am responsible for the amazing piece of work, this masterpiece that captivates every beholder, but I did not create it. I just complied, while someone or something acted through me to bring it into being.

The final image of the canvas on Anselmo's phone was the finished painting, which he had entitled *Garden Before the Fall*. The overall effect was of light and life. The garden seemed alive. Look at it. Now look again a couple of minutes later, and you might see that the bloom in the corner has swollen a little, a flower has turned its face closer to the light source, and the branch of a sturdy tree has inched a little further into the space around it. But most of all, the painting was a triumph of light. The entire canvas was light struck, with every element of the garden bathed in luminosity. At the same time, every blossom, leaf, stem, and branch seemed lit from within. This created an aura of colored light pulsing around each object. The effect was almost of a laser light show in soft focus. Anselmo's garden was made of light, struck by light. It captured and emanated light. Breathtaking! Claire whispered, thinking that Anselmo's painting might possibly be the most beautiful and powerful of the three works.

When the artist and the trio of canvas hunters had finished discussing his painting, Claire invited a more upbeat Anselmo to take a walk with her. She wouldn't make the same mistake she'd made with Sebastian and miss the opportunity of grilling the artist to find out if he had lived through the same uncanny episode she had. Freed from his torment, he was happy to go with her and get out of the studio that had been his prison, or worse, his hell, for the last few days.

Now, sitting across from Anselmo in Il Campo, Claire sipped the strong dark coffee through the foam of her cappuccino and thought about how to begin. "Besides dreaming of the garden, have you experienced other dreams?" she asked.

"Yes, but not until after I sold my painting," he explained. The feeling of despair he felt after selling his painting had been immediate and crippling. As soon as the buyer left with the masterpiece, the artist had fallen into bed, assuming he'd sleep off his dark mood and feel better in the morning. But when he woke up, the loss and dread only grew worse. And then, the next night, instead of a dream, he had experienced what would become a recurring nightmare. Keeping his eyes fixed on the stone floor of Il Campo, Anselmo was somber as he spoke. "I stood in the garden I had painted and saw a man. He was radiating light, and I realized that he was the source that lit the paradise. Every petal, leaf, and grass blade was made from the light that emanated from this being. It was magnetic and pulled me to him. I wanted to get close but I couldn't. Some force kept me away. I stood on a threshold where dark ended and his light began, but I couldn't cross the boundary."

"Why not?" Claire asked.

"I don't know. I knew that time was running out. The darkness around me was growing, eating into the light like a cancer. I was paralyzed and couldn't cry out to the man, so I reached out to take his hand. As the darkness expanded, I felt terrified, and then suddenly the light went out, and the man was gone. I was in a blackness that had consumed every photon of the light that had been so abundant only seconds ago. I crouched in a sea of inky black stillness and knew I was forsaken."

Anselmo looked shaken, the color in his face gone again. "Afterwards," he said, "every night when I fell asleep, I'd think maybe tonight will be different. Maybe I'll reach the man, take his hand, and escape the darkness. But the dream always ended the same way. I was left crouching in a terrifying darkness." Anselmo examined the dregs in his coffee cup like his past was written there. "I sold the painting when I was supposed to hold onto it."

"Is that why you think you're having the nightmare? Because you sold the painting?" Claire asked. While Anselmo was recounting his nightmare, she had thought about the power of a guilty conscious to trouble the mind and torture sleep.

"I'm not sure," Anselmo said. "I do know that the nightmares started right after I sold the painting. Depression and the nightmares felled me when the buyer took the canvas from my studio."

"Why hold onto the painting?" Claire tried to sound nonchalant, but she really wanted to hear Anselmo's answer. She had felt the same prohibition, an inner voice warning her not to sell her work.

"Who knows?" Anselmo whispered. "Maybe I was supposed to keep it till someone like Father Brandt came along. I know I wasn't supposed to sell to the wrong person for profit."

"Why was the buyer the wrong person?"

"Because it was just an object to him, a collectible, a material possession, whose spiritual value he overlooked." Anselmo grimaced.

"Why the look?"

"While I was painting, I never thought of it as a spiritual endeavor. I'll be honest with you, that painting was better than anything I've ever done, and my ego got caught up in creating a work so amazing. I thought it was the beginning."

"Of what?"

"Fame, money, the recognition I felt I deserved. Do you really think Brandt can get it back?"

"Sure," Claire reassured him. "Brandt needs the painting for his work, so he'll do everything he can to retrieve it." Anselmo smiled and let out a long, satisfied sigh.

Back at the studio, they saw Richard had returned to the hotel and Brandt was alone. Buoyed by the morning's turn of events, Anselmo began hunting for the uncashed check among the uproar of his studio, in the stacks of papers, books, and unopened mail. "I know it's here somewhere," he said, bending to retrieve a spray of papers he had scattered earlier in his rage and frustration. "There's no name or address on it, but there is an account number you can probably trace. When you find him, give the check to Mr. Anonymous. Tell him the painting is mine, and I want it back."

Anselmo repeated that the buyer had said his office was in Milan, although that could have been a lie. "But I do know that he learned about my work through a mutual friend from Milan called Gio Monte. He's out of the country right now, but I'll find out what he knows about Mr. Anonymous."

The studio door opened, as Richard came in and handed his phone to Anselmo. "Is this who bought your canvas?" The artist scrutinized the photo and shook his head. Peering over his shoulder, Claire clocked the man in the photo and smiled at Richard, who grinned back. It was none other than Gray's companion at Claridge's. The mystery lunch guest was one Antonio Baggio, the Italian from Halou's list. Finally, they had a clue. Maybe Baggio was their man, she thought, and he could lead them to the stolen parchment and all three paintings. What if Gray hung a replica of *Absent a Miracle* because Baggio has the original? And maybe Baggio used Mr. Anonymous from Milan to buy Anselmo's work in the same way he used Gray to buy mine? That left Sebastian's painting. Brandt had got to it first, so it made sense that since Baggio couldn't buy it, he'd be forced to steal it.

Anselmo showed them out. "Don't worry, I'll find the check and bring it to you," he promised, and with no warning, he grabbed the stocky Bavarian monk in a hug. "Thank you so much!" Brandt grinned and patted the young man's shoulder. "Have no fear, friend. We'll get your painting back."

Out on the street, as the three friends headed back to the hotel, Claire thought she heard a voice calling Brandt's name. She stopped, turned, scanned the street, and spied a barefoot Anselmo across the busy road on the opposite corner. He was calling to them and waving the recovered check. As the traffic light changed to green, it looked like he might have enough time to dash across the road before the stationary cars at the stoplight pulled away. But a fast-moving car that Anselmo couldn't see was advancing down the far lane. It sped through the green light and hit him with full force.

***

The medic held up his hand like a stop sign. Claire and Richard could not ride in the ambulance. As a spiritual advisor, the monk was allowed to accompany Anselmo to the hospital and pray next to his bed. But the gravely injured patient didn't respond to the power of Brandt's prayers. He remained in a critical condition throughout most of the night, moving in and out of consciousness, until the early morning hours, when he opened his eyes. Brandt put his ear to Anselmo's colorless lips to catch his whispered, almost unintelligible words. Once he'd pieced the message together, the monk hurriedly summonsed a nurse to act as a witness. Possessed by a force that ignored his broken body's command to give up and surrender the ghost, Anselmo dictated his will. Not really a will, it was a garbled but insistent instruction that bequeathed his painting to Father Karl Brandt. "Get it back," he pleaded with Brandt, who had momentarily ceased praying and now held the dying man's hand. "Please get it back, or there'll be no peace for me."

***

In the way that sudden tragedy often does, Anselmo's accident ripped away the illusion of control and reminded Claire how death can jump any one of us, at any time, anywhere. A seemingly perfectly healthy young schoolteacher might secretly harbor a rare blood cancer that announces itself only when there's no time left to fight it. A distracted painter, excited at finding a misplaced check, might race barefoot across a busy road, not knowing that death is hurtling toward him.

Claire didn't want to be alone, and knowing that the surest way to ward off thoughts of death is to hunker down with the living, she spent the night in Richard's room, where they stayed up talking into the early morning hours before finally falling asleep. At 6 a.m., she awoke to find she had passed out, fully clothed, next to Richard, on his bed, and now lay on top of the bedcovers, stiff, achy, and with the beginnings of a headache. Richard had covered her with a blanket and was asleep beside her, his arms wrapped tightly around her, his chin resting in her fragrant curls. Claire kept still, staring at the thick blond hair on Richard's forearms, realizing how much she wanted to stay in his embrace.

The pair had talked and talked the night before, when Claire had come close to telling Richard about her health problems, and almost confessed that she knew the truth about Hilde, that she was his wife and not his sister. But she hated to spoil the closeness they enjoyed during their makeshift picnic of wine and pizza topped with the salty anchovies they both loved.

Their happiness at tracking down Baggio had been demolished by the violence of Anselmo's shocking accident. He had been conscious when they watched the ambulance transport him at high speed, sirens wailing, to a nearby hospital, but Brandt had called later to say that the painter's injuries were far worse than medics had originally thought. The news prompted Claire to voice a growing worry, "What if Anselmo dies? That will make two dead painters." Richard had the same concern. Out of the three painters they were tracking, one was dead, and one was near to death. The third was sitting cross-legged on his bed, and becoming more important and irresistible to him with every passing day.

"Did Brandt share any details from the scroll about the three painters?" Claire asked Richard, as they sat on his bed after dinner, with a discarded pizza box and an empty wine bottle littering the floor. "Did it predict they'd be alive when the paintings were found?"

"Honestly, I don't know," Richard said, "but I intend to find out." The thought of anything happening to Claire alarmed him. Brandt had hedged about his findings, picking and choosing what he shared with Richard and Kushner. That was the monk's prerogative, but things were different where Claire was concerned. Richard was the one who had pulled her into this situation, so it was up to him to protect her, and he intended to get a detailed briefing from Brandt.

Lying close to Richard in the early morning hours, Claire thought more than once about what would happen if a casual touch led to an embrace and ignited urges that drove them to undress and slip beneath the covers. Between stiff white sheets, under the weight of a hotel comforter, she would discover the answer to a question she had harbored since she first laid eyes on Richard. What would it feel like to make love to him? But all thoughts of love making had been chased away by a growing anxiety, as Claire took stock of her situation. One painter is dead, another is seriously injured, and I'm racing around with a potentially life-threatening aneurysm. I shouldn't have left for Europe without consulting Dr. Bentley. Avoid all upset, the doctor had warned. Rest and stay quiet. And I've signed up for the mother of all stressful, hectic, and exhausting road trips. If I suffer a medical emergency, no one will know what's going on or how to help me. I should come clean with Richard and Brandt about the diagnosis. But then they'll want to ship me back to the States and I don't want to go back. I want to help find the paintings. The paintings? Who am I kidding? She knew it was Richard and her attraction for him that was keeping her bound to this improbable scavenger hunt for religious scrolls, amateur artists, and elusive masterpieces. She got up and went into the bathroom. On a slip of paper, she listed her doctor's phone numbers and prescribed medications. In case of emergency, contact Dr. Bentley, she scribbled, before slipping the note in her purse.

Now, in the morning light, she enjoyed a few more delicious moments, cradled in Richard's arms, until she sensed that he was awake and not moving. Maybe he wants to stay close to me. Turning her head, she looked up at him, bleary eyed. He looked at her lovingly, gave her soft, warm body a final squeeze, and there was no mistaking its message. It said he wanted to keep holding her, to do more. She warmed inside. The signs were all there, mounting proof that he cared for her. She sat up, indifferent to the sorry sight she knew she must make with messy hair, rumpled clothes, and stale makeup. "Do I have raccoon eyes?" She fluttered mascara-smudged eyelids and lashes at him, while he looked impossibly fresh on only a few hours of sleep.

"Yes, ma'am, you do. Do I?" he teased.

"You look handsome and perfect as usual." She turned away to hide the desire in her face, aware that her careless comment had revealed too much. Close to the point of no return, it was time for a quick getaway before things got out of hand. She scooped up her shoes and headed out.

In the hallway, as she closed the door to Richard's room, she heard the ping of the elevator, and there was Brandt, rounding the corner with a look that could only mean one thing—Anselmo was dead. She stopped in her tracks. Another accomplice and fellow painter was gone. Anselmo had seemed tormented when they first found him yesterday. But within hours, with the promise of regaining his lost painting, he had looked like a man with everything to live for. Now, less than a day after their coffee together in Il Campo, the young Italian artist was no more.

Claire was embarrassed. *Lord knows what Brandt must think, seeing me sneak out of Richard's room, when he's spent all night ministering to a dying man.* "We stayed up late talking and I fell asleep in Richard's room," she stammered in Brandt's direction, but the lame attempt to explain herself to the exhausted monk only made her feel grubbier. *Who worries about their reputation at a time like this? Brandt looked weary. I doubt he's been wondering what Richard and I have or haven't been doing all night,* she thought. *He's had so many setbacks, and he has no one to turn to. Well, he has God, I suppose, but he doesn't have a flesh and blood person who can hold him through the night.* "I'm sorry," she told the dejected monk, who just nodded.

"We should try to find Anselmo's family," he said, his voice trailing off.

"I meant sorry for you," Claire muttered, as she watched the monk stumble, exhausted, into his hotel room.

Claire didn't feel right going through Anselmo's papers. Luisa had come to the studio to help clean up and sat on the couch looking queasy and upset. The girl wasn't twenty yet, and her friend's death had hit her hard. The only family Luisa recalled the painter mentioning was a brother in Parma, and she couldn't remember his name. Now they were hunting through his phone's contacts for relations who could come manage the dead man's affairs and make funeral arrangements.

Claire picked up a sketchbook, it's cover soiled and stamped with sticky rings from coffee cups and wine glasses. Inside, she found a series of drawings of a captivating figure, a Christlike character who radiated light. In the near corner of all the sketches, she saw another figure in darkness that she recognized as Anselmo. He was curled up and crouched close to the ground, covering his head with both arms, his fingers clawed and exaggerated. *These must be based on the nightmare he told me about,* she thought, as she turned the pages to find more renditions of Anselmo's painful dreamscape. Over and over, he had drawn the same scene, each time with more energy, violence, even, the pencil point almost slicing through the paper. Was he pouring out his disgust with himself because he'd used the painting he thought of as a sacred object for profit, and in service of his ego? Like a Judas with his thirty pieces of silver, she thought, a reward for his betrayal. The biblical comparison came uninvited, and she brushed it away. *I've been hanging around Brandt too long.*

Claire studied the composition's central, Christlike figure. *Who is he?* Anselmo had described him as a master, and she remembered Josie's claim that all the great archetypes — the goddess, the Virgin, and even the Christ — live deep in the psyche, a complex of energy waiting to be triggered by outward symbols. *Is the Christ who lives in my dreams the same one that lived in Anselmo's dreams, and in Sebastian's, for that matter?*

Claire wandered over to the window and peered down at the street, trying to arrange her disjointed thoughts into a coherent explanation. She noticed a tall man with a shaved head standing on the opposite side of the street. He was rubbing his palm over his smooth scalp and seemed to be looking up at the window where she stood. She caught his eye, and he casually turned away. *Maybe he's Anselmo's friend or a neighbor. As word gets out about his death, people will probably start showing up here at his studio.* Luisa had volunteered to keep her eye on the place and start packing up the dead artist's belongings, until family could take over.

Claire mulled over her strange circumstances. Even though she was along for the ride with Brandt, she wasn't sure that she bought into his convictions about the Angel Scroll and its prophecies. But there were certain facts that she couldn't deny. *All three of us, Sebastian, Anselmo, and I, have dreamt about or painted a Christlike figure and his disciples. We've all produced unusually stunning works of art that seem to be based on similar* dreams or psychic material. Are we collectively fulfilling the scroll's prophecy and creating a visual gospel as Brandt believes? Or was each of us just at an emotional crossroads, reaching deep into the unconscious to find meaning? I'm mourning Jake. Sebastian was grappling with his imminent death from lung cancer. Anselmo was lost and struggling with his selfishness, aware that he was failing.

She looked over at Brandt. He's a good man, who believes with his whole heart in the scroll and its prophecy. He's devoted his life to being a monastic and serving Jesus, but maybe it's getting harder for him to live on faith. He's too desperate for the scroll to be more than just disintegrating parchment, written by an ancient man, who, more than two thousand years ago, was probably dreaming his own dreams, and struggling to give meaning to his own life. Brandt needs to believe Jesus the priest's prediction of three artists and three paintings. Events in my life and inner world certainly seem to dovetail nicely with his beliefs, but does that really signify anything other than coincidence?

Claire saw how she'd become seduced by the idea of the scroll, hoping it would allow her to glimpse beyond the veil and prove that Jake lived on in some way, so she might find him again. But Jake is dead, she told herself now, and it's time to let him go. He wouldn't want me to tie myself up in a wild goose chase, or convoluted rationalizations and superstitions to avoid the brutal fact that he's gone and never coming back. And then another uncomfortable truth hit her. Her growing attraction for Richard was undeniable, even though she was troubled by her fickleness. Can I really transfer my affection so easily to another man after the hole Jake's death created almost swallowed me? But maybe that's the real miracle in all this, she realized, that love might save me.

She turned from the window and saw a despondent Luisa sitting on the couch. She strode over and took the hand of the striking, sad-faced girl, Anselmo's young muse. "It's very sad, but Anselmo would want you to be happy, you know, and remember your good times together."

"I made fun of his paintings with my friends. I said they were ugly." Luisa looked contrite.

"Some of them are ugly." Claire smiled and nodded toward a row of self-indulgent canvases propped against the wall. They revealed an artist struggling to find his own style and falling into the trap of posturing and cliché.

"His last painting was gorgeous," Luisa sighed.

"It was," Claire agreed. "Anselmo was starting to get it right. Given enough time and effort, we can all get it right." She looked at Anselmo's sketchbook in her hand. "Would it be wrong for me to take this?" she called to Brandt.

"I think he would want you to have it," the monk replied.

Chapter Nine

Surprises

Richard placed the last of their bags in the SUV's cargo hold, slammed shut the hatchback and climbed in. Next stop, Milan. The trail was going cold on Sebastian's stolen painting, and Brandt was eager to meet with Baggio in hopes the art dealer was the key to the missing scroll and paintings. They'd racked up plenty of miles in the last few days, Claire thought, and now they faced a four-hundred-mile trip north to Italy's fashion capital. She looked down at her tired uniform of jeans, white cotton shirt, and hoodie. She certainly wasn't wowing Richard with glamour.

Richard, their group's most capable driver, was once again at the wheel. Claire rode shot gun and looked out, transfixed by the almost fairytale quality of the Tuscan landscape: rolling green hills, sharply pointed mountains in the distance, sporadic rows of rocket shaped poplar trees, vineyards, and stone villas with magical gardens. All of it drenched in the delicious warmth of a reliable sun that staved off cold for most of the year.

Brandt carefully studied the information on Baggio that Trevor had forwarded. Antonio Baggio, the monk announced to his traveling companions, was forty-two, handsome, and eligible. The middle son of an eminent Milanese family, he was a gallery owner and broker of fine art and antiquities, who was routinely written up in the society pages. He had a degree in fine arts from the Sorbonne, and a master's degree in art history from San Francisco's School of Art. His clientele included the wealthiest and most influential business professionals, politicians, celebrities, and noblemen in Europe. As they analyzed his credentials and noted his pedigree, it made no sense that a guy so legitimate, who was living out a lifestyle that bordered on fantasy, would be caught up in anything so shady as assault and larceny, not to mention the brokering of stolen artworks and antiquities.

Once in Milan, the trio checked into yet another small, budget-friendly hotel, where Brandt grew restless. Posing as a collector of manuscripts seeking rare finds, he had set up a 7 p.m. appointment with Antonio Baggio, at the art dealer's office in the city center, and he was anxious to head out and get the meeting under way.

"You should let me come with you," Richard repeated for the third time, as Brandt emerged from the hotel bathroom in fresh street clothes. Claire was resting, and Richard was annoyed at being left behind, insistent that he should accompany his friend. Despite his sterling credentials, Baggio was definitely shady, and might even be dangerous.

"I'll be fine." Brandt waved away his friend's concern. "Maybe this Baggio guy has nothing to do with the scroll's disappearance."

"Come on!" Richard said. "Baggio was on Halou's list, so he was definitely after the scroll. Then, right after it goes missing, we see him lunching with Gray, who had just bought Claire's painting, probably on Baggio's behalf. And who should buy Anselmo's painting but an anonymous "businessman" from Milan?"

"I know, I know." Brandt checked his pockets to make sure he had his wallet, cell phone, watch, and the rosary he always carried. On the ride north, the three friends had gone around and around, discussing Baggio, analyzing the thefts, exploring all the angles, covering the same ground. Brandt was tired of speculating. He knew he had to meet Baggio face-to-face to get a feel for him. Only then would he know how accurate his suspicions were, and whether the Italian art dealer was a serious player in the drama that was underway, or just a hapless bit player.

"I'll walk you down to the lobby," Richard offered.

"No need." Brandt was sharp and then softened. "Take some time off. Why don't you take Claire for some sightseeing and a nice quiet dinner?"

"What's that supposed to mean?" Richard snapped.

"What do you think I mean?" Brandt spoke softly but held his friend's gaze, until Richard looked away and muttered an apology.

"I won't be long." Brandt pulled the door of his room shut, leaving his friend inside to pace.

Out on the street, Brandt realized that the art dealer's office was only minutes away by cab. Once there, he'd have at least a half hour to kill. Better to nix the cab and set out walking to kill time and burn off nervous energy. He navigated his way through streets and alleyways that brought him closer to the main avenue where Baggio's office was located. As he headed south on a short, narrow, one-way street, a small Fiat pulled up and parked a few meters ahead of him. He noticed two men get out of the car, chatting, but walked on, sensing no threat. As he passed them, the smaller of the two, and the one closest to him, suddenly reached out and caught Brandt's hand in a wrist lock that was excruciating and impossible to escape. He struggled to pull away, but his assailant used his tight grip on the monk's arm to yank him into the back seat of the car, handcuffing him to the headrest of the seat in front, as the Fiat took off.

**

Vincent Malveau made his way to the rendezvous and found himself becoming sexually aroused, as he anticipated the rewards his visitor was bringing. The priest's complexion was more sallow than usual, with vivid purple shadows encircling his eyes. He was the first to arrive at the pre-arranged meeting place, a small secluded cemetery, behind a nondescript church, in a working-class section of Rome. He was inconspicuous, he thought, and didn't look out of place in his dark suit and dog collar, as he sat on a bench beneath a group of poplar trees, contemplating the quiet graves, many of them mossy and overgrown.

Malveau's fetish for human bones, dug up from their place of rest, had developed, like any worthwhile hobby, over a long period of time. It seemed so long ago that it had all begun, back when he was a child, growing up in the lonely woodlands of northern France. Who, Vincent thought, could fathom it? His family? Totally normal. His mother and father? Good Catholics and diligent parents to three boys. His school life? Normal and uneventful. But Vincent? No, he was not normal. His spectacular bouts of blinding rage began at around age six or seven. With little or no provocation, the demented child would lash out and rain kicks and blows on one or other of his two brothers, both taller and heavier than he, but nevertheless afraid of their stick-thin and vicious younger brother. Punished with his father's belt or sent to bed without supper, Vincent soon learned a more secretive way of venting his fury and releasing the incredible tension that built up in his tall, scrawny body, until his legs grew almost rigid, and his muscles cramped.

He remembered the joy of his new release, catching small animals — rabbits, squirrels, and stray dogs, then tying them to a stake, and pelting them with rocks, until they twitched and expired. Next, he would bury them, and then came the best part, visiting those small graves or mounds to exhume the decaying creatures or small skeletons. Vincent recalled how he would return again and again to the clearing in the woods, where he had made a burial ground of ten or so graves. He shuddered with pleasure at the memory of ritualistically digging up his kill, lining them up for inspection or play, before reburying them in the cool, moist earth. The decay didn't bother him, neither did the stench, nor the occasional appearance of wriggling maggots. His pleasure and curiosity during these ceremonies far outweighed any ugliness.

Vincent was nine when he found a piece of an Iron Age ax buried in the earth, alongside the rotting carcass of his brother's dog. He had killed the dog out of a nonchalant spite, buried, and then dug it up again. It was in this moment that Vincent's two fetishes, his sadism and his passion for buried objects and creatures, became inexorably linked. "When I grow up, I'm going to be an archaeologist," he used to tell people. It seemed a good calling for the tall, awkward, bookish boy, who played alone for hours in the woods, but was, his grateful parents observed, no longer prone to violent rages.

By age sixteen, Vincent had decided that the priesthood would be a perfect home away from home. Girls bored him unless they were the objects of the violent pornography he consumed. Training as an ecclesiast and antiquarian would allow him to indulge a favorite pursuit legitimately, collecting artifacts, especially the buried or entombed. At the same time, he could hide out from the rest of the world and its ridiculous expectations and conventions. A lone wolf, a confirmed bachelor, and twisted eccentric, Vincent would use the priesthood to escape social pressures and censure. And that was pretty much the way it had gone, but with one surprise. Who would have ever guessed that one day, the antisocial youth, who blossomed into a reclusive and vituperative adult, would make it to one of the Church's top slots as an antiquarian? Vincent liked to joke with himself that while other professionals were committed to their work, he was passionate about his.

Today, the human remains that his contact was scheduled to bring belonged to the victims of violent crime. Vincent grew even more excited as he thought about poring over the injuries, running his fingers around bullet holes, or exploring the cracks caused by bludgeons or knives. These weren't like the bones he ferreted out for himself and his personal collection, or the human artifacts he curated professionally for the church—the relics of saints and such. These were a type of reward or trophy, a nuance that aroused him immensely.

Vincent and the man he was about to meet had a simple agreement. Vincent would use his position in the Vatican to gather and pass along information about the scroll project. In return, his associate would reward him with the bizarre and gruesome collections he most enjoyed.

Sitting on the bench, the priest watched his accomplice, dressed casually in jeans and a sweatshirt, approach. He was carrying a metal case like the ones photographers use to tote equipment. The man set the case down next to Vincent, joined him on the bench, and smirked. "There you go. Enjoy."

"I hope I'm not the only one getting what I want." Vincent eyed the silver case, longing to liberate its contents.

"Well, it's tricky business, but so far so good." His companion's impatient tone belied his banter.

"Do you have the third painting yet?" Vincent looked straight ahead as he spoke.

"I like it better when you give me answers instead of asking questions." The man sounded flinty.

Vincent's temper flared, but he squashed it and kept staring ahead. This was a special day, and he didn't want it spoiled. He really didn't give a shit what happened to Brandt and the project. He stood up before his mood was ruined, anxious to cart off his prize.

"Keep up the good work," the man said.

"As long as the incentives make it worthwhile," Vincent, already up and carrying off his spoils, called over his shoulder.

It was not far to the small, two-roomed apartment in the rundown neighborhood that the priest rented when he wanted to explore his bone collections in secret. Italian men, he thought, were infamous for late-afternoon trysts with their mistresses. Well, here in the secret room he reserved for macabre assignations, Vincent enjoyed his own altogether unique and exciting pastime. And in addition to being erotic, it was infinitely more peaceful than any encounter with the living.

***

Despite slim pickings in her duffle bag, Claire managed to dress up for dinner with Richard, pairing dark blue slacks with a pale-yellow boyfriend sweater, and silver strappy sandals, in place of the go-to trusty sneakers that had been stuck to her feet. She applied a little makeup, including the coral pink lipstick she had debuted in Jerusalem, and wore the amber-studded earrings she had picked up from a street vendor in Siena. She even managed to shake out a couple of drops from a perfume sample buried at the bottom of her toilet bag. A flush of anticipation took care of the rest.

The pair found an upscale trattoria, a few blocks from the hotel, and Claire lingered over the menu posted near the entrance, poring over every dish on its list of delicious offerings. What a great change of pace from the pizzas, baguettes, and cheese, the daily rations that had been fueling the intrepid trio's European adventures. Inside, the hostess guided them past well-heeled guests to a small table at the rear where Richard held the chair for her. Sunlight tamed by early evening lit the dining room, and jazz throbbed quietly under the hum of patrons, as the muffled clink, rattle, and scrape of the room's glasses, cutlery, and chairs signaled the work of convivial diners.

This feels like a real date, Claire thought, and Richard, in an open-necked white shirt, dark unstructured blazer, and crisp khakis, looked the most handsome she had seen him yet. It was almost a magic trick, she thought, the way he managed to pull fresh, smooth, and pristine garments from the confines of his small canvas carry-all, and wear them on his tall, lean frame with a casual elegance that marked him as intelligent, sophisticated, and urbane. When Claire remarked how impressed she was with his packing chops, Richard had playfully bragged that this was a talent perfected by battle-tested veterans of world travel like him. "Not only do we have to know how to pack for any occasion," he joked, "but more importantly, we must know what to leave behind, because it's not needed, or can be sourced locally at minimum cost and bother."

Tonight, the two of them were relaxed, their conversation unhurried, as they sipped red wine. Given her aneurysm, Claire knew she should go on a wine diet, but not tonight on this special occasion. Richard touched his glass to hers, producing a perfect clinking note to match his toast. "To you, Claire, the bravest woman I know."

"Come on," she laughed, casting her eyes down, and lowering her lids with a sweep of long, lovely lashes, "you know what a crybaby I am."

"I know this hasn't been easy for you. It's been wrenching, and I hope you don't hold it against me for strapping you into this roller coaster for such a hairy ride?"

Claire looked away, ignored his question, and paused for a beat before speaking. "Richard, what do you really think about the scroll and the prophecy?" He swirled the rich red liquid in the paper-thin glass of his expensive wine goblet and tried to recalibrate. He wanted this to be an intimate affair, but his lovely dinner date seemed intent on turning it into a business meeting. "Honestly, I don't know," he said finally.

"Do you really think you have found three inspired works or three works that are just unusual?"

"Does it matter?"

"Of course it matters."

He took a minute to form his answer. "There is great beauty, vibrancy, and poignancy in the paintings we've found," he said. "They are all masterpieces that genuinely affect, maybe even heal people."

Claire reprised the argument she had made to Brandt in Vermont. "Isn't that what art—the good stuff—is supposed to do? Touch us by expressing what is universal? I was suffering when I painted *Absent a Miracle*. I didn't fully realize at the time, but I was trying to express my despair when no cure came for Jake. That's all there is to it."

Claire wanted to squash the idea that her painting was somehow supernatural. She recognized the strange conditions surrounding its creation. The same conditions that Anselmo acknowledged were at play when he painted his canvas, but she was weary of the scroll, its bizarre predictions, and Brandt's theories. She wanted to live in the realm of the probable and not the miraculous. She wanted a practical and not a far-fetched explanation for what was happening in her life. "Is Brandt right, that the scroll really does predict three miraculous paintings? Predicts my painting?" she pressed her date.

"Yes, in a way," Richard replied. "Claire, the scroll's predictions don't have to be either completely rational and true, or completely irrational and false. Life itself is simultaneously magical and mundane. Isn't it a miracle that we're sitting here, enjoying dinner, on a spinning rock warmed by a distant star? Where did we come from? Where are we going? Don't our lives feel familiar and normal, and yet completely mysterious at the same time? Why does it surprise you that Brandt, who has spent his life contemplating the sacred in mundane, day-to-day existence, should believe so completely in a miracle predicted by the scroll? To a man like Brandt, prophecy is a fact of life, and finding the divine in all things is his job."

Claire tried a different angle. "Do you believe in God?"

"Sure, I believe in God, the God of my own understanding. I see proof of His existence everywhere. The beauty in nature, and our human experience, the workings of a complex universe, and love of course." Claire remembered how in Vermont he had confessed so sweetly to believing in love.

"Love," Richard went on, "is the fundamental law of a basically sane world. Maybe when Jesus the priest, whoever he was, wrote the scroll, he simply understood that love is the central truth of human existence, the message of all messages. Love redeems, is the only thing that redeems. And love will find a million ways to assert itself in each day of every millennia. Maybe that ancient scribe was wise enough to predict that great art will always play a role in inspiring love that moves, heals, or guides us. You said yourself that art expresses what is universal—the good, the true, and the beautiful. Perhaps the author of the Angel Scroll was able to predict your work, because he foresaw that a kind of divine inspiration will always, in any age, make masterpieces like yours possible."

Dinner arrived, and Claire tactfully changed the subject. Richard watched her rejoice over her cannelloni, relieved to be on less thorny ground.

As they lingered over a dessert of fresh berries drizzled with honey, Claire felt the thrill of being close but not touching. The would-be lovers unfolded their past for one another, like they were each dusting off and unpacking a hope chest, an important event here, a turning point or vivid memory there. Stories from childhood, hers in Massachusetts, his in Pennsylvania. Notable differences, she had been outgoing and popular, he was solitary and introspective. And striking similarities, both had mothers who were homemakers and fathers who were academics, hers a professor of literature and his of economics. In the drama of connecting, she experienced how each small act became infused with newness and pleasure, like paying the bill followed by a meandering promenade. They held hands and succumbed to the pull of store windows with their artful displays of expensive garments, accessories, and jewelry.

Back at the hotel, they checked on Brandt, but he hadn't returned. "It's 9:30, he should here by now." Richard frowned.

159

"Maybe he needs alone time and went for a quiet dinner," Claire suggested.

"No, he wouldn't do that. He knows we're anxious to hear what happened." Richard called the monk, and when no one answered, he left a message. By 11:30, he had left numerous messages and alerted Trevor and Kushner that their colleague was missing in action. Around midnight, Richard tossed Claire her jacket. "Put this on. We're going to Baggio's place."

Baggio's place was an imposing three-story, spot-lit townhouse in the most exclusive section of Milan. Elaborate stone moldings and arches graced all the building's windows. The figures of two almost life-sized nude nymphs, sculpted onto the façade, held up a balcony above the main entrance. Claire stared up at the second-floor windows where soft light was visible. "It's past midnight. You can't just knock on his door and interrogate him," she whispered.

"Looks like he has guests." Richard nodded toward a sleek blue Mercedes, with a sleeping driver, parked at the curb. Just then, the house's lower floor lights came on, and they heard voices, and a woman's throaty and seductive laugh. Richard pulled Claire close and put his arms around her, hoping they'd pass as a couple smooching on the sidewalk. Baggio exited the house in bare feet, playfully pulling along his date, a brunette, with ample cleavage, curly tresses, and long toned legs that were showcased to perfection in her sequined mini dress. He helped her into the Mercedes' luxurious backseat. While the parting couple laughed and indulged in lingering goodnight kisses through the car's open window, Richard and Claire snuck into the house, through the front door that Baggio had left ajar. Loitering in a small masculine study off the main foyer, they waited for the owner to come back inside.

"Signore Baggio." Richard tried to sound friendly, like he was hailing an acquaintance on the sidewalk and not breaking in after midnight. The Italian art dealer and playboy, sleepy and with his expensive shirttails pulled out of his pricey pants, was startled by Richard's greeting and spun around to see the intruders. Richard took a few steps toward him. "Get out of my house," Baggio demanded, more angry than afraid.

Richard stopped and held up both hands in the international sign for don't panic. "We will leave. We're not here to steal anything or to hurt you. We just need to know what happened to our friend who came to see you this evening, Johan Lenz." Richard used the alias Brandt had assumed for his meeting with Baggio.

"He never showed," Baggio snapped. "I waited for thirty minutes at the office and then left. Now get out."

"Did he call?" Richard was measured and calm, but Baggio was out of patience. "No, he did not, and there was no message on my cell to say he was running late."

"Signore Baggio, I sincerely apologize for our intrusion. It's just that Signore Lenz left earlier to meet with you and was supposed to join us after for dinner, but we haven't heard from him, and we can't reach him."

"A grown man is missing for a few hours, so you break into my house? Go to the police if you are so worried. In fact, why don't I call them?"

"No, don't do that," Richard said. "There's more to it. Do you know an Amman art dealer called Ansari Al Halou?"

"Not well." Baggio sounded uncertain and uncomfortable.

"A few months ago, you inquired about a parchment he was selling, shall we say, quietly?"

"I was representing a client."

"Which one?"

"None of your business." Baggio stepped further into the study and perched on the arm of a club chair, realizing now that his unwanted guests were here on a tiresome business matter and not a home invasion. In unison, Claire and Richard sat down on a taupe linen couch, while Richard proceeded carefully. "The Angel Scroll was recently stolen from the man who bought it from Halou."

"That's a shame. Hope he was insured." Baggio smirked, knowing the parchment was a black-market buy and pretty much uninsurable. "For a fee, I was asked to inquire about the scroll. The asking price was high, so my client withdrew his interest."

"And how do you know Lucien Gray?" Richard pushed.

"Time for you to go." Baggio stood up.

Richard was undeterred. "I bet the same client that wanted the scroll asked you to arrange for Lucien Gray to buy a painting called *Absent a Miracle* in New York, on his behalf."

"I need the bathroom." Claire looked at Baggio, guessing he was too well brought up to inconvenience a lady, even one who had snuck into his house uninvited. This was her second unlawful entry in one week, first Gray's place and now Baggio's. Life certainly had become exciting.

"It's through the foyer, second door to the right, and come straight back please," Baggio said, and Richard detected he was nervous now. "Antonio, I know how it is with clients. It's important to be discreet, but this guy you've been representing is bad news. We think he had something to do with an assault and theft of the scroll. How did you meet him?"

"We didn't meet. He lives in Madrid and only works by phone. He calls me on a burner."

Richard could tell that Baggio was telling the truth. "He asked you to fly to London to settle with Lucien Gray after he bought *Absent a Miracle*, right?" Baggio nodded. "So where is *Absent a Miracle*, the painting you obtained through Lucien Gray?"

"It's in a small storage room off the hallway, all wrapped up. Looks like it came from New York," Claire announced, and then she looked at Baggio. "Sorry, it's rude to snoop."

"Antonio, we're going to have to take the painting," Richard declared, like it was a foregone conclusion.

"No way!" Baggio held up a hand to defend against the outrageous proposition. "My client has spent almost two million dollars to acquire that painting. He's sending a courier to pick it up in the morning. I can't just let you take it."

"You have no choice. To our knowledge, your client is involved with robbery and assault and the possible disappearance of Johan Lenz." As he spoke, Richard felt worried about Brandt's safety. If his friend was still missing in the morning, he knew he'd have to involve the authorities.

"How do I know you're not lying?" Baggio asked.

"How do I know you're not lying?" Richard shot back. "Maybe there is no client, and you stole the scroll and hurt Lenz."

"No, I didn't. I told you, I only inquired about the scroll for a client in Madrid who wants to remain anonymous. If I let you take his painting, I could get hurt."

"When your client contacts you," Richard coached the worried art dealer, "tell him that the painting was stolen while you were out tonight, and you thought you should consult him before calling the police. Believe me, he won't be surprised that it's gone, and he will not want you to involve the police. He will have a fair idea who took the painting, and he'll come looking for us not you. He used you as a legitimate front, but now that we know about you, he's done with you."

"How can you be sure?" Baggio asked.

"Because I know it to be the case," Richard said dismissively. "Did you look into buying any other paintings for your Madrid client?"

"No, just the one." Baggio sounded tired.

"You sure? You didn't just make a purchase for him from an artist in Siena?" Baggio shook his head emphatically.

"You have a big car?" Claire asked.

"Range Rover."

"Good. You can take us and the painting back to the hotel."

On the ride through the deserted streets of Milan, Baggio relaxed and spoke more freely. Just as Claire suspected, Gray had agreed to display a replica of *Absent a Miracle* in New York and ship the original to Baggio in Milan, who was instructed to hold the canvas for pick-up by Madrid man's courier.

It was very late when they got back to the hotel, and only the night desk manager saw Claire and Richard haul the large package into the elevator and up to the fifth floor. Claire was worried about Brandt, but at least her painting was safe, swaddled in multiple layers of foam and bubble wrap and hidden under the bed in Richard's room.

***

Locked in the small bedroom of an apartment on a seedy block behind the Milan train station, Brandt had pulled out his rosary and whiled away several hours in prayer, before falling asleep on the room's only single bed. It was dark outside when he was awakened by the door opening and a bare bulb going on overhead. Bleary eyed, Brandt surveyed his visitor. "You didn't bring me dinner by any chance, did you?"

"It just so happens that I did, pasta fagioli." Monsignor Robert Fitzpatrick set down the takeout container of hearty soup on a nightstand next to a ravenous Brandt.

"You may have to feed me. I think my wrist is broken." Brandt raised both bushy eyebrows and rubbed his sore wrist. "Was there any need to be so rough, Bobby?"

"I asked you nicely quite a few times to drop in for a chat. How else could I get you to comply?" Fitzpatrick frowned, despite his relief at catching up with his runaway friend. "Have you any idea how much trouble you're in?"

For two hours, the friends sat side by side on the bed's cheap floral bedspread and discussed the missing scroll and the three elusive paintings. Fitzpatrick asked how Brandt had learned about the painting in Saint Michel.

"I got a call from someone at the Vatican," Brandt said. "He didn't give his name. He said a friend in Rome wanted me to know about a painting in Saint Michel that I might find interesting. I thought it was a message from you, Bobby. I thought you directed the guy to call me, because you wanted me to get to the painting first."

Fitzpatrick shook his head. "The call wasn't made on my say so. I had no idea that such a painting existed. The only person at the Vatican who knew about Sebastian and his canvas is Vincent Malveau. Why would he tip you off about the painting and then tell me you had stolen it? What's he up to?" Brandt shrugged. He barely remembered Malveau.

"Malveau led you to Sebastian. Who or what led you to Anselmo and his painting in Siena?" Fitzpatrick asked?"

"Claire did. She's a visionary who resists her calling."

Fitzpatrick watched his friend's face light up. The Benedictine was very susceptible to a belief in the visionary and the mystical, but then again, Brandt was a translator of ancient manuscripts. All things prophecy was his stock in trade.

In the early morning hours, as Brandt embraced his old friend and ally goodbye, Fitzpatrick took him by the shoulders. "Karl, I need you to go back to Jerusalem and stay out of this mess. The Vatican has a fortune tied up in the parchment, and we'll find a way to get it back, but there is absolute agreement that your involvement must be terminated."

Brandt shook his head. He couldn't do that. He'd rather face expulsion from the Church than abandon his mission. There was no other course for him other than to finish the translation and assemble the paintings to experience their message for himself, whatever it might be.

Fitzpatrick watched Brandt's stubborn expression. "I can't protect you, Karl," he said, knowing full well that there was no getting Brandt to quit. The monk would race the Vatican to find the lost treasures, and he would not turn them over until he had personally deciphered their secrets. Fitzpatrick resigned himself to providing whatever cover he reasonably could for his intractable friend.

"This way, Father." Like the politest concierge, Frank, who only hours earlier had snatched Brandt from the street, now returned the monk's cell phone and graciously opened the Fiat's rear door so he could climb into the back seat.

***

At 3 a.m., Richard looked over at Claire sleeping soundly on one of the two double beds in his room, while, too edgy to sleep, he read on the other. He was thinking how content he felt with Claire resting nearby when he heard a knock, and on opening the door beheld an exhausted Brandt. The two men talked in whispers, but their low voices penetrated Claire's sleep, and she woke up with a smile as wide as a coat hanger when she saw their missing friend was back. The weary monk joked that while he had only managed to get himself kidnapped, Claire and Richard had successfully intercepted her painting and despite the late hour, he wanted to see it.

Richard dragged the canvas out of its hiding place and began carefully cutting through layers of protective wrapping, but before the last of the covering was removed, Claire knew there was a problem. The painting wasn't hers, and Richard was unwrapping what looked like a large, amateurish portrait of a woman. Gray's name was on the shipping label, but once again, he or the man paying him had thwarted their efforts to reclaim Claire's painting.

Awakened from a deep sleep by Richard's call, Antonio Baggio swore he had no clue where Claire's painting was. His instructions had been to hold the package from Gray, until a scheduled courier picked it up. That's all he knew.

At 9 a.m., there was another knock on Richard's room door and Mike Kushner appeared. Worried for Brandt's safety, he had come looking for his friend, and was relieved to find him unscathed and napping on Richard's bed. Over a room-service breakfast, Brandt briefed his colleague, confessing that when it came to getting their hands on the paintings, the tally was not so good. Sebastian's painting had been stolen on the very same night they acquired it. By the time they tracked the third painter, Anselmo, to Siena, he had already sold his painting to an anonymous buyer from Milan. Last night, they were sure that they had intercepted Claire's painting, but it turned out to be a decoy. As for the scroll, all they knew was that Antonio Baggio had looked into buying it for an interested party in Madrid. They had no clue who this Madrid man was, but they did know he had used Baggio to buy Claire's painting through Gray.

Mike looked up from taking notes. "Complicated."

"Dizzying," Claire said.

Another city, another church, Claire strolled around the hushed interior of Milan's elaborate duomo with Richard. She gazed down the long tiled center aisle with its countless rows of humble wooden pews, bordered by a skeleton of towering, sculpted columns. She linked Richard's arm and studied the warm tones of the orange and purple stained-glass windows beyond the altar. Despite red herrings, heart-pounding encounters, and mounting disappointments, Claire was happy because of Richard, and the enjoyable alone time they spent together. A slow fuse was burning on their growing romance, and they both knew it was inching toward a passion that was bound to ignite sooner or later.

As they left the cathedral and came outdoors, Richard took Claire by the shoulders and turned her to face him. "There is something I need to tell you about Hilde," he said, and Claire took a long, deep breath. Finally! He was ready to take down this obstacle to their relationship and clear up the lie that had filled her with caution. Then his cell rang, and Richard held up a single finger to keep her in place while he took the call. "Gio, great! Thank you so much for getting back to me. Out of the country? Yes, I understand. You're in Milan now? Great! Where can we meet? Forty-five minutes is fine. Ciao!"

Claire knew it was important to meet Gio to find out more about Mr. Anonymous and what he'd done with Anselmo's painting. But, at this moment, more than she wanted to find the paintings, she longed for Richard to tell her the truth about his dead wife. "Richard, what about Hilde?" she asked.

"I'll tell you later." He took her hand, pulling her along as he hailed a taxi.

***

Malveau could see that Fitzpatrick was exhausted. His superior's face was gray, his eyes puffy and red. The monsignor was strolling around Malveau's small office, staring in disdain at the objects showcased on shelves, plinths, and glass cases. "You called Brandt and told him about the painting in Saint Michel," Fitzpatrick said without warning as he shifted from perusing Malveau's odious objets trouvés to scrutinizing the collector's dark eyes and cruel mouth.

"I did not!" Malveau, an experienced liar, managed to squeeze just the right combination of upset and faux outrage into his denial.

But he didn't fool Fitzpatrick, who had whiffed Malveau's rank nature on the handful of occasions they had met, and now caught its full stench. "You are lying." The older man was deliberately harsh.

"I am not lying." Malveau's voice rose in an indignant whine. "This morning, I spoke with Father Bertrand in Saint Michel," Fitzpatrick continued. "He said he met with you here in Rome."

"I only brought him here to help the project. I was afraid to admit that I had gone out of bounds when you and I spoke."

Malveau knew his excuses would sound plausible to almost anyone, but they didn't placate Fitzpatrick. The monsignor could see through him. "I don't believe you, and I want to know why you deliberately entrapped Father Brandt. You set him up to take Sebastian's painting and snitched on him when he did. And then, you left my office an anonymous message about Brandt's whereabouts in Milan. How did you know he was there?"

Fitzpatrick was shaking. As a boy in Ireland, he had been an amateur boxer. Reflexively, as the adrenaline coursed through him, he curled his right hand into a fist.

"Are you going to hit me, Monsignor?" Malveau smirked.

"Answer me." Fitzpatrick struggled for composure, not wanting his infuriating subordinate to see him lose control.

"I didn't leave you a message," Malveau lied again. "I don't know where Brandt is, and I don't care. He is an arrogant, ill-mannered, self-righteous bastard, who does not respect the work we do here."

Malveau was taking a different tack now. By openly condemning Brandt, he hoped that Fitzpatrick, who was a veteran of the Vatican's political wars, would believe Malveau was fueled by professional jealousy and politics.

"You are not fit to kiss the boots of Karl Brandt," Fitzpatrick shouted, a small blue vein throbbing in his temple. He saw the small smirk slip across Malveau's face and knew he was still manipulating. The odious bureaucrat had not acted out of professional jealousy, it was something else, something far more destructive, but Fitzpatrick didn't want to signal that he knew there was more to it. He strode out of the office and slammed the door, sending a small but priceless piece of chipped Etruscan pottery crashing to the floor.

***

Claire studied the young man as they sat in the small bar where they had met for drinks. Sparkling water for Claire, because she wanted to avoid triggering the persistent headaches that were dogging her. Gio Monte looked to be in his late twenties and was not just handsome but beautiful. Rich brown hair, expertly cut, fell below his ears in well-formed ringlets, not unlike her own. Tall and slender, he smelled delicious, thanks to what Claire guessed was an outrageously priced cologne. And despite being dressed casually in t-shirt and jeans, the uniform of the street, he nevertheless exuded immense style. It was evident in the luxurious cotton of the short-sleeved tee that showed off his muscular brown arms, and the faded and ripped designer jeans that accentuated his long lean legs. There was no mistaking the signs of the enormous wealth that backed the socialite: the perfectly even, year-round tan, soft leather loafers worn without socks, expensive watch, and discreet accents of gold jewelry. Gio radiated the well-groomed, pristine quality that marks only those fortunate enough to have spent their entire lives elevated beyond material struggle. He exuded a feeling of relaxed entitlement so complete that his enjoyment of the finest things was never tarnished with anxious thoughts about how to pay for them.

Just now, though, the dazzling young man was somber, as Richard watched and waited, giving him time to absorb the news that his friend from Siena was dead. Claire listened as Gio did what survivors do, remember and recount fragments of his relationship with Anselmo, a prank here, a funny story there, plenty of assertions about their tight bond and mutual respect. Finally, gauging that the time was right, Richard homed in on the meeting's purpose and said, "Anselmo sold his painting, the one of the garden."

"That painting was crazy, man!" Gio exclaimed, taking his appreciation for the work up a notch because the artist was gone and could never paint another.

"He sold the painting to a businessman in Milan who had a photo of the work that you gave him," Richard went on.

Gio looked puzzled, then remembered something. "My parents had a thing, a few weeks back, society party, plenty of high-profile people. I took the photos and showed them around. I told Anselmo that'd I'd rep his work, take a percentage if I found a buyer. You know, maybe get a business going. He had the talent and I know the market."

Claire was willing to bet that Gio didn't have to work for a living. He could while away leisurely days beneath the drip, drip of generational wealth that washed away every want and lubricated endless adventures. But instead of envying him, she thought about how quickly affluence can kill ambition and make it hard for someone like Gio to find lasting meaning in life. Or maybe she was wrong. Gio had won the genetic lottery. He'd inherited enormous beauty and social status, with enough money to insulate him from struggle and ensure pleasure on every day of his charmed existence.

Richard pressed him, asking who had asked about Anselmo's painting, but Gio couldn't remember. He knew that he'd shown the photos around and texted several to a few interested parties. People were impressed, but he didn't remember anyone saying they wanted to acquire the work. "Why are you looking for the buyer?" he asked, and Richard's answer was only partially true. "Anselmo regretted selling the painting. He never cashed the buyer's check, and he was so serious about getting the canvas back that he dictated a will in the hospital. He bequeathed his work to a friend of ours. We're helping him to track the canvas down."

Gio was a little surprised but understood why his friend might have a change of heart when he was dying. "Sure, man, I get it. Makes sense that Anselmo would want to control what happens to his one and only masterpiece."

Standing to leave, the handsome Italian insisted he'd be heading down to Siena for Anselmo's funeral and would call them if he got a bead on who had bought the painting. His parents would probably know. They practically ran the town. He shook Claire's hand. "Ciao, Signora Markson." He had mistaken her for Richard's wife, and neither she nor Richard corrected him.

Chapter Ten

Crimes

Lincoln Swelt rubbed a palm over his bald head and then scratched it hard like he was trying to fire up the neurons in his brain. He was rusty, no doubt about it. He had quit thieving about five years ago. He'd just grown sick of being in and out of the joint, and his knees weren't up to it anymore. These days he worked for a company in Florida, installing cable TV, also bad for his knees. It would be easy to combine both professions, burglary and cable fitting. They were a good combo. Yep, every day on home installations, he saw money and jewelry just lying around, begging to be lifted, but he never did, because that would be wrong. You're gonna be a thief, go for it, but don't be one thing and pretend to be another, that was Lincoln Swelt's position. Not that he couldn't use more money. He and Annie did okay with what he made and what she picked up working as a cashier at the local grocery. People trusted Annie with money because that girl was as honest as the day was long. She'd been around other people's money all her life, and never in her thirty-two years had she ever lifted a cent.

A trip to Italy, Swelt smiled. Annie had never thought that was on the cards, but here she was, having a ball. He'd left her by the hotel pool drinking a white wine spritzer. Not much fun for him, though, with the job weighing on his mind ever since they'd arrived a couple of days back. Yeah, he was rusty, not really up to it, but it was like he told Annie, a situation where he couldn't say no. Some debts you can ignore, and some you just have to settle or suffer the consequences.

So, here he was, out of retirement for a limited engagement, sitting in the dark blue rental van, parked outside the Villa

Fiori. He'd driven out last evening to do reconnaissance. He'd been briefed on the villa and knew that it had a basic security system and was the smallest and least used of four weekend retreats. Its wealthy owner paid a housekeeper, Nettie, and her husband, Gianni, to live in the guest cottage on the property and keep their eye on things.

Last night, Swelt had arrived before dark to get the lay of the land. After nightfall, he'd managed to get inside the villa, where he found the alarm system switched off. He saw why. Not much to steal really. The place was rustic, nice furniture, but no family silver or nothing. He had found the painting easy enough, hanging on the largest wall in the master bedroom. He'd sat on the bench at the bottom of the bed, shone his flashlight on the canvas, and contemplated it for a bit. Got a real nice feeling, too, calming, like sitting in a real garden, not just looking at a painting of one.

Today, he pulled the rental van along the far side of the villa, off the driveway and onto the grass, out of sight of the guesthouse. He was all set to break a pane in the French doors, but found them unlocked. Great! Inside, the house was quiet, nobody around. He darted up the staircase and into the bedroom. He lifted the unframed painting off the wall and moving fast for a man as large and ungainly as he was, he carried it downstairs, through the drawing room, back out the French doors, and deposited it in the back of the van. He reversed, leaving a swathe of crushed grass, and made his getaway, out of Villa Fiori's main gate.

Hearing an engine start, Nettie looked out from the kitchen window of the small two-bedroom guesthouse, in time to see the back end of a blue van turning right out of the property. No workmen and no deliveries were expected, she thought. Signore's painting was not scheduled for pick-up and transfer to the big house in Rome until tomorrow. She called for Gianni. Better have him check inside the villa.

***

Claire had a splitting headache, the worst one so far. She lay on the bed with a cold washcloth across her eyes, fighting nausea. She had only a few minutes to get ready for her late lunch with the others. It was nice having Kushner around. With his unassuming manner, dry wit, and deadpan delivery, he lightened the vibe, and even got Brandt belly laughing. She heard a knock and Richard came in, beaming at her. We're like teenagers, she thought, reveling in the first tentative gestures of courtship, long looks and handholding, but neither of us brave enough to voice the heavy-duty feelings. Richard looked worried. She removed the washcloth. "Don't fret, I'm OK and done resting." He sat beside her and stroked her hand. Claire couldn't help herself. "Richard, what were you going to tell me about Hilde this morning?"

"Nothing important."

"I think it's very important," she said, and as Richard stared at their entwined hands, he understood the difference between holding back and not telling the truth. "Hilde was my wife, not my sister," he said with no preamble, and Claire let out a long breath that she felt she'd been holding since Josie let slip the truth as they stood on Glastonbury Tor.

"Why didn't you tell me before?"

"Too painful," Richard whispered. His answer was short but adequate. "I can't talk about her, not yet." He sounded tentative, not stubborn.

"I understand." She felt him tug his hand away and she opened her palm to release it. "See you downstairs." He managed a smile and left.

"Now we can begin," Claire whispered after he'd gone.

***

Richard was first to the table in the hotel's small but folksy dining room. Kushner came next, and then Brandt, who had been to mass at the duomo. While they waited for Claire, Richard's phone rang. "Gio, how are you? You do? That's fantastic! Let me get a pen." Kushner handed Richard a pen and an envelope so he could scribble down the information Gio gave him.

Unable to make out what Gio was saying, Kushner and Brandt did catch his animated tone. Richard hung up and looked from one friend to the other. "Gentlemen, Mr. Anonymous is one Gilberto Brazzini, successful entrepreneur, and connoisseur of all things collectible. Gio says the guy is loaded and," he made air quotes, "an insane collector, who travels a lot for business. He has a small office here in Milan, but his main office is in Rome. Gio's mother heard Brazzini at her party going on about Anselmo's painting and how he was certain he would buy it."

"But Gio's not certain that Brazzini is the guy, right?" Brandt said, bursting Richard's bubble. He had a point. Brazzini's big talk at the party didn't mean he'd followed through and actually bought the work.

"Has Trevor tracked the check yet?" Kushner asked.

"He's working on it," Brandt said. "If we can trace the account back to Brazzini, then we know we have our man. Maybe it's just easier if I fly to Rome and talk to him in person."

"If you go to Rome, I go with you," Kushner piped up. "The last time you left for a rendezvous, you weren't back in time for curfew." All right, Brandt relented, Kushner could go with him.

Richard checked his watch. Claire was fifteen minutes late. Not like her. "You guys go ahead and order and I'll see what's keeping her," he said, as he headed for the elevator.

Richard called Claire's name and tapped on her room door. No answer. Inside, he found her sprawled on the floor, like she'd collapsed on her way out. Pushing off panic, he crouched beside her, where she lay breathing but unresponsive, before hurrying to the bathroom for a wet cloth to place on her pale face. Then, grabbing the room phone, he directed the front desk to summon an ambulance, pronto. He put a pillow under Claire's head, and knelt beside his new love, holding her hand as he waited, minute after tense minute, for help to come.

***

Richard snatched up Claire's pocketbook and followed the medics, who maneuvered the stretcher carrying the unconscious patient downstairs to the ambulance. Catching sight of Brandt in the crowd that had gathered to investigate the commotion in the hotel lobby, he signaled for him to follow them to the hospital. Once in the ambulance, he checked Claire's purse for medications. Peeking out from a small inside pocket was a slip of paper, and its message filled him with panic. "My name is Claire Lucas. I have a cerebral aneurysm. In case of an emergency, contact Dr. Bentley."

The neurologist found Richard in the hospital waiting room and shook his hand. Ms. Lucas was lucky on two counts, he said. The aneurysm had leaked only a small amount of blood into the fluid area in the subarachnoid space surrounding the brain. It was a small rupture and slow leak. Had she complained of a bad headache? Richard nodded. She'd been plagued with headaches, and the one this morning had laid her low. A sentinel headache, the doctor explained. It usually signaled a bleed. In some cases, the patient was lucky and the rupture was small, like Claire's. If undetected, it was often followed by a major hemorrhage. When severe enough, this caused blood to travel into the brain substance and back up into the ventricles or caverns where the spinal fluid is produced. More often than not, these bleeds were fatal. Seventy percent of patients died before they even made it to an emergency room or within thirty days of the rupture.

Claire was lucky on another count. Not only was her bleed small, but the neurologist's team was trained to perform a minimally invasive endovascular treatment. "We're going to pass a tiny catheter through the blood vessels in her neck," the doctor explained. "Through this, we'll direct tiny coils to the area of the rupture to occlude the vessel and help it heal. We're going to get her ready for surgery now, okay?" Richard nodded, and after the surgeon strode off, he sank into the waiting room chair. Burying his face in his hands, he could only wait in a state of misery, not knowing how long Claire's ordeal would last.

***

Gilberto Brazzini was sophisticated but also savage, Brandt thought, immediately detecting ruthlessness in his host. He saw it in the forceful way the man strode across his large, exquisitely furnished office in an exclusive section of Rome to receive Kushner and Brandt, who wore his monk's habit and introduced himself as Father Karl Brandt. Brazzini's greeting was not warm, as he herded his visitors toward a designated area for fear they might roam around the space, paw priceless objects, and disrupt the ambience of exclusivity. His gaze was dispassionate and calculating when he gestured for them to sit across from him at his sleek, museum-quality desk. And he was chilly and dismissive, as he fielded questions about Anselmo's painting. Of course, Brandt realized, Brazzini was upset, as he related how that very morning, the painting his guests were inquiring about had been stolen from his Villa Fiori in Milan, right before it was scheduled for shipment to his main residence in Rome. Hadn't Brandt and Kushner just flown in from Milan? he asked. What a coincidence!

Questioned by Brandt, Brazzini admitted that he'd recently bought the painting from an unknown artist in Siena. "Now it seems like all kinds of operators, thieves, and con men are coming out of the woodwork to get their hands on it," he added. "Who'd have thought it?"

Brandt ignored the snide commentary. "Do you have a receipt for the painting? Surely you'll need one for insurance purposes."

Brazzini bristled. "My canceled check is the receipt."

"You mean this?" Brandt held up the uncashed check, a simple piece of paper that had caused Anselmo's barefooted sprint into oncoming traffic. Brazzini reached out to snatch it but Brandt held the check away from his reach. "Signore Brazzini, Anselmo changed his mind about selling his work to you. When he couldn't locate you, he asked for my help to track you down."

"Well, now that you've found me, you can tell Anselmo" — Brazzini said the name like it was an ugly word that had no place in his vocabulary — "that he and I had a deal, a verbal agreement, and we shook hands on it. Asking for the painting back is a breach of that verbal contract, and I have no intention of returning it."

"But you don't have the painting." Brandt wanted to see what effect this simple statement would have on his host.

"I will get it back." Brazzini gestured like he was swatting away an inconsequential detail that didn't trouble a man of his means. "The police think the thief was an amateur who took the painting because he couldn't find anything else of value in the villa. He left tire tracks all over the property, and probably fingerprints."

"Anselmo is dead, a traffic accident," Brandt announced.

"Shame." Brazzini's tone suggested he couldn't care less. As though he was secretly pleased that the world was littered with one less tedious and inferior specimen like Anselmo.

"And now the painting belongs to me, because Anselmo willed it to me," Brandt continued, pressing his advantage.

"Really?" Brazzini gave a sly smile, delighted that the latest problem to cross his desk was so easy to solve. "Well, why don't we just tear up the old check you have there, and I'll make out a new one directly to you. This way, there's no need to go through all kinds of legal gyrations to get the money that is rightfully yours. My lawyers will have to validate the will, however. Did you bring it?"

"I want the painting, not the money," Brandt said, slipping the folded check into his jacket pocket.

"Believe me, the money will do you more good." Brazzini was a little confused at the monk's bravado. He was sure that he had read Brandt correctly, with his ridiculous monk's costume, and his butchered hair that stood up in outlandish spikes. The man was a bumbling mediocrity who should be easy to manipulate.

Brandt had calculated that the check, written in euros, was the equivalent of half a million dollars. "You paid such a lot for a painting by a gifted amateur," he said.

"Yes, I overpaid." Brazzini stood up. He was in control of everything, including this unpleasant conversation that he was now ready to terminate. "Listen, let me know when you're ready for me to make out a new check in your name. Maybe I can throw in a little extra for your trouble. I can see why you'd feel sentimental with the artist being dead, but I ask you, is it worth it to have an expensive, protracted, and upsetting legal battle that you can't win, just for the sake of sentiment? You won't get anywhere near what I paid for the painting if you're thinking of selling it to turn a profit. I am, how shall I put it? idiosyncratic. I paid too much for the canvas, simply because it appealed to me, and I can afford it. Yes? And besides, the painting has been stolen. If you return the check, I'll have the money, but you still won't have the painting."

"That's why I intend to keep in touch," Brandt said, standing to face Brazzini. "We'll talk when you have retrieved the canvas, if you do." He held out his hand, but Brazzini did not take it.

Instead, he walked across the parquet floor and opened the office door so that Brandt and Kushner, who had not uttered a single word, could file out. "God bless you, my son," Brandt said with his most pious smile to Brazzini, who received the blessing like a spit in his face.

Brandt and Kushner remained silent on the ride down in the elevator, as though Brazzini's super-sized ego and mania for control had tagged along, forbidding them to discuss the matter further. But once outside on the sunny Roman sidewalk, the spell was broken. "Brazzini bought Anselmo's painting in person, but he could still be Madrid man," Kushner said.

Brandt wasn't sure. "If he is Madrid man, why didn't Brazzini use an intermediary to purchase Anselmo's painting? Why did he buy it in person with a check, if he wanted to remain truly anonymous and untraceable?"

"Maybe he bought the painting, but then arranged to have it 'stolen' to throw us off the scent and look like he no longer owns it?" Kushner countered.

Brandt thought about it. "How ironic," he said finally, "if a man devoted entirely to acquiring possessions is hijacking the scroll and paintings just to own priceless objects he's incapable of understanding,"

"It wouldn't surprise me," Kushner said. "Brazzini is the kind of jerk who will hoard the finds of the century in a private space solely for his personal consumption. What an asshole! What a shit show!" Brandt frowned at his friend's spicy recap, but Kushner just shrugged.

***

Richard stood over Claire's hospital bed. She looked fragile but still beautiful, as she lay unconscious, despite the trauma of the operation, the starkness of her room in the critical care unit, and the various IVs she sported. Her face was ashen in contrast to the rich brown curls that framed it. The procedure had gone well, and the neurologist was confident that with proper rest, she'd make a full recovery in only weeks.

Despite his relief, Richard felt anguished, convinced that Claire had almost died because of a fundamental flaw in himself that he couldn't fix. *This is like Hilde all over again. My inability to take emotional risks has hurt the person I love. It lost me Hilde forever, and now it's almost cost me Claire. I should have told her the truth about Hilde sooner, and let her know how much I care for her. Then she would have shared how serious her condition was. I would have recognized the headaches for what they were and gotten help.* His phone vibrated and he saw it was Brandt. He felt obliged to answer, his voice husky and raw. "Hello."

"Dear boy." Brandt was extremely gentle, as Richard fought back tears. He was overwhelmed by the misery he still felt over Hilde's death and the events leading up to it, and panic at almost losing Claire.

"Is Claire all right?" Brandt sounded alarmed.

"Yes, she's in recovery and doing fine," Richard mumbled, as runaway emotion made it hard for him to speak. "It's my fault she almost died."

"I don't think so," Brandt said gently. "You're a man of very few faults, Richard."

"You don't know me. How distant I can be. How I hurt others. I hurt Hilde."

"I recall that Hilde hurt you too." Brandt was calm to offset his friend's intensity.

"But I couldn't forgive her. She died because I couldn't forgive her." Richard sounded bereft, as Brandt tried to soothe him. "She died because she couldn't forgive herself. The question is, Richard, can you forgive yourself? I don't know what you've told Claire, but I know her well enough to know that she will understand."

When there was no answer, Brandt went on. "Do you know that the reason we go to confession has as much to do with self-love as penance? We confess because our real or imagined wrongdoing contaminates our life force when we let it fester in secrecy. When we confess ourselves out loud before God and in the presence of another human being, we humbly acknowledge our humanity and refuse to separate ourselves from the love of God. It is ego, pride, and self-loathing that make us nurse our faults and hold onto them. Nothing opens us more to ourselves and to others than recognizing that we are better than perfect, that we are gloriously human and imperfect, always changing, always improving. When she wakes up, talk to Claire, Richard. Confess to her. When you see understanding and acceptance in her eyes, maybe you will learn to understand and accept yourself."

"Did you see Brazzini?" Richard changed the subject, unable to stay vulnerable, or accept another kind word.

"I did, and I'll tell you all about it when I get back, but first I have some other business in Rome."

***

It was almost dusk as Brandt stood gazing at the architectural marvel that was St. Peter's in Rome. The massive dome atop the basilica was testament to Michelangelo's genius, which seemed to know no bounds in the creation of superhuman works of painting, sculpture, and architecture. It amazed Brandt that in his ninetieth year, the greatest of Italian masters still had the vitality, the inspiration, and the audacity to envision a new grandeur for St. Peter's.

Brandt remembered clearly the first time he had stood before the structure, topped by its enormous cupola and adorned with statues of the apostles. Now, like then, the Latin invocation ran through his head: "Tu es Petrus et super hanc petram, aedificabo meam ecclesiam. You are Peter the rock and upon this rock I will build my church," Christ's words to his apostle, Simon Peter, the Church's first pope. And for over two thousand years, cardinals had chanted the same words at the anointing of each new pope.

How fragile the gospel had been after Christ's death, Brandt thought. It had been carried forward in the face of overwhelming odds by so few men and women, Christ's disciples, and their early converts. All of them believing that their messiah would return to them soon, within forty years of his death. But over two thousand years had passed and still He had not come. Nevertheless, the good news of the gospel had spread through twenty centuries, and billions of souls had heard and been transformed by it. Brandt was convinced that the three paintings prophesied by the Angel Scroll were a new expression of the same good news. With his help, they would be brought into the light of day to bring comfort to the faithful and salvation to the lost.

Minutes later, Father Karl Brandt entered through a back door into one of the buildings in the shadow of St. Peter's that housed Vatican offices. From memory, he was able to make his way down a series of corridors to a particular office he had visited only once before, belonging to a man he barely knew, who was on the periphery of the scroll project. Brandt knocked and hearing no answer, he entered. The small room was in shadow, lit by a Tiffany desk lamp. Brandt took in the crowd of artifacts on display in cases and shelves. He walked around the room slowly, trying to get a feel for its occupant. He trailed his fingers against rough, unglazed pottery and picked up an arrowhead, blackened and smoothed by time, fingering its blunt tip. He detected the faint odor of incense that clung to a black jacket hanging on a closet door. But the overall smell was of mustiness, of objects that, despite being brought above ground, still retained the odor of the earth where they'd been buried for so long. A thick ancient book caught Brandt's eye. It was a Celtic manuscript containing exquisite images in brightly colored illuminated inks. Brandt was gingerly turning the yellowing pages, when it dawned on him that he had seen this exact book before.

Minutes later, it was pure luck that brought Vincent Malveau back to his office to pick up a few favorite pornographic magazines that he kept locked in a slim secret drawer in his ornately carved desk. He exited the building, left the environs of St. Peter's, and set out through the streets, free of heavy tourist traffic now that it was early October. He was headed for his cache of bones in the small, dingy apartment, in a rougher section of the city, that was nevertheless a virtual paradise to him. Senior Vatican antiquarian, pervert, and dissembler, Vincent Malveau strolled the Roman streets. Close behind and unseen, a short, stocky man with spiky white hair, who looked just like a regular working stiff, now that he was back in department store clothes, was following him.

***

Lincoln Swelt sat in his rental van, outside a hotel in the heart of Milan, waiting for his mark to exit. He'd been in place for over three hours and felt edgy. Had he missed the guy? Swelt's bald head glistened with sweat despite the light rain, as he bit into a pastry, showering his lap with flakes. He brushed off the debris, and when he looked up, he spotted the mark handing his ticket to the valet, who took it and returned with a maroon minivan. "Let's get this show on the road," Swelt muttered, pulling out into traffic, a few car lengths behind his mark who was finally on the move.

First stop, a Federal Express depot on the outskirts of Milan. Swelt watched from a distance as workers slid the large, heavily wrapped, flat six-by-four-foot package into the mark's minivan.

The car took off and looked to be heading toward the city center, before taking an unexpected detour off the main highway. After a few minutes, it stopped at a mini-storage facility. Swelt parked and followed on foot, as the van stopped before a storage bay, eighth in from the end of the row. Unseen, Swelt watched the mark unlock and raise the metal door, transfer the package from the van into the bay, then close and lock the door again. The man got back in his van and was off, but this time Swelt didn't follow. Instead, he waited five minutes before slowly pulling up next to the bay.

A man, Swelt mused, might enter the joint as only a mediocre thief and come out an expert. If you'd been in and out of prison as often as he had, you'd know how easy it was to get a higher education in the various aspects of larceny. The proper way to case a joint, pick a lock, forge a document, even make explosives. "Child's play," Swelt muttered, as he teased the padlock meant to keep intruders out, and it clicked open in less than a minute. What he saw inside made Lincoln Swelt smile and rub his palm back and forth across his bald head in jubilation. Just as he'd hoped, not one but two identical packages sat in the otherwise empty bay. With these two paintings, and the one he had taken from Villa Fiori, he now had all three items he had been hired to steal.

All his fretting about whether he could handle the job had been for nothing. The whole caper had been a breeze, and almost made him nostalgic for the old days. Lincoln headed back toward the highway, thinking about the nice dinner he was gonna buy Annie.

Chapter Eleven

Visions

The first thing Claire saw on waking was Richard, bleary eyed and unshaven, holding her hand, his chair pulled up as close to her bed as he could get it. Drained and unable to speak, she felt the searing pain of a headache that persisted despite the painkillers. She tried a smile, but her face refused to cooperate. Seeing her awake, Richard relaxed the frown he had worn since they had arrived at the hospital, and managed a concerned smile. He kissed her forehead, her cheek, the tip of her nose, and then, softly, her lips. She felt the relief and the tenderness in his kisses that told her better than any love letter what she meant to him.

"How do you feel?" he whispered. She tried to shake her head to indicate she felt so-so, but the smallest movement sent waves of pain cascading through her brain.

"The aneurysm leaked, but just a little. You had surgery, and it went well. You're fine. I was so worried," Richard gushed. Claire crinkled her eyes and nose to signal she was okay. She managed to lift a limp hand to shoo him by flicking her fingers. He looked exhausted and she wanted him to go rest and freshen up, knowing he'd come right back in the morning. He kissed her, letting his lips stay gently pressed against her forehead for a moment, and then he left.

A nurse came in and out, chatting and cooing in Italian, brisk and efficient. Claire couldn't understand a word, but she felt comforted and reassured that she was out of danger. She looked around the room. It was as bland and unremarkable as any American hospital room, except all the signs and equipment were in Italian. She squinted out of her left eye. It wasn't dark. She saw a blur of light. Concentrating too hard hurt. She relaxed, peering through the egg-shaped bright spot, until she was able to make out an impossibly long cylindrical tunnel with a brilliant light at its end. It looked just like the kind of tunnel that she'd heard survivors of near-death experience describe. But she wasn't dead or near death. She was worse for wear but alive and awake in an Italian hospital bed.

The better Claire controlled her breathing, the more stable her vision became. Slowly, she breathed in for five and out for five. Soon, she realized that what she'd thought was a tunnel was in fact a long, long road, stretching far beyond any conceivable horizon to a brilliant point of light at its end. The road was familiar. Where had she seen it before? It was the road in Sebastian's painting, but it was deserted with no sign of travelers saying farewell. She softened her gaze, and the road was no longer confined to the small opening of the mandorla. Instead, the vista expanded until it filled her entire field of vision. She felt her physical self fading away, along with the sensation of existing everywhere at once, as the atoms of her being dissolved into the space all around her that was filled with clear light. She rested in the light with no sense of time, until she finally became aware, once again, that the hospital room was back in view. It was 4 a.m., and nearly five hours had passed in almost an instant.

The next morning, her neurologist visited and determined that she was making excellent progress. By mid-morning, Richard was back, rested and clean shaven, with the latest news. Brandt had returned from his trip to see Mr. Anonymous in Rome. "His name is Gilberto Brazzini. He bought the painting from Anselmo and has been storing it at his villa in Milan, but guess what?"

"The painting has gone missing?" Claire said.

"Correct." Richard smiled weakly and Claire rolled her eyes. Talk about the can't shoot straight gang, they were always a day late and a dollar short.

"I'm starting to think we don't stand a chance against whoever it is that's fighting us for the paintings. We'll never get our hands on one canvas let alone all three." She was tired and her voice was a little hoarse, but she was feeling stronger.

"I wouldn't count Brandt out yet," Richard said.

Claire shrugged. She didn't want to think about Brandt. She'd had a scare, and it was time for her to bail on the monk's ill-advised venture. All the chasing around had exhausted and stressed her out, and probably caused her bleed. She was lucky she'd come out of it alive and without any serious complications. How would she feel if she never again set eyes on her own canvas? She knew she'd be perfectly fine. She'd satisfied the overwhelming urge to create a work that had become an object of fascination, as well as a magnet for all kinds of unsavory characters, but now its fate was beyond her control. If Brandt needs to keep hunting for the scroll and the paintings, best of luck to him, but I'm signing off.

Richard was watching her. "You look tired. You want me to come back later?"

"Yes, I need to rest." Claire tilted her chin up. The first time that she'd ever sought a kiss from him. He leaned down and catching his distinctive scent, she felt it stir her. She gave him a loving look and he caressed her face. "See you later, beautiful."

Beautiful? Good lord, had she ever looked so exhausted and worse for wear? It must be love he's feeling because it's definitely blind.

Alone again, Claire focused on the mandorla, controlling her breath, until the familiar roadway appeared and straightaway filled her entire field of vision. She concentrated on the far-off light, hoping it would absorb her like before. But this time, a figure caught her attention, an Indian woman, petite, fine boned, and dressed in a beautiful purple sari that shimmered in the ambient light. As the woman's face came into focus, Claire recognized her as the dying wife from *Absent a Miracle*, but now she was alive and alert. Claire watched her walk along the road, past the banks of a river, and a row of small mud plaster houses, down a small alley way, and into a clearing. She passed through an elaborate brass gateway, into the courtyard of a splendid two-story home. In the courtyard, five men, seated cross-legged on large silk brocade pillows, were waiting for her. Claire recognized the men from her dreams. The woman's handsome husband was in animated conversation with the young master and his three followers. The woman greeted them and went into the house, returning with a large jug of lassi. She looked flushed, her upper lip moist with a light sweat, and her small hand trembled from the strain of hoisting the heavy jug. The young rabbi placed a hand on her brow, and the woman closed her eyes, as though his touch was cooling an inner blaze. Claire felt her own face and temples flush. The young wife excused herself. She didn't feel well and needed to lie down. Climbing to an upper floor, she lay on the low platform bed so familiar to Claire from her recurring dream, and as the woman closed her eyes, Claire was instantly pitched into darkness.

When she woke up, Richard was standing beside her bed. How long had she slept? Had she been dreaming? She scanned the mandorla, but it was dark.

"You're doing great. The doctor is pleased," Richard said with the kind of relief that comes after the worst fears have failed to materialize.

Claire swallowed, trying to find her voice. "Can I go home?"

He looked sympathetic. "No, not for a couple of weeks, I'm afraid."

Her face fell. Where would she stay? She'd had her fill of hotels, even the good ones. Richard looked pleased with himself. "I hope you don't mind, but Lake Como is no more than fifty miles from here, and I've managed to rent a villa with lake views. The least I can do is keep you comfortable while you convalesce."

There it was again, the businesslike tone that implied he was acting out of duty or obligation. Claire frowned and Richard caught himself. "I want to be with you, Claire, if it's all right with you. I want to be somewhere romantic and wonderful. I want to hold you every day and tell you how grateful I am that I found you and was spared losing you."

He's gone from holding it all back to letting it all out, she thought and smiled. "It's okay with me," she told him. Sitting up in the bed, she reached up for him, so that he could wrap his arms around her and become entangled in the wires that tied her to the monitors.

She patted the covers, inviting him to sit, and taking his chin in her fine artist's hand, she angled his face to look directly into hers. "It's time," she whispered and saw resignation in his eyes, as he acknowledged that he could no longer avoid what had gone unspoken between them. And then, sitting on her hospital bed with Milan's busy street noise drifting in through a window, Richard told Claire about the long, painful saga that had almost demolished his life.

He had fallen very in love with Hilde. She was ten years his junior and active in the more glamorous regions of his business. She consulted to the best New York galleries, helping to locate and authenticate manuscripts, art, and antiques; connecting buyers and sellers. Theirs had been the perfect attraction of opposites. She was gregarious, vivacious, and outgoing. He was introverted, inexpressive, and studious. These differences fueled their passion initially but eventually they led to conflict. Hilde loved to dress up and go out and about, always active in the New York social scene. She had to do it really, to be successful in her work.

For the first few years of their seven year marriage, Richard was content to accompany her when she went out. Just being with her and watching her charm everyone she encountered was exciting. It made all the small talk and social chitchat he so hated bearable. But after a while, he needed less time with Hilde to appreciate her. He didn't need to attend every party or event with her. He trusted her, he said, so why not go without him? He would be there, waiting for her at home, absorbed in his books, his work, and the solitary pursuits that entertained him far more than the social whirlwind she relished. Hilde didn't like the arrangement and complained about it all the time. She knew he loved her, but that wasn't good enough. She wanted more of his time, more of his attention. And then suddenly, she stopped complaining. She seemed happy to socialize without him after all.

For nearly a year, they were content again, almost as happy as when they had first met, despite their respective lives running on different tracks. He spent his time quietly hunting down the manuscripts he collected, studied, and sold. She spent hers gaining more and more notoriety as a smart, beautiful, and accomplished woman about town.

After a while, it was Richard who began to miss Hilde, as she scheduled more weekends away with a wide circle of friends. In the summer months, she went, like many fashionable New Yorkers, out to the Hamptons of Long Island, for boating, tennis, shopping, sunbathing, and restaurant hopping. In the winter, there were cozy weekends upstate, in the Berkshires, or out in Pennsylvania for skiing, antiquing, and socializing with monied contacts on sprawling estates. She had so many friends, and a glut of invitations. You can come if you like, she would say on Friday nights, as she packed another weekend bag. But Richard preferred to stay home, and more and more he wanted Hilde to stay with him. The pendulum was swinging too far in the opposite direction for his liking. He had been content with distance in their relationship, but somewhere along the line, distance had turned into remoteness. Hilde was hardly home anymore, and Richard missed her.

One fall night, during a quiet dinner for two in front of the fire in their New York apartment, Richard asked his wife to text him her plans for the coming weekend. He should know where she was in case of an emergency, he said. But, in truth, he was hatching a plan to surprise her. Hilde thought he was headed to Boston for a one-day conference on Anglo-Saxon manuscripts, and had no clue that he intended to show up unannounced to spend the weekend with her and her friends on their latest outing. He smiled to himself as they finished their dinner, sipping the last of his wine before the warmth of the fire and plotting his surprise. He imagined Hilde's eyes shining, her hands brought to her cheeks in surprised delight as, in an act of long-awaited romance, he finally turned up for weekend festivities, delivering spontaneity right when his wife least expected it.

Hilde told him she was planning to attend a birthday party in Westchester County, New York, for her old pal Patsy Miller, who had been a few years ahead of her at Brown. "Patsy won't mind if you join us, and afterwards, a few of us are going on to spend the rest of the weekend at her new place in Armonk. Are you sure you don't want to come?"

Richard shook his head. "I'm headed to Boston for the conference early Saturday morning. It's too good to miss. I just need to know where you'll be in case there's a problem."

Hilde kissed the top of his head. "What problem? Why are you always so gloomy?"

Her remark got him thinking. Was he gloomy? She lectured him constantly about his reticence. Why was he so introverted? Why couldn't he be more spontaneous? Well, this weekend he would show her that romance and spontaneity was something he could muster.

Come Friday evening, just forty-five minutes after Hilde had left their Upper East Side apartment, Richard climbed into his car and settled in for the hour-long ride out of Manhattan and through the small, picturesque towns where many well to do Manhattanites maintained their weekend retreats. He pulled up to the rambling two-hundred-year-old colonial house that had been converted into The Spyglass Inn. It was a cold November night, as Richard walked into the cozy bar. Heated by a roaring fire, the place was decorated in classic New England style, with dark woods, rich leather Chesterfield sofas, and chairs upholstered in a traditional flame stitch, while hunting scenes hung in gilded frames on the walls. Richard told the hostess he was looking for Patsy Miller, party of ten, and the statuesque blond sentry checked and rechecked the computer, before announcing finally that there was no such reservation. Was he sure he had the right date and location? Richard reread Hilde's text. Yes, it was definitely The Spyglass Inn, Armonk, New York, Friday at 8 p.m.

Richard looked around the bar and then ducked through a low doorway into an elegant dining room that hummed with the quiet chatter of dinners. The room was lit with brass candle chandeliers and filled with tables dressed in cut lace cloths and delicate stem ware. Seeing no large parties, he turned to leave, but then turned back. He saw light reflect off the large silver pendant the woman at the corner table wore. He knew the pendant. He knew the woman. It was Hilde. But he couldn't fathom the rest. There was no party, no large table with excited guests and birthday girl at the head. There was just Hilde and Richard's good friend, Trevor Dunne. Such a handsome couple in a perfectly romantic setting. They were holding hands, and they looked very in love.

He wanted to flee, get back in his car and drive home. He needed silence to absorb the shock and process the information. No matter what the problem, he always looked for alone time, quiet and calm, so that his mind in all its wonderful efficiency could break down the issue and slowly digest it. Tonight the problem confronting him was painful and overwhelming, and he had no idea how to dismantle it so it would hurt him less.

Too late, Hilde, facing the doorway where he stood, saw her husband, and released Trevor's hand. Her lover turned in his chair to follow the direction of Hilde's open-mouthed stare, until they were both looking in shocked recognition at Richard. This just made the mess harder for him to handle. First, the shock of finding Hilde and Trevor together, and now a scene of some kind. Richard turned and fled the restaurant, taking long, quick strides back into the November chill that jolted him out of his shock.

His flight from the inn was one of the things that Hilde reproached him with later. Confronted with a challenger for her affections, what had he done? He hadn't stayed and fought for her. He'd simply walked, no he'd run away. Indignation, anger, even violence would have been preferable, she said. Anything but his withdrawal, the distance that he habitually created in their relationship.

Richard was not looking at Claire. He had turned his face to one side and was looking at one of the room's white antiseptic walls, unable to tolerate eye contact. Like it was easier just to recount these humiliating events in a low, measured voice with no hint of emotion.

The affair, Richard told Claire, had been going on for almost a year. Hilde was planning to divorce him and be with Trevor. In the worst of clichés, Hilde's lover was Richard's friend and colleague of fifteen years, and resembled Richard only in that they shared the same area of study. In every other way, Trevor was a more perfect match for Hilde, handsome, adventurous, outgoing, warm, demonstrative. He paused and clamped his lips together. Claire saw how he tortured himself with comparisons, convincing himself that he didn't measure up to Trevor and had lost his wife to a better man. She had seen Richard's rival only once and very briefly, the day he held the door for her in

Vermont. What was her impression? Handsome? Yes, but too well-groomed, too slick maybe. Who knows? Trevor had hurt Richard, lied and betrayed his friend, so he was definitely the lesser man in her book.

"Did Hilde leave you?" Claire asked.

"No, she didn't. When it came to crunch time, she decided to stay. She broke it off with Trevor, told me she regretted the affair, and begged for my forgiveness."

"Did you give it?"

"I tried. I wanted to. I just needed time to work it through. Hilde thought that I was deliberately withholding my forgiveness and punishing her."

"Were you?"

"I don't think so. I was..." He paused, as though unable to describe his feelings with any of the words that sprang so readily to Claire's mind. "You were hurt," she prompted him.

"Hurt." Richard contemplated the word, turning it over in his mind, like one of his artifacts, inspecting its meaning to see if it lined up with the anguished, empty feeling that had filled him in the weeks and months after Hilde's betrayal. "Yes, I was hurt," he said finally.

"Why did she kill herself?" Claire went right to the heart of the painful wound that had kept them apart and ripped off the bandage.

"Because, after the affair, life was different, hellish and painful," Richard said. "Infidelity shatters a relationship. It's like a crystal ornament that's been dropped. It can take forever to find all the pieces and glue them back together, make them fit. Who knows if you'll ever find all the slivers and shards? And it can't really be beautiful in the same way it was, not when there are cracks and joints with chips and pieces missing. But maybe with time, with enough patience, it's possible, if you really love the thing, to see past the damage and hold onto its essence."

"Was Hilde scared your relationship wouldn't recover?" Claire asked.

"Perhaps. Probably. I'm more patient, painstaking. I was willing to go through the process of finding all the pieces and cementing them together, but Hilde was different. She wanted our marriage to be magically restored the minute she gave Trevor up, and that just wasn't possible. She was depressed and despondent, and then she was dead."

Claire watched Richard stand, walk to the window and back again, like he needed to put distance between himself and his past that hung in the air, thickening and weighting the space between them. He had told his story, and Claire felt him mentally close the book, but she sensed there was more, something he wasn't saying. He was still holding back.

"That's it?" she asked.

"Isn't it enough?" he snapped, like he had heard her question as criticism. He had been forced to tell her a saga in which he was not the hero but the cuckold, and now she was complaining because she didn't like the way it ended? Claire sensed how raw he was beneath the composure he always affected.

"I have to go," he said, standing at a distance. Claire held out her hand to take his, and because she was bed bound, he had to come closer. She took his warm hand and squeezed it. "You are a good man and I love you. Thank you for telling me this. I know it wasn't easy. Come back when you're ready. Take all the time you need."

She could feel his strong need for self-protection pulling him away from her, but he pushed through his resistance and embraced her, holding her tightly. She felt his heart, pressed almost against her own, beating fast, before he released her, turned, and left. *I see now how fragile he is, Claire thought, but that's okay. I have no intention of dropping him.*

The two-story villa sat on a bluff above the lakeshore. Claire curled her fingers around the elegant black wrought iron rail that bordered the second-floor stone terrace overlooking Lake Como. Behind her was the picturesque village of Santa Maria Rezzonico. Built on the sunny west side of the lake, the village nestled into the rock, with winding cobbled streets that descended to a beach overshadowed by a beautiful, second-century castle. She thought wistfully of Jake and their honeymoon on another lake, Lake George, in Upstate New York. They had rented a cabin on its shores and spent their time hiking and canoeing and splurging on dinners at the fancy Sagamore Hotel.

After Jake's death, a friend had tried to reassure Claire that the initial agony of grief would eventually subside, and that with each rotation of the earth, her pain would lessen. A time would come when whole hours might pass without her feeling nauseous from a grief that she would gradually learn to subdue. After a long while, it would be possible to push the hurt to the back of consciousness where it would exist as a background ache. Pain would flare up without warning, of course, but it would be manageable. Eventually, her friend said, it would come to pass that the young widow might recognize the beginnings of nostalgia, which is to say, she would experience remembering without pain. Claire had wept at the lie and shook her head. She knew none of this could possibly be true. She knew her grief would always be a searing attack on her senses, a constant, hateful companion that was with her every second of every day. But here she was, looking out over Lake Como, with some measure of time and space separating her from the first brutal impact of Jake's death. Her pain was easing, and perhaps nostalgia was dawning. She was bound to heal. No point clinging to the sharpness of grief. Better to let it soften and transform into something she could absorb into her being and carry with her as she moved forward.

She thought about Jake, allowing the memories to come, gentler and easier to handle now. Their love had been tried and true, deep and rich. Her love for Richard was exciting and new, only lightly tested. There was no way to compare the two loves, and she recoiled from the idea. She gazed at the water, like she might find Jake there, on a boat, in a sunshine yellow slicker, smiling up at her. Bodhipaksa had told her to find him everywhere, on the ground underfoot, and in the sky. She kissed the tips of her fingers and stretched out her hand to find Jake's face. She touched the air, knowing he was out there, somewhere. She relaxed, caressed by the breeze, and soothed by the sounds of the lake.

Visions were coming almost daily now. To trigger them, Claire had only to focus her intention, stabilize her breathing, and wait for the familiar scenes to arise in the mandorla before filling her gaze. Successive visions told her more about the fate of the young Indian wife, with the latest one revealing the most so far. Once again, Claire had seen the Christlike figure depart the sick room and leave the dying woman, not long before she closed her eyes and succumbed to death. She studied the woman's motionless corpse as it lay unattended in the bedroom, and what happened next filled her with amazement. The dead woman opened her eyes, sat upright, and swinging her legs over the side of her low bed, she stood. And then, the resurrected woman left the house, walking through the courtyard, into the narrow alleyways, and onto the main street. She hurried past the river, and onto the long dusty road, until at last she was moving toward the brilliant light that was her destination. The light drew closer until, like a benign fog, it swallowed the woman. As she watched, Claire, too, was engulfed by the same light, wrapped in a sensation of freedom, weightlessness, and indescribable happiness. And then the woman was gone, and in her place on the roadway, Claire saw the young rabbi. Just like in Sebastian's painting, he was saying goodbye to his three followers. Claire watched as the master pointed to the light. "I am the light of the world," he said, repeating the words she had seen written in mosaics, in the book that the Christ child held in Dormition Abbey.

Claire felt lifted out of time, precisely aware that no time existed. There was only this light and her presence within it. A strange epiphany was upon her. Everything and everyone somehow lived in the eternal now. How can I grieve for Jake when he is right here? she thought. Everything he has been and ever will be, right here, right now, always with me. And then, Anselmo's garden appeared, and Anselmo was there, looking like he had in his sketches, wretched and tormented, crouched in shadow and encroaching darkness. Only now his face began to shift, his features morphing into endless new appearances. How many times? A hundred? A thousand? Soon she no longer recognized it as a face, but as a blur of evolving shapes and features, sometimes tantalizingly real and recognizable but ultimately ephemeral and changing. It occurred to her that form itself was irrelevant. Beneath form was the clear, brilliant light of creation from which everything manifested.

Standing on the villa's terrace, Claire contemplated how her dream life and waking life were uniting. She knew Anselmo and Sebastian as painters, but she also knew them as the disciples from her visions. Who am I? I am the third painter, but am I the third disciple? she wondered out loud, but the answers eluded her.

Throwing off the mystery, she decided on a closer look at the lake. Narrow stone steps cut into the rock on which the villa sat formed a path down the steep, rocky slope. She counted forty-four, as she descended to the pebbled shore below. The doctor in Milan had cautioned her to rest, avoid stress, and be alert to unusually bad headaches. She shouldn't really be going off alone, but she wanted to explore and give Richard a break. He was indoors waiting for Brandt to arrive. He had been a tireless nurse over the last couple of days, cooking and reading to her, and taking her arm as they went for gentle strolls around the simple but immaculately groomed property with its captivating lake views.

She decided to walk the hundred yards or so to investigate the villa next door, and arriving, she saw the place looked deserted, no tenants. She peered through the windows at the rustic but tasteful interior, before turning to walk back and ascend the rocky steps. Nearing the top, she could hear Richard. "Claire almost died, Karl. I need to understand what is happening. Tell me what the translation says about the three painters." Claire stopped and remained still, perched just below the terrace.

"Richard, I understand that you're upset, but I can't give you a clear answer. The translation is imprecise and the meaning ambiguous." Claire recognized Brandt's familiar calm tone.

Richard was out of patience. "Please stop hedging. This woman means too much to me."

Claire realized her heart was beating faster, as she heard Richard voice a worry that had been preoccupying her. Two of three painters that Brandt believed the scroll prophesied were both dead at a young age. Was she facing the same fate? In her rational moments, she could throw off the fear as just superstition. But there was something in Brandt's conviction that the scroll's predictions were factual that unnerved her. As long as Brandt believed so completely in the scroll, its prophecy had the power to influence her and make her fear what it foretold.

"The words can mean many different things, not just one interpretation." Claire heard Brandt's impenetrable cool giving way.

"Karl, please just tell me what it says," Richard implored. There was a long silence, and then Brandt relented. "The text says that when the paintings are gathered together all three painters will be dead."

"No!" Richard gasped, and his mind ran in two directions. Commonsense told him that Brandt was indulging in superstition and this pulled him toward reason and calm. But his fear that the past was repeating itself, and he was destined to lose Claire as well as Hilde, pushed him into irrational panic. Claire pressed both palms against the bluff to steady herself on the narrow step.

"It doesn't necessarily mean physical death," she heard Brandt argue. "The word in the text can be translated to mean dead in a spiritual sense, devoid of hope. Anselmo was certainly desperate when we met him."

"Karl, Anselmo may have been spiritually dead, but now he is physically dead too." Richard was infuriated. "Why didn't you tell me this before? We need to get Claire back to the hospital."

"I don't want to go back to the hospital." Claire felt her face turn pale as she stepped onto the terrace where Richard and Brandt sat facing each other, on sun-bleached deck chairs. The sun was out, the rippling water was a cerulean blue, and the breeze was still warm. It was a near perfect day, meant for pleasure, and none of its beauty was disturbed, as Claire stood before the two men, struggling with the idea of her own mortality.

Her visions had given her a taste of what she might describe as expanded consciousness. Perhaps they were only dreams, or hallucinations, or a neurological tic from the effects of the aneurysm, but whatever they were, they had allowed her to transcend day-to-day reality, mundane consciousness, and the gross heaviness of the physical plane. These remarkable visions had felt as real as waking life, but at this moment, such other-worldly experiences seemed remote and irrelevant. She wanted to live on as a flesh and blood woman, and not as illusion or play of light, or whatever fanciful notion she had concocted in her tripped-out state. She wanted to stay with Richard. She loved him.

He came toward her and held her. "It's not real," he whispered into her hair. It's all just silly superstition and wishful thinking.

It's coincidence and conjecture, like empty predictions from a fairground fortune teller. We don't have to take it seriously. To hell with the scroll, and the paintings, and all the stupid make believe."

Claire looked past Richard at Brandt and his worried expression. He believes the prophesy, Claire thought, every last word of it. Life was shocking in what it could take away so carelessly, with little disruption to the flow of things. She heard the water lapping on the shore below and felt warm sun on her back. Nature was beautiful and steadfast, untouched by the grief that was everywhere, unmoved by her plight. As Claire held on to Richard, she recognized an inner voice she couldn't silence. It said the prophecy was true and she might die.

***

Lincoln Swelt was in a great mood and whistling away happily on the entire drive to his appointment. He and Annie were scheduled to fly home the day after tomorrow now that the job had gone off without a hitch. In the back of his van were three large packages. One he had lifted from Villa Fiori, and the other two he had snatched from the storage place. Lincoln didn't know what the packages were, and he didn't care. The boss wanted them, and his job was to deliver them. He stopped the van, set the hand break, and marveled at the beautiful view of the lake. Bet there's great fishing in there, he thought. And the stone house looked classy. Amazing how the other half lived. He climbed out of the van's cab and cracked a smile as he saw a short, energetic figure approaching. "Father Brandt!" He towered over the monk, unabashedly gripping the shorter man in a tight hug, tears springing, as he acknowledged his treasured bond with his mentor, the man he loved like a father. Lincoln saw Brandt was out of his habit and laughing. "Come on, Lincoln, no crying, man. This is a happy time." Brandt poked a finger into his friend's strong, wide chest.

"I know." Lincoln wiped a sleeve across his runny nose and gently brushed a palm across his bald head. "I'm just happy to see you, Father."

Claire thought she recognized the big bald guy that Brandt had escorted into the villa's kitchen and was introducing, but she didn't know from where. Finally, it came to her. She'd seen him, from Anselmo's window, standing on the street corner in Siena. "Some iced tea, Mr. Swelt?" Lincoln nodded, took the glass Claire offered, and said how nice it was to hear voices from back home speaking English. Italians talked too fast. Not that he could understand them if they talked any slower.

Lincoln filled Brandt in on his news. He lived full time in Florida now with Annie, and the weather suited him better than up north in New York. Claire had no clue how Brandt knew this tough guy, but she did notice how the monk beamed at him, like he was the prodigal son returned to eat the fatted calf.

"So how did you two meet?" she asked.

"I grew up in an orphanage in Queens," Swelt explained, "and when I was fourteen, I went to Israel as part of a youth program. That's where I met Father Brandt."

"I caught him trying to pilfer the money offered for candles at the abbey, but I knew under all the misbehaving that Lincoln was a good boy." Brandt smiled at Swelt, and the big guy grinned like a kindergartner whose dad had turned up for show and tell.

"Father Brandt got permission for me to stay in Jerusalem for six weeks and work on a dig he was directing."

"He worked very hard," Brandt said with pride. This was too comical, Claire thought. The learned Brandt appeared to have an unbelievable soft spot for their surprise guest. But why was he here?

"I visited Father Brandt every summer for three years, till my first stint in the joint stopped me from going," Swelt continued.

"First?" Claire raised both eyebrows.

"Yeah, I was in and out of prison for a bit of thieving, you know, larceny. No drugs. No violence. I wouldn't let Father Brandt down like that."

"It could have been much worse." Brandt pinned Claire with a judge not lest ye be judged look.

"Oh, yeah," Swelt sounded chipper. "Most of the crowd what I ran with is dead now — drugs, murder, all of it. Remember Bernie Marchello, Father?" Brandt nodded. "They found him out back of a Chinese takeout with his throat cut."

Swelt looked at Claire. "Father Brandt saved my life." He turned back to the monk. "And like I said in my letters, many times, Father, I'm sorry I done time in prison and let you down like that, but I'm going straight now. My knees are blown, and no good for thieving. But it's not even that. I've got Annie to look after, and it's like you always say, it's better not having bad shit on your conscience. I've done my time, paid my debts to society. I wouldn't come out of retirement and do no job for nobody but you. I told that to Annie. I'd give my life for that man, I said. Do time and everything if I had to, but, as it turns out, no need. Job went smooth as butter."

Brandt patted his protégé's hand. "Well, Lincoln, I appreciate your help, and I want to reassure you that you have only helped me to recover items that rightfully belong to us."

Claire caught sight of Richard, who had just come in from outdoors with a puzzled expression. She shrugged. All self-pity at her predicament evaporated, as her mind whirred, trying to figure out this latest development. Swelt had retrieved "items" for Brandt. Paintings? How many?

Lincoln was making moves to leave, so she shook the enormous hand he extended and walked through the living room with Richard and Brandt to see their visitor out. Hallelujah!

Leaning against the wall, near the front door, were three large, equal-sized packages. Under Brandt's direction, Lincoln Swelt had apparently performed a miracle and recovered all three paintings. What was he going to do for an encore? Pull the missing scroll out of his ear?

"There is just one more thing I need you to do for me, Lincoln," Brandt said, as he linked Swelt's arm and led him away, out of earshot.

Minutes later, Claire heard the van pull away as Brandt came indoors, grinning and very pleased with himself.

"Are those the paintings?" Richard asked.

"If I'm not mistaken." Brandt said.

"How did you find them?"

"I will tell you later."

"Can we open them?" Claire moved toward the packages.

"Not yet." Brandt's command was firm. Then he softened. "Please, it's important that we don't open them just yet. We should wait for the right time and place." Claire stopped and looked at Richard, who nodded. Brandt had engineered the paintings' return, it was only fair to let him control how and where they were unveiled.

"Did you retrieve the scroll too?" Richard asked.

"No, but we will, very, very soon." Brandt picked up his cell phone and pressed speed dial. "Kushner, you back in Jerusalem yet? Good. Wait for me there." He paused. "Yes, I'll come there soon...Yes, things are going very well...You take care too." He hung up the phone and rubbed his hands together with satisfaction. "How about an early dinner? I have a big evening planned, and later, I'm expecting a guest."

***

As the afternoon light faded, Swelt approached the pick-up spot and scratched his head. He had done as Brandt requested, calling the mark and offering to tell him the whereabouts of his missing paintings in exchange for fifty thousand dollars. He had suggested they meet at the mini-storage, so the man could see for himself that his packages were no longer there. "You place the money in front of the storage bay, where I can collect it and drop off the directions," Swelt directed him on the phone.

Pulling up to the mini-storage, Swelt spotted the mark's car parked at the far end of the row. He quickly pulled on a knit cap, got out of his van, and picked up an oversized envelope that was propped against the metal door of the familiar bay. He looked inside. Yep, there was a good bunch of money. He could tell from eyeballing the wad that was fastened with an elastic band, and doing a quick calculation, that all fifty thousand dollars looked to be there. Growing up, he had hardly attended school. He'd bunked off nearly every day and couldn't recall ever sitting through an entire math class, but when it came to money, Lincoln Swelt could count just fine.

Now it was his turn to deliver, so he set down his small envelope containing directions to the villa on Lake Como, got back in his vehicle and took off. Only later, at a gas station farther down the highway, did he stop and carefully count the money, before calling Brandt. "It's all here, Father, fifty thousand dollars. What do you want me to do with it?"

"Keep it," Brandt instructed.

"Shit, I can't do that, Father!"

"Lincoln, you are a good man, and I am proud of you. Now keep the money and use it to take care of Annie." Brandt hung up, leaving Swelt to rub his bald head like a bewildered child.

***

Claire served spaghetti in colorful bowls in the villa's comfortable country kitchen. She made an excellent marinara sauce that was good enough to rival the natives. Richard sliced the fresh baked bread he had bought earlier in the village and served it into a wooden bowl, as the three friends sat down to eat, totally at ease together.

Earlier, Richard had taken Claire for a stroll. They had walked and talked, calming each other's fears, reasoning their way through worries about her health. The surgeon who had operated on her had averted a crisis and assured her she would be fine. Maybe she had dodged a bullet, and this was where all the coincidences that seemed to validate the scroll's predictions ran out. Yes, Sebastian and Anselmo were dead, but Claire was on the road to recovery.

As they finished dinner, Claire decided that now was a good time to tell Richard and Brandt about the mandorla, and her recent and most fascinating visions yet. She'd made a list of all the visual disturbances that had occurred since the opening had appeared months earlier. What had begun with simple flashes of light had developed in recent days into full-blown picture shows.

Brandt set down his fork to listen, transfixed by Claire's revelations. "I'm taking Josie McLean's advice," Claire told her friends. "I try not to judge or label these strange waking dreams or visions or psychic disturbances. I just accept them at face value, accept that they are happening to me, and I don't know why. The visions bring a mysterious sense of knowing with them, sensations and intuitions that I understand but can't validate. Explaining them is like describing dreams that make absolute sense while you are having them, but sound totally irrational when you try to convey them to someone else."

Richard had told Claire about a theory that claimed the historical Jesus had spent time in India as a young man. It was supposedly during an unrecorded period of his life, before He began His ministry, which ended with His death around age thirty-three. Claire's visions had begun with a Christlike figure in India. She confessed now that she didn't know if this was significant, just coincidence, or simply her imagination piecing together the random flotsam and jetsam that floated around in her psyche.

In Benares, India, Claire continued, the young master attracts at least three devoted followers, and he's befriended by a wealthy man whose wife dies from a sudden illness during his stay. "I don't know why the master won't perform a miracle. Maybe he isn't ready to begin a ministry of healing. Perhaps he is trying to reassure his followers that death is an illusion, a man-made fear, because I see the woman rise from her deathbed and travel down a road toward a brilliant light that absorbs her." Claire paused to see if her friends were following along. "Any questions?"

Richard went to say something, but Brandt interrupted. "No questions. Please continue."

"In my vision, Anselmo and Sebastian are two of the master's followers. They're in the rich man's house that I painted, and later, I recognized them on the road that Sebastian painted, saying farewell to their master. They want to go with him, but they have to stay and fulfill their purpose. I think their purpose is to create the paintings. According to the logic of the vision, the dimensions of time and space as we know them don't exist. Events aren't linear and somehow take place simultaneously. Anselmo and Sebastian are the painters we just met, and at the same time, they are the disciples in Benares. Make sense?"

Brandt nodded. Richard shook his head, then nodded, then shook it again, trying to process what he'd heard.

"Are you the third follower?" Brandt asked. Claire herded stray breadcrumbs on the table, pushing them around with her finger. "I don't know. That's a conundrum the visions don't answer. I watch the action unfold. I'm not part of it."

She spent the next hour trying to answer her friends' questions, and when the subject was temporarily exhausted, Brandt stood up to load the dishwasher. "And now, if it is all right with you," he said once he'd finished, "I want to park the cars out of view and turn off the lights, so that the visitor I'm expecting sees no signs that we are here."

Time passed slowly, as Claire waited with Richard and Brandt in silence. Night fell and the monk still refused to say who was coming. "Just trust me," he said cryptically. Richard encouraged Claire to go to bed, but she wanted to stay downstairs where the mystery was unfolding, and eventually she fell asleep, propped against Richard on the large, comfortable sofa. Close to midnight, she awoke to the sound of a car in the driveway and the glare of headlights that shone through the front window and danced across the living room wall. The engine died and moments later, Claire heard someone try the locked front door. Next, came the sound of footsteps, followed by the French doors rattling, just beyond where they waited. The doors, left unlocked by Brandt, opened, there were footsteps on the terracotta tiles, and then the lights went on. Claire blinked, trying to rouse herself as Brandt stood up. "Mike, come in, we've been waiting for you," he said. Claire grinned, delighted that Kushner, who she thought was already back in Jerusalem, had caught up with them. Then she saw an expression of shock combined with fury darken their visitor's face.

"Come sit down," Brandt instructed him. Claire could see Kushner's thoughts racing, as he set his keys on the table and joined them in the living room, lowering himself into the chair opposite Brandt.

"The thug you hired to steal the scroll from my office in Jerusalem could have killed me, Mike." Brandt's admonition was calm but icy.

"He wasn't supposed to hit you so hard, or with something so sharp. You kept the office locked. I couldn't take the scroll myself, so I was forced to make other arrangements." Kushner sounded equally cold.

"Please tell me that this is a joke," Richard said, as both he and Claire looked from Brandt to Kushner, seemingly gone from the closest of friends to bitter enemies.

"Not a joke, unfortunately," Brandt said. "Shall I fill them in, Mike?"

Kushner shrugged. "Go ahead."

Brandt explained how it had taken him longer than it should have to put the pieces of the puzzle together, perhaps because it was such a disappointing picture for him to face. Initially, Kushner had not wanted the Vatican to buy the parchment. He had retained Baggio to explore buying the scroll from Halou. That's why Baggio and not Kushner appeared on Halou's list of interested parties. "But the asking price for the scroll was too hefty," Brandt said, "so Kushner came to me. He knew how much the scroll would mean to me. Knew I could access Vatican funds to buy it. Knew I would be tasked with translating the text, and that I would invite him to help me with the work."

It was lucky for Kushner, Brandt explained, that Vincent Malveau, the Vatican's chief cataloger, was on the committee overseeing the project. The priest was a degenerate, so it was easy for Kushner to keep one step ahead by bribing him for inside information about the scroll project and paintings. Brandt scowled at Kushner. "When we visited Rome, I went to Malveau's office and recognized a valuable Celtic manuscript there. It was yours, Mike. I knew then what you had done, that you, the last person I would have ever suspected, were responsible for the thefts. That one small clue forced me to see what would have been obvious all along if I hadn't let our friendship blind me. You used valuable artifacts to bribe Malveau. And that's not the worst of it. I followed him to an apartment and saw for myself the filth that he takes there. The man is a pervert, and you supplied him with vile objects, with human remains that have been violated."

"I gave him discarded remnants of research cadavers, that's all," Kushner scoffed. "He found Sebastian's painting, didn't he?"

"Yes, Malveau discovered Sebastian's painting," Brandt said. "You directed him to tell me about it. Then once we'd retrieved it, you stole it from us, and sent Malveau to tell Fitzpatrick I had taken it. After Richard found Claire's painting, you had Baggio hire Lucien Gray to buy it for you and display a reproduction. When we found out about Baggio, and you could no longer use him as a middleman, you had Gray send the canvas directly to you in Milan. All told, you paid two million dollars to acquire Claire's painting. That's a lot of money, Mike. Where did you get it?"

"Plenty more people besides you are interested in the scroll, Karl, and they are willing to fund more open research."

Claire could hear that Kushner was indignant, not repentant. "You didn't have the guts to fight the Vatican. If I waited for you, the scroll would never be opened for genuine debate by people who deserve the opportunity to study it. It would wind up as just another Vatican find, under their agenda and control, hoarded away from the light of day and the greater good."

"You have no patience, Mike." Under his calm tone, Brandt was struggling with Kushner's betrayal and accusations. The two friends, Claire saw, had wanted the same thing, to share the scroll with their peers for broader analysis. But Kushner wanted it at any price, even at the cost of breaking the law and ruining their friendship.

"It was just a fluke that Brazzini bought Anselmo's painting," Brandt explained. "He was a legitimate collector, who saw how special the work was from Gio's photo, and had the money to acquire it. He wanted to remain anonymous, but he was traceable thanks to his check and Gio Monte."

Brandt had called in Lincoln Swelt to lift Anselmo's painting from Brazzini's Villa Fiori, and once he figured out what

Kushner was up to, he directed Swelt to find out where the traitor was hiding Claire's and Sebastian's paintings.

Kushner nodded toward the three large packages in the hallway. "You had Swelt follow me to the storage unit in Milan and snatch the two canvases. Congratulations! You have all three paintings, Karl, but you don't have the scroll."

"You will give it to me, Mike." Brandt sounded cool.

Kushner sneered at his friend. "What makes you think that?"

"Because I have faith that you will do the right thing."

"Oh, for God's sake, Karl!" Kushner exploded. "Your faith is a ridiculous security blanket that you cling to like a child. Sometimes you have to step up, be a man and take action, instead of being a coward who prays for answers."

Brandt's glare was incendiary, as he let out a roar and smashed his fist on a side table so hard that Claire flinched and clutched Richard's arm. "It takes monumental courage to live on faith," he yelled at Kushner. "To not charge into things, clutching and grabbing. To live gracefully and allow events to unfold and not force them, even when you are aching for an outcome. It takes incredible humility, learned over a lifetime, to kneel every day and accept that this world operates beyond our understanding. To surrender and pray that a more divine will, not our own, will be done. To stem desire for things we are not meant to have. To sit on hands that long to meddle in affairs, on impulse, with no forethought or understanding of what will come to pass in the long run. Do not talk to me of being a man, you sniveling boy. Yours is the aggression of a bully. Your conviction is faithless and comes from ego. Your desire is selfish and lacking virtue. Don't you dare mock my faith. It is only my faith that stops me from choking the life out of your miserable carcass."

Brandt was trembling, and Claire could see spittle had collected in the corners of his mouth. Kushner stood, picked up his car keys, and walked out the way he had come in.

"Return the scroll, Mike. It doesn't belong to you," Brandt called after him.

"Screw you!" Kushner slammed the door behind him.

Richard, who had remained silent, trying to process the incredible scene, stepped toward his friend. "Leave me alone, please." Brandt held up his palm, and Claire watched him sink, spent, into the chair. She took Richard's hand and led him upstairs, leaving the strong Bavarian bear to wrestle with loss and betrayal.

It was around 2 a.m. when Brandt rose from praying and glimpsed a figure passing by the French doors, where Kushner had exited earlier. Maybe Mike was still out there, hanging around, wanting to come in but too proud. Hope rose in the dispirited monk. Perhaps his good friend wasn't lost to him. Did he regret what he had done and was ready to make amends?

Brandt opened the French doors and looked over the railing in time to see a dark figure scurrying along the shore below. Descending as fast as he could on the narrow, rocky stairs, Brandt followed the person, barely distinguishable in the light of a slim crescent moon, as he made his way to the villa next door. The neighboring building was in darkness, and a door stood open, with glass from a broken pane glinting on the ground.

"Mike?" Brandt called as he entered the vacant house, trying to adjust to the deeper darkness within. He felt along the wall for a light switch, sweeping his arm up and down, until there it was, and he flicked it on. The head he saw charging toward him looked like a devil's, with black eyes, encircled with purple, sunk in a gaunt face. Pale lips were drained of blood by a rage that contorted his assailant's face into a twist of mangled features.

"You bastard!" Malveau rammed Brandt against the wall, where the monk slammed his head and slid to the floor in a blur of dizziness.

"Where are my finds? You took my finds and I want them back!" Malveau emphasized the last word with a kick to Brandt's chest, and the monk collapsed against the wall, inhaling sharply, certain his ribs were broken.

"My finds!" Malveau began kicking again, as Brandt twisted this way and that to avoid the vicious blows. The demented, ranting priest punctuated his words with kicks aimed at the older man's face, chest, and abdomen. "You came to my office when I wasn't there, and you took my treasures. Where are they? Where are they?"

"I buried them," Brandt gasped, hardly able to speak with the wind kicked out of him. The deranged attacker instantly stopped. "You buried them? Where?" Already he could feel the thrill of digging up his lost bones, clawing through the dark, moist earth to retrieve them.

"I won't tell you," Brandt said with disgust, as Malveau pulled out a gun, perfectly prepared to shatter the monk's bones if he wouldn't talk.

"Get away from him!" Lincoln Swelt charged across the room, as Malveau turned, coolly trained the gun, and fired into the center of his wide barrel chest. Lincoln hit the tiles like a massive tree crashing to the forest floor. Malveau smirked, one eye squinting shut, almost a wink, teeth bared, like an animal. Fear rushed through Brandt like a faucet had been turned on inside to send panic pumping through his body.

Mike Kushner was tough and skilled, trained in hand-to-hand combat during his time in the Israeli Defense Force. Swelt had called out to Malveau, inviting his lethal attack, but Kushner understood the power of stealth and surprise. Unseen, he moved in and delivered a swift blow to the madman's throat. As Malveau dropped, Kushner kneed him in the face and sent him sprawling, before finishing him with a kick to the groin. He bent, retrieved the gun, and then booted the priest again. "How do *you* like the taste of shoe leather, you psycho?"

Summoned by the sounds of a gunshot and the commotion, Richard rushed into the chaotic scene to find Brandt slumped against the wall and Malveau curled in a fetal position, demolished by Kushner's attack. The Israeli stepped over him and headed for the door, refusing to look in Brandt's direction.

Brandt was in too much pain to rise. Instead, he crawled to where Lincoln lay in shock, shivering on the floor, his knees tucked into his body, and his pants soaked with blood from his chest wound. "I didn't like the idea of giving your address to some guy we just ripped off. I thought I should come back and make sure you were all right," Lincoln whispered, his teeth chattering.

"Thank you, son." Brandt stroked the dome of his friend's smooth head.

***

In the chill of the morning, with the lake still covered in mist, Claire stood outside the villa, wrapped in a blanket, watching as Frank the driver opened the back door of a black Mercedes so a shaken Karl Brandt could climb inside. During the early morning hours, the Vatican clean-up crew, dispatched by Fitzpatrick, had arrived to restore order, following the unexpected violence. Malveau was sedated and carted off, and no one Claire questioned would say where. The three paintings had been loaded into the back of a van for a road trip to the Vatican City in Rome. Before he died, Sebastian had freely given his painting to Brandt, and Anselmo had willed his canvas to the monk, which meant that of the three paintings, the only one Brandt didn't own was Claire's. He asked her permission to take the work.

"My painting was sold to Lucien Gray," Claire told him, "and apparently Kushner supplied the money for the purchase, so I have no say over what happens to it." Brandt nodded. At some point, he would have to settle with Kushner, retrieve the scroll, and work out ownership of Claire's painting. He would also have to deal with Brazzini, who would not accept the return of his uncashed check and was still looking for the thief who had stolen the painting from Villa Fiori. Unfortunately, that well-meaning thief was dead. A private ambulance had taken Lincoln Swelt's body to a morgue in Milan. Brandt's priority, before flying back to Rome, was to visit Annie at her hotel and tell her the devastating news of Lincoln's death. He had retrieved from Swelt's van the fifty thousand dollars his friend had earned in the exchange with Kushner. Annie was entitled to the money, and she was going to need it. But the cash was lousy compensation for the loss of the man she loved.

Claire read the guilt that had seeped into every pore of her friend's bruised and battered face. I'm sure Brandt believed there was little or no risk in asking Swelt to help him recover the paintings, she thought. How could he know that Malveau would stalk him, once he found out that the monk had taken his bone collection? And Brandt probably never counted on Swelt returning to Lake Como to make sure he was safe. Maybe Kushner stepping in to help was a consolation, a sign that his loyalty to Brandt wasn't completely extinguished.

***

Just two weeks after Lincoln Swelt was shot dead at Lake Como, Claire's doctor in Milan pronounced her well enough to travel. She was excited about flying home to America, but first, Brandt had invited her and Richard to view the paintings in Rome, where they'd been assembled into a pre-ordained triptych. She set her suitcase on the bed and began to pack, pausing now and then to look out and soak up as much of the lake view as she could. Who knows if I'll ever see this stunning place again? The time spent with Richard in the villa had been special, but she

217

was ready for home. They'd walked daily along Lake Como's shores. They'd talked, dined, read, and luxuriated in each other's company and their evolving romance, trying to restore calm after the frantic chase around Europe that had ended so catastrophically.

Living together, off the beaten path, the pair had learned about each other's daily rhythms, and Claire had to admit their coupling felt like a fit. Like her, Richard had a strong interior life. He needed time and space to be alone like she did. One warm afternoon, he had surprised her with a traveler's set of watercolor paints and paper. From then on, she spent time each day on the terrace with her new implements, trying to paint the lakescape with as few brush strokes as possible. Not overworking was the secret to watercolors that were less forgiving than oils.

Aside from long kisses, warm embraces, a shared bed for nighttime spooning, and an often overwhelming and uncontrollable physical attraction, the pair were foregoing sexual intimacy. Claire was still recovering, and Richard was governed by his self-appointed role as her protector and nurse. The scroll's prophesy of "three dead painters" still cast a worrying shadow, but they waived if off as superstition. Or maybe the ancient prediction had been thwarted by the wonders of modern medicine that had saved Claire's life.

Richard had confessed his past and taken down the walls, but Claire's growing intuition told her that he hadn't revealed all. And by holding back an important chapter of his story, he had created a subtle barrier. It wasn't as thick and impenetrable as before when he'd misled her about Hilde; still, it remained like the finest of veils that hung between them, almost transparent, often undetectable, but always there. And while it was there, Claire could not give herself over to her growing desire for the handsome, caring, long-limbed, blue-eyed man, who found new ways every day to make her love him more.

She was tired of mysteries, guessing games, and unfathomable puzzles. Sick of all the questions and what-ifs that the last year had brought to her door. Would Jake survive his illness? How had she managed to paint such a masterpiece? Should she keep or sell it? Were her visions and waking dreams real, a product of her imagination, or just a malfunctioning brain playing tricks? Was the scroll true prophecy or primitive prognostication? Was a dutiful and faithful Father Brandt wise and knowing, or just hoodwinked by the religion he'd devoted his life to? Would she live or die? What would become of her romance with Richard? Would he revert into the withdrawn, secretive recluse that had driven Hilde away, to her death even? Or become, with her help, a gloriously open book?

Too many unknowns kept Claire from surrendering completely to their love affair. She couldn't commit to Richard as a lover, as long as secrets hung over her like a sword that threatened to cut through her peace of mind. Slowly, she was starting to piece together the remnants of a once happy existence that fate, or just the unpredictability of life, had ripped apart with its cruel surprises and unsolved riddles. She longed for Richard's touch, to give into desire, to lose herself in passion and sexual ecstasy, but she wouldn't, not until her man of mystery had given up every last one of his secrets.

Claire zipped up her suitcase. All good things must come to an end, and she was ready to leave. Life with Richard in the idyllic setting of Lake Como was one thing, but how would it work with this sensitive, complicated man once they were back home? And what could be less like the tranquility of Lake Como than Manhattan?

Claire and Richard boarded a flight for the short hop to Rome. "Arrivederci," she whispered, as the plane ascended and she watched Milan shrink. Richard touched his lips to her neck. "We'll be back." Hopefully he was right, but nothing seemed certain. Each morning, she woke up feeling happy yet faintly surprised to be still alive. The mandorla in her left eye had gone dark and all visions had stopped. She was about to enter a new chapter in her life, but what with her health problems and the bizarre prophecies surrounding her, she couldn't help but wonder if it might be her last.

In Rome, Brandt had sent a car to pick them up and was waiting for them at the Cicero Hotel, only a stone's throw from the Vatican. He looked rested and less stressed, but clearly the loss of Lincoln Swelt still preyed on his mind and probably always would. The reunited friends ordered refreshments in the hotel bar, and Claire asked Brandt how his meeting with Annie had gone. He said it was heartbreaking, as he knew it would be. When he met her at the hotel in Milan on the morning of the shooting, he found her frantic, because Lincoln was missing and hadn't answered his phone all night. Before leaving to deliver the paintings to Brandt, Lincoln had assured Annie that the job was over, he'd done right by his beloved mentor, and he would be back in time for a special celebration dinner. But then he'd called again to say he'd be late, because he had to make sure Brandt wasn't in any danger.

"It was impossibly hard," Brandt said, "telling Annie that Lincoln was dead. She didn't want his body flown home, because Lincoln had once confessed that he feared burial was like being left alone in the dark, and cremation seemed less frightening. She asked me to perform his funeral service, take his ashes, and scatter them somewhere peaceful."

And so, two days after he was shot dead, Lincoln Swelt was cremated at a private service in Milan, attended by only two mourners, his great love, Annie, and his surrogate father, Karl Brandt. "I loved him like a son, but I know that I am responsible for his death." Brandt rotated his small espresso cup on its saucer. "I have his ashes. I will take them to Jerusalem and scatter them there. That's where we met and began our friendship, and where Lincoln spent so many happy times."

"No coroner's inquest or police investigation? Lincoln was murdered, after all." Richard's bluntness broke through Brandt's recriminations, but the monk just shook his head. A Church physician had signed Lincoln's death certificate, and the Church would deal with Malveau. Brandt set down his cup and fell silent. Claire could see that he didn't want to acknowledge or discuss how the Church had incredible power to skirt the law and sometimes operate according to its own will and agenda, just as Kushner had pointed out on that awful night of violence that they all wanted to forget.

Brandt changed the subject. Before dinner, he'd love if they would come to the Vatican and see the paintings that had been hung in a small private chapel near the office that Fitzpatrick had assigned to him. For the first time that afternoon, Claire saw her friend happy and animated, as he described the incredible effect the paintings created.

"Any miracles yet?" Claire couldn't resist asking.

"Wait and see." And with that, the monk stood up to say goodbye.

"What are you going to do, Karl?" Richard asked, and Brandt gave him a quizzical look. "About the paintings and the scroll?" Brandt looked down at both his hands and pumped his short, strong fingers. "The Church bought the scroll and will take possession once it's retrieved. It was arrogant of me to think I know what's best. When the scroll is returned, I'll be allowed to continue my work on it here in Rome, where the paintings and the scroll will be safe."

"And will the world hear about this work?" Richard asked.

"All in good time. Monsignor Fitzpatrick and I understand each other. Right now, the most important thing is to get the work back on track, complete the translation, and study the paintings."

Claire felt nervous and wanted to enter the chapel alone. Brandt held open the polished wood door for her, then closed it, and waited outside with Richard. The paintings hung on the front wall of the simple chapel that was no more than thirty feet by thirty. It was one that busy Vatican staff used when they needed quiet time for prayer and contemplation. Several rows of highbacked red and gold tapestry chairs were set before a simple cherry-wood altar. The altar was dressed in only a white linen altar cloth, and silver candlesticks, with ivory tapers that burned with a thin, bright flame.

Behind the altar, Claire beheld the triumph of the three paintings. She had seen two of them, her own and Sebastian's, either propped on easels and leant against walls, or hung in a busy gallery. Here in the simplicity and sanctity of the chapel, she was overcome by their magnificence. She gazed longest at Anselmo's *Garden Before the Fall*, marveling at the canvas that she'd only seen in photos until now.

Whoever had hung the three works, from left to right, had done so according to the chronology of Claire's visions. Her own painting, *Absent a Miracle*, was placed first on the left. Chapter one, a Christlike figure watches a young woman on her sick bed in Benares, as she surrenders to dying and new life after death. Chapter two, Sebastian's *Farewell on the Road*. The master bids farewell to his three followers. He is journeying to a place where they will eventually follow when they have fulfilled their purpose. Chapter three. Anselmo's *Garden Before the Fall* symbolizes the Eden from which Adam and Eve were banished. It is the paradise men and women dream of, and the home to which life's weary travelers long to return.

Claire studied all three works, inviting them to tell their collective story. We are born to die, but we can cultivate faith. By following the path of truth, set out by a prophet or messiah, we are able to transform ourselves, until we find redemption, defeat death, and return home to paradise. Understood in this way, she thought, the paintings do herald good news, and deliver a message of faith, transformation, and resurrection, just like Brandt had hoped.

Displayed together, the paintings were glorious, and Claire tried to see them through the eyes of an observer who knew nothing about their enigmatic origins. What might some uninitiated stranger take from this unusual triptych that emanated warmth from a mysterious heat source? She tried to look past the Christian symbolism, the religious overtones, and her personal connection to the works, so that the paintings could speak simply and directly to her. Their power and beauty stopped the chatter of her anxious mind, allowing her to enter the space they created and discover a deep peace there.

Her own canvas had a special message for her and all who mourn or fear death. It reveals, she thought, the grace in dying. The master is calm and reassuring. The sick woman is unafraid and at peace, even though her death is imminent. It's only the husband who is bereft and clinging to hope that his life will go on unchanged and untouched by suffering. Only he is unable to see the miracle that death represents for the faithful, the triumph of the spiritual being over the physical body.

Claire remembered the young master's words from her dream, "To thwart death is not to conquer it." She thought she better understood their meaning now. To raise a man from the dead is a fine miracle, but to convince all men not to fear death is an act that can redirect the course of human history. Jake died. Hilde died. Sebastian and Anselmo died. As I sit here, death is at work everywhere. But in the actual moment of dying, who knows? Maybe there is no dread, only release, and the realization that death is perhaps nothing more than a short walk down the road, until we dissolve into the light.

She closed her eyes as the surge of electricity rose up through her spine and neck to radiate throughout her skull. The mandorla next to her left eye opened and expanded until all she could see was a vision of space shot through with strands of light, glistening like a spider's web across infinity. In that moment she knew that all beings were interconnected and ever present. There is no separation, no passing of time. All of us are part of the eternal throb of creation, rising and falling. Our essence is divine energy that relays and transforms but is never extinguished. The vision subsided and the mandorla shifted from the corner of her left eye. It relocated to the space on her forehead, between her eyes, the traditional location of the third eye, so well-known to mystics. Now in its proper place, it closed and went dark.

Claire lingered a while, and when she left the room, Richard and Brandt seemed to her, in her blissed-out state, to be vibrating with stress and anxiety. Richard reached out to take her hand but she recoiled. "You are both very dark," she said, instantly regretting her words when she saw Richard's pained expression.

"It's a common reaction among the few we've allowed to see the paintings," Brandt reassured his friends. "In a deep meditative state induced by the paintings, negativity and stress are burned off. Blood pressure and heart rate drop, and alpha waves in the brain increase. Respondents emerge completely relaxed and hypersensitive to their surroundings, and even the slightest amount of tension in others." Brandt looked at Richard and gestured to the door. "Shall we?" Claire waited outside. Pacing the long Vatican corridor, she tried to hold onto the indescribable feeling of lightness and expansiveness that the paintings had aroused in her.

An hour later in Brandt's office, the three friends sat before a fire, preparing to say goodbye. "Claire, I know that this has not been an easy journey for you," Brandt said. "I sense you have resisted it, resisted your destiny, and I want you to know, it is your destiny as a visionary and an artist. It was ordained and foretold that you would deliver this very special gift to the world — the painter's gift."

Claire smiled and didn't argue. She couldn't deny that she was one of three painters who, without knowing it, had created one-third of an incredible triptych, but her story had diverged from the others. Sebastian and Anselmo, who had become her friends in life and characters in her dreams, were both deceased. And she was still no closer to understanding her own role in the allegory or mythic vision that she had tried to paint. She wasn't convinced that her experiences, even though they were enlightening, were anything more than the delusions of a woman made a little crazy by illness and grief. But why spoil Brandt's happiness? *He has the ending he wants to the story he desperately needs to believe,* she thought. *He's arranged all the puzzle pieces of the paintings and the scroll into a picture that aligns with his vision of this world and the next. He's a good man, and if the worst that faith does is lead a man to do better, to try harder, then faith is worth cultivating.*

There was a knock at the door. "Come." Brandt's baritone summoned the visitor on the other side of the heavy wood paneling. The door opened and in walked Mike Kushner. Both Richard and Claire stood, unsure how to greet their friend, while Brandt remained in his armchair. Mike strode over to him, and without a word, set down a large metal case, before turning and walking back toward the door.

"Mike, wait." Brandt rose as his visitor turned to face him. "Come with me. There is something that I want you to see."

Chapter Twelve

Revelations

Not for one minute had Claire thought about the money. She'd been so caught up in the drama, she had forgotten that after Deirdre Vetch took her cut for commissions and expenses, she had almost one point two million dollars coming to her from the sale of her work.

Back in New York, Claire had received Deirdre's invitation to come collect her check, kiss and make up. She tapped on the office door and entered. It had been only a couple of months since she was last there to meet with her agent and Gray, in a sorry episode that seemed like forever ago, and now she felt like a changed woman.

She wasn't nervous or intimidated as she sat across the desk from her agent and exchanged pleasantries. On a credenza, Claire caught sight of a black and white photo, in a silver frame, of a striking man in his late forties that she'd never noticed before. Beside the photo was a round crystal vase of tightly bunched white roses. "Who's that?" she asked, pointing at the photo, and Deirdre glanced at it. "That's my late husband, Harry. He died when we had been married for only five years. He was the love of my life."

Claire saw her agent's expression crack wide open as though, just for a second, she was experiencing the loss all over again. "I'm so sorry," Claire said.

"Yes, well, of all people, you would understand." Deirdre tried to smile and Claire softened. She'd been bracing herself for this meeting with the woman she thought of as her nemesis, but now all the tension drained out of her, and Claire suddenly saw her agent in a new light. Deirdre was just doing her job by selling my painting for top dollar. I've been self-centered and fickle.

If I really didn't want to sell, I should have just stayed holed up with the canvas, but there was a part of me, like Anselmo, that wanted reward and recognition. And when Deirdre went and got them for me, I acted like a child who wouldn't take responsibility for my part in the situation.

"I'm sorry for making the deal so hard to do," Claire said. "I owe you an apology and a thank you. You're a good agent."

For a second, Deirdre looked thrown off before quickly recovering. "Well, you're a talented painter, a good negotiator, and a hell of a woman." She pointed to Claire's outfit. "And let me tell you something else, kudos to whoever convinced you to up your fashion game. You look fantastic."

Claire had dressed in a soft, honey-colored suede skirt with an oversized belt of silver disks, a brown sweater, and boots. Her hair hung in loose ringlets that grazed her shoulders. Her romance with Richard made her feel beautiful again, and she wanted to celebrate her femininity.

"Listen," Deirdre said, "in the spring, how about we arrange a show? It'll be a good time to present your abstracts."

"Really?" Claire couldn't believe her agent's sudden largesse. "I thought you weren't keen on my abstracts."

"Darling, it's all about perception." Deirdre stood and walked around the desk to sit next to Claire. "You sold a major work for big money. You've arrived. Show up to your opening looking like you do today, classy and beautiful, make nice with the punters, and your stuff will fly off the walls."

"The work's good enough?"

"Sure it's good enough. We're gonna retire on what I sell." Deirdre winked.

Ten minutes later, Claire stood to leave and hugged her agent. "Thank you so much, Deirdre." She caught sight of Harry's photo again. "And I'm sorry about Harry."

"Don't ever be sorry about Harry. He was the best thing that ever happened to me. Don't forget this." She handed Claire the check that totaled well over a million dollars. "What are you going to do with it?"

"Some good, I hope." Claire folded the slip of paper that had completely changed her status from starving artist to relatively well-off art world darling, returned it to its envelope, and put it in her purse. Early next week, she had an appointment with a financial advisor. After taxes, she figured she'd pay herself three hundred thousand dollars to buy some time and breathing room. She'd use the rest of the money to establish the Jake Lucas Fund. She didn't have a specific cause in mind, but her gut told her she would know where to donate the money when the time was right.

Back on the sidewalk, she hailed a cab. Richard had forbidden her to take subways, until she made a complete recovery. Her balance was off, and she was still sensitive to light and noise.

It was almost 6 p.m. when she arrived home. After changing into comfy clothes, she made herself a small white wine spritzer. Alcohol was still a bit of a no-no, but this evening she wanted to celebrate. She resisted calling Richard. She was spending almost every night at his place, and needed to spend more time alone to create at least a semblance of independence. But being with him was so easy, except for the abstinence. "Are we crazy?" she had asked him a few nights earlier, as she pulled away and halted a particularly passionate make-out session. "We're two formerly married adults, fumbling around and foregoing sex, like chaste virgins from the bible belt."

He smiled suggestively. "Ready when you are." But Richard knew and fully accepted that she wasn't ready to take the final step in consummating their relationship. She was uncertain and a little afraid about moving forward across the new landscape of her life. Her broken heart was only lightly mended. Her leaky brain was still causing headaches and mild symptoms. And thanks to her escapades with the Angel Scroll, she was coming to terms with an altered psyche that produced strange dreams, intrusive thoughts, and unasked for intuitions. She smiled at him. "I'm sorry. I don't mean to be a tease." He enfolded her in the safety of his patient arms and kissed her fragrant hair, the smell he now loved most in the world.

Claire looked around her apartment. It was so familiar, and the backdrop to a story that had ended in the tragedy of Jake's death. Change was happening faster than she wanted and rearranging the pieces of her life, but change, she knew, was unstoppable. She stretched out both arms and slowly raised her palms, as if signaling to imaginary stagehands that it was time for a change of scenery. She remembered a line from a favorite poet: A loved one is the custodian of our solitude. She savored the long nights she spent in comfortable silence with Richard, as they pursued their personal interests, or sometimes just wallowed in the luxury of doing nothing together.

At Richard's place, there were no souvenirs or artifacts from Claire's past to trigger memories of Jake and their old cozy routines that were being replaced by fresh routines with a new love. Richard had removed all traces of Hilde from his apartment, long before he met Claire. Still, the new woman in his life could sometimes sense the ghost of the previous one wandering in through open windows and drifting about the place. Hilde's ghost lingered between bed sheets, loitered in rooms, and reminded Richard of what had been.

A call from Richard interrupted her pensive mood. "Think of the devil and you see his horns," she joked.

"Want to come for dinner and tell me all your news? I'm serving quesadillas made with my own expert hands." Richard dangled his tantalizing offer, and Claire wanted nothing more than to skip over to his place, celebrate her pay day, crow about her upcoming show, and eat homemade Mexican. Then, she'd curl up with a good book, while he searched online for news of a rare find. But no, tonight it would be better if she stayed home. "I have to wash my hair," she joked, and then she told him about the show Deirdre had proposed, while he cheered for her.

Richard is good at being happy for me, Claire thought after she hung up, almost as good as Jake was. Her husband had been her number one fan and cheerleader. Being a teacher and a coach was his true calling. He loved nothing more than to inspire the kids he taught, to see their potential, and help them fulfill it.

Every Saturday morning, when Jake was alive, the couple would leave their Upper West Side apartment for their Saturday ritual. They'd pick up the paper on the corner and duck into their favorite diner to read over a breakfast of coffee, toast, and eggs. Then came a leisurely stroll down the wide avenue that was Broadway, as they looked in store windows and waved to familiar vendors manning the carts that sold hotdogs, coffee, falafel, or fruit. This was a residential section of the city, where young professionals tried to raise families in the quieter neighborhoods between Central Park and Riverside Park, and where the manic Manhattan energy and fast pace was a little slower.

Next came the best part, a stroll around Zabar's, located between 81st and 82nd. New Yorkers made a weekend pilgrimage to the renowned deli to pick up the best lox, cheese, chopped liver, and every kind of cooked meat, fish, and delicacies to tempt the palate. Here, Claire and Jake bought bagels and cream cheese for their Sunday brunch routine, and afterwards, they made their way to Central Park. In summer, they might take a picnic. In cold weather, they walked, or biked, or sat, bundled up, people watching. Without fail, a kid from the nearby middle school where Jake taught history would spot them and come over. "Oh, hey Mr. Lucas, how's it going?" And Jake would jump up and go in for his customary high five. "Zach, my man! Headed for soccer practice?"

"Yes Mr. Lucas."

"I saw you tearing up the pitch last week. That's some set of legs you're building. You working out?" Jake showered the kid in approval.

"Yeah. I've started with some weight training, and I'm jogging around the reservoir every day after school."

"Keep it up! I see a big improvement. You're killing it."

The kid would give a bashful smile and then head off, walking just a little taller, determined to work just a little harder if Mr. Lucas thought his efforts were paying off.

Money was tight and Claire knew she really should work a steady job instead of the temping and casual gigging she did to help make ends meet. Living in New York on a teacher's salary was a struggle, but Jake insisted she paint. He believed in her talent and exclaimed over every small sale or commission she managed to snag. "What! Twenty-five hundred dollars for *Raindrops*? That's amazing. Come and kiss me, my Michelangelina." He would wrap her in an inescapable hug, as she rested her head on his strong chest under his chin.

"You sold *Raindrops*? Man, I can't believe you let that one go. You know it's my favorite."

"I'm supposed to sell them. That's the whole point. We need the money." She punched him in his arm that had the thick, strong, muscular heft of a chronic gym rat and outdoors man.

"Yeah, but your paintings look so pretty all lined up in the hall, don't you think? Aw look, now there's a hole where *Raindrops* is supposed to live." Jake tickled her and she fell back on the bed, where he fell beside her, and slowly his tickling turned to caressing and kissing, and then she was under him, his weight and smell stirring her. Their lovemaking always came on with a rush of urgency and excitement, and when it was over, she rested in the crook of his arm with the most comforting feeling of safety, peace, and gratitude that she had been blessed with such a love as this.

Claire studied her favorite wedding photo on the bookshelf. She had white rosebuds pinned in her curls, and Jake posed with the stem of a rose between his teeth. This was the goofiest picture from the whole album, and the one they chose to memorialize their unforgettable day of love and dancing, celebration and friends. In a familiar ritual, she kissed her fingertips and touched them to her husband's smiling lips. "Ah Jake, how good you were. You and your encouraging words, and your secret ways of making others believe in themselves." Looking around the room, she gazed deeply into the space around her, trying to penetrate beyond what was visible, but the mandorla and its visions were quiet. She trailed her fingers across the photo. "Stay with me always," she whispered.

In a corner of her bedroom was a beat-up cardboard box containing Jake's letters and diaries, the last of his belongings and the most private. Most of his clothes, his bike, and carpentry tools, she had given to friends or to charities, but she'd been unable to bring herself to sift through his personal papers and journals. It was time to face culling through these intimate reminders, so she dragged the box into the living room, summoned the jazz station that had been their favorite, and sat on the floor. Outside her window was a chill November night in New York, when the air was cold but clear; the best of the season, bracing but not dismal. Claire opened the box and sifted quickly through memorabilia: high school yearbook, freshman swimming certificates, awards in Tae Kwan Do, a set of Eagle Scout badges. Then came letters from Jake's parents, both dead, and love letters from her. She read a few. Who was this panting, infatuated twenty something woman, who wrote page after page about her longing for her handsome lover? Here were the stubs of James Taylor concert tickets, their first big outing as a couple. A photo Jake had snapped of her. She looked ruddy and happy after reaching the summit of some minor peak in the Adirondacks.

Near the bottom of the disorganized box, she came upon a sketchbook. On the first few pages were woodworking sketches of a kitchen cart with butcher-block top. Jake's Valentine's Day gift to her one year. A love letter in wood, he had called it. She turned the pages and came upon drawings of unusual figures. Four men in robes. They were very good. Who knew he was such a talented draftsman? Claire turned another page and pressed a hand to her mouth. The sketch was entitled *The Sick Bed*. It showed a single figure, a pretty woman lying on a low bed. On the next page, a drawing entitled *The Holy Man* revealed a young man sitting cross-legged on the floor. On another page was *The Husband*, a sketch of a young man beside his wife's sick bed, his head resting against hands that were clasped in prayer. Here in pen and ink drawings were all the elements of her painting, *Absent a Miracle*, but Jake had created them.

Claire felt the familiar shudder run up her spine. She lay on the floor, closed her eyes, and watched the bright light that played behind her eyelids. Brandt's words from the terrace of the house in Lake Como snaked through her memory: "three dead painters." She saw it clearly now, partly through intuition, partly from the evidence in the sketchbook, and partly from her dream in France when Jake had come to her as one of the three Indian followers in the courtyard. She understood that Jake was meant to be the third painter—Sebastian, Anselmo, and Jake. Her husband was supposed to paint *Absent a Miracle*, but he died before even attempting a canvas. And it's me, his wife and proxy, who fulfilled his purpose and delivered the work.

Collapsed on the floor and too overwhelmed to move, Claire tried to stop her mind. Thinking was hopeless and had nothing to do with reality. Thinking, she realized, was just made-up stuff that got in the way of knowing the truth. She thought about Josie, Brandt, Bodhipaksa, and Dr. Bentley. They each lived in different worlds with different rules. They each used different theories to decipher her unfathomable experiences and explain what was happening to her. Finally, she dozed off to escape the exhausting tumult in her mind, but not before she had one last thought. If Brandt and his scroll were to be believed, then it was Jake, and not she, who was the third of the "three dead painters." This left Claire very much alive, with the promise of more life to come.

***

Bodhipaksa exited one of the outbuildings. He wore the familiar cable-knit sweater over his red robes, and green rubber boots splattered with mud. He was smiling as usual, and the sight of him immediately put Claire in a good mood, despite the solemn reason for her return to Apple Valley. Carefully packed in the bag that Richard was now removing from his SUV's trunk were Jake's ashes. She'd kept them out of sight at home for over a year, but it was time to give them a final resting place.

Like Lincoln Swelt, Jake had requested that his ashes be scattered someplace peaceful, maybe Lake George, where they had spent their honeymoon. But how could she let it all end in the place where their life together had begun? To Claire, Lake George would always be the joyful spot where they'd honeymooned, so sure that they'd live happily ever after and grow old together. She recalled those last, strained, and painful conversations in the hospital when Jake was dying. "I need to talk to you about financial stuff. Important stuff," he had pleaded. "I want to tell you my wishes for a memorial." But Claire couldn't. She just couldn't. She would run from the room every time he tried to speak of his death that was racing toward them like a freight train, while they braced for impact. Finally, it was Jake's best friend, Alistair, who had sat with him to help get his affairs in order and plan the funeral that his wife could not bring herself to contemplate.

Bodhipaksa had told Claire to find Jake everywhere in the phenomenal world around her. The more she thought about this, the more she realized what a great comfort it would be if Bodhipaksa assisted her in scattering Jake's ashes in the orchards at Apple Valley. The monk had agreed, and the ceremony was scheduled for the next morning.

That evening, Bodhipaksa invited Claire and Richard to join him for a simple evening meal by the log fire in his small study on the ground floor of the farmhouse. They ate around the scratched circular, candlelit table. At the far end of the study was an altar adorned with candles, fresh flowers, and burned-out incense. At the center of the altar was a large serene, bronze Buddha sitting in the lotus position.

Claire sensed no aggressive curiosity in Bodhipaksa. He was totally present and unobtrusive, as they ate a dish of fresh vegetables and rice, but a few minutes into the simple meal, she decided to engage the monk in what had been an inner dialogue. As yet, she hadn't even told Richard about Jakes's sketchbook and her intuition that it was her husband who was supposed to paint *Absent a Miracle*. "Bodhipaksa, I want to tell you what happened in Europe."

"Of course," he said, and as usual, his smile invited her to keep the loosest of holds on her experiences, as she told him about the mandorla at the corner of her left eye that eventually emerged as a fully open third eye. She recounted all her dreams and explained her visions of a Christlike master in Benares, India, his followers, and the resurrected woman.

"It is very propitious," Bodhipaksa said when Claire had finished, "that your visions are set in Benares. Not far from there, at Deer Park in Sarnath, is where Lord Buddha Shakyamuni, after attaining enlightenment at Bodh Gaya, preached his first discourse to set in motion the 'Wheel of the Dharma.' This is one of the holiest sites in Buddhism, because it was in this place that the stream of the Buddha's teaching first flowed."

"What happened at Bodh Gaya?" Claire asked.

Bodhipaksa folded his hands and closed his eyes. When he opened them, he was ready to tell her how the story of the Buddha had, over millennia, transformed and directed the course of millions if not billions of lives. "One night," he began, "more than five hundred years before Christ, the Indian prince Siddhartha Gautama, who was destined to become the historical Buddha, sat down beneath a fig tree to meditate. He vowed not to rise until he had discovered the answer to human suffering. Come the dawn, the Indian prince had become bodhi, which means awakened. He was able to pervade all phenomena and experience his ultimate nature. He had been tempted by every illusion of mara or the deluded mind, and was able to recall his countless rebirths, or incarnations. When Lord Buddha arose at dawn," Bodhipaksa continued, "he was committed to taking the middle way, avoiding the excesses of both poverty and wealth. He would teach the dharma based on four noble truths: there is suffering, suffering has a cause, the cause is removable, and there are ways to remove the causes. To remove the causes, the Buddha prescribed an eight-fold path of right speech, right action, right livelihood, right effort, right mindfulness, right concentration, right attitude, and right view. This is the core teaching that Buddhist practitioners still follow today."

Claire listened. How seductive it is, she thought, to believe that an ancient guru succeeded in penetrating the mysteries of the universe and could somehow provide answers to the questions about existence that every human, since the proverbial dawn of civilization, has been desperate to know. But she didn't say any of this. "I don't know if I believe in reincarnation," she announced instead.

Bodhipaksa shrugged. "That's okay. Lord Buddha taught that no one should accept his teachings on faith but must investigate for themselves. If the teachings do not bear truth for you, then throw them away. There is no dogma, nothing to be taken on faith alone."

Interesting, Claire thought. Bodhipaksa dismisses faith, but Brandt has built his world around it, and yet both monks are chasing the same conclusions. "Do you believe in reincarnation?" she asked, and the monk nodded and smiled. "In my vision," she went on, "the painters Sebastian and Anselmo were also the master's followers in India. My husband, Jake, was the third follower, and he was supposed to be the third painter, but he died before he could paint his masterpiece, so I did it." Claire didn't look at Richard, but she sensed his surprise at her newest revelation. "If you believe in reincarnation, do you remember your past lives?" she asked the monk.

Bodhipaksa shook his head. "Sometimes people can recall past personalities," he said, "but only a Buddha can remember all his incarnations and clearly see the truth of interdependent co-arising."

"What's that?" Claire asked.

"Everything depends on something else for its existence. Everything and everyone are interconnected. All our current choices affect future conditions. The law of karma says that for every action or cause there is an effect. Because this is this way, that will be that way. Because this is not this way, that will not be that way. So every decision, even the smallest, has consequences. We do not plant an apple seed and get an orange." He reached for the fruit bowl and held up an apple. "Everything that we are today is conditioned by past actions. Past actions determine how a person will reincarnate, the body they will have, their good or ill fortune, their faults and virtues."

Claire sighed. "What a sobering thought."

"Yes, but also a liberating one," the monk countered. "Once we become mindful of this reality, the true interdependence of everyone and everything, we realize how important right living is. Why it is important not to contaminate the field with wrong thinking and action. We work to clean our mind of the three poisons of ignorance, anger, and greed. As we do this, we encounter our true nature, our Buddha nature."

"And what is our Buddha nature?"

"Our essence or inborn capacity to be open, kind, spacious, connected, and compassionate, without negativity."

"Looks like you're pretty far along that path," Claire kidded him.

The monk smiled. "Nothing," he said, "exists independently from its own side. Everything arises from the one, from the ground of being. We are both form and formless at the same time, separate and yet part of the whole."

Yes, Claire thought, she had experienced this during her visions. She had dissolved into a feeling of formlessness and oneness that brought bliss. "What do my visions mean?" she asked now.

"I don't know," Bodhipaksa said simply.

"Are they real?" she pressed him. Surely, he had an explanation for her.

Bodhipaksa thought carefully before answering. "Everything you have experienced is both real and unreal. Every thought is a product of the conditioned mind, the play of the mind. Good thoughts, bad thoughts, holy and sacrilegious thoughts, painful and blissful, all just a play of our mind. Sometimes thoughts arise from our gross, deluded mind. Sometimes they arise from a more subtle and enlightened mind. It is not necessary to seek or reject a particular thought or experience. Just understand it simply as thinking, the natural play of mind, and release it."

Claire was more confused than ever, as she looked into Bodhipaksa's small, fine-boned face, and he let out an impish laugh.

The apple trees were bare and the dormant grass, beneath a thick layer of fallen leaves, was a pale green, not the lush emerald it would turn come spring. A soaking rain in the night had drenched buildings and landscape and created an icy dampness. A light mist clung to their ankles as Claire, Richard, and Bodhipaksa tramped in rubber boots through acres of orchard, occasionally kicking at what remained of a rotting apple, until it tumbled and rolled out of sight.

Richard and the monk said nothing and walked behind Claire, waiting for her to find the perfect spot. After a few minutes, she stopped, indicating she had found it at the crown of a small rise, where she stood and surveyed the army of apple trees lined up on the hillside below. They were bare of fruit and foliage now, like soldiers standing sentry, awaiting spring, the warm sun, rising sap, and boughs that would be transformed by blossoms, and later, made heavy with fruit.

"Here," she said to Richard and Bodhipaksa. Like a water diviner who has detected an underground flow, she could feel that this was the right place for her purpose. She set down her backpack and removed the white square plastic container that held Jake's ashes. She had fingered them once before and felt slivers of the merest hints of bone buried in ash, like teeny shells in fine, pale sand.

She looked first at Richard, who nodded in understanding, and then at Bodhipaksa, who did what he did best, smile. She took the lid off the box and carefully placed her hand through the opening. Wrapping her fingers around a palm full of ashes, she cast them down the hillside, where they dusted the moist ground and leaves with their silver grains. Walking back and forth like a farmer casting seed, Claire scattered the ashes of her departed husband. She had no urge to shake out the contents and let the light wind catch and carry them off. She wanted to spread every particle and return it lovingly to its source.

As she walked, her friends filed behind her, a small but attentive procession. Bodhipaksa had told her that he would recite the Heart Sutra, the profound illumination expressed by the Buddha, and she heard him now reciting the teaching in a low chant: "There is no birth and no cessation. There is no impurity and no purity. There is no decrease and no increase. In emptiness, there is no form, no feeling, no perception, no formation, no consciousness; no eye, no ear, no nose, no tongue, no body, no mind; no appearance, no sound, no smell, no taste, no touch." Claire let the chant wash over her. "Therefore, the great mantra of prajnaparamita, the mantra of great insight, the unsurpassed mantra, the unequaled mantra, the mantra that calms all suffering, should be known as truth, since there is no deception. The prajnaparamita mantra is said in this way: OM GATE GATE PARAGATE PARASAMGATE BODHI SVAHA."

Claire thought about Glastonbury Tor, and the Druidical choirs that Josie said had chanted day and night, literally enchanting the hillside. Now, first Claire, and then Richard, recited the last line of the mantra in Sanskrit. The monk had given her a rough translation of the words: Om. Go, go, go beyond, go far beyond. Awaken. Hallelujah! The widow allowed the rhythm of the strange, foreign words to give a sound to the feelings of heavy longing, sadness, and grief. This was the last act in her marriage to Jake. She would enchant this simple Vermont hillside, the final resting place of the man she had loved so dearly and lost so young.

That evening, Bodhipaksa gave Claire and Richard the private use of his study, away from the bustle of the sangha. Claire sat in one of two worn plaid, wing-backed chairs. Richard sat in the other. The monk had built a log fire for them and lit fresh candles and incense at his altar. It created a soothing and exotic atmosphere. After the gravity of the morning's ceremony, Claire felt lighter and unburdened now. Richard, on the other hand, had withdrawn into himself, He was pondering something that absorbed his full attention.

Claire watched the fire and occasionally stole glances at her companion. It's selfless of him to come with me, she thought, and stand with me while I tend to another love. Taking a page from Bodhipaksa's book, she decided to let him be. She had coaxed one painful confession from him in Italy. Anything else he would have to give freely. The second she thought this, he said her name. "Claire, there's something I need to tell you."

"OK." She looked at him gently, no penetrating stare. Richard gazed into the fire. "No one knows what I am going to tell you, not even Karl, who has been my closest confidant and adviser." There was a long silence, but Claire still said nothing. If Richard wanted to hold back, it was his choice, but after three or four minutes, he began to talk. He focused on the fire, careful not to make eye contact and break the spell that made it possible for him to speak.

"After her affair," Richard began, "and after she left Trevor and decided to stay with me, Hilde discovered she was pregnant. We both knew it was Trevor's baby. At first, I asked her for a divorce. I knew that in time I could forgive her affair, but I doubted that I could handle raising a child who would be a constant reminder of my humiliation. Believing it would save our marriage, Hilde decided to terminate her pregnancy. It was a tough decision, but eventually she saw it as the best course of action. Perhaps because she had given me a way out, I had a change of heart. If Hilde wanted to keep the baby, I would support her, but she didn't trust my turnabout. She was afraid to have the baby and risk me rejecting both the child and her. We were trapped in a no-win situation, and Hilde was in an agony of indecision. The weeks went by, and time was running out."

Richard fell silent for several more minutes before he began again. "One day, without telling me, she drove herself to the clinic for the procedure. I hadn't done enough to reassure her that keeping the baby would be OK. Truth is, I still wasn't sure myself. Sometimes I found the whole mess completely workable. Hilde would have a sweet baby, and I would get over myself and love it as my own. At other times, I felt terrified that having the child would signal the end, that feelings I couldn't control would ruin all our lives. I knew as soon as Hilde returned and told me what she'd done that we were doomed. The crystal had shattered into a million pieces that we could never put back together. Within weeks, my wife was in the grip of a clinical depression exacerbated by hormonal changes. It was like she had stepped into quicksand and was slowly sinking. The worsening depression triggered a psychosis, and she refused to take her medication. There was nothing her doctors and I could do to pull her out of it. She refused all help. She hated herself, and me, and eventually life itself. I'd had my chance to support and reassure her and I'd failed. Now she was lost and impossible to reach. She left in the middle of the night while I was asleep. She was wearing a pair of her favorite pajamas decorated with penguins that I'd given her as a gift. I never saw her alive again."

Richard continued gazing into the fire, like he saw his painful story in the movement and shapes of the flames as they devoured the logs. Claire knew there was no point approaching him. He was mortified and would throw off any comfort she offered him. She looked past Richard's chair at the altar where the bronze Buddha sat fixed and immovable, gleaming in the flicker of candlelight. A wisp of smoke rose above his head, and his bronze fingers lightly touched the ground that bore witness to his remarkable discoveries.

As she sat and waited, Claire pondered the situation. Richard always tries to do the right thing, she thought. He's quiet, methodical, painstaking. He needs time to analyze and come to a decision, but when he does, it's usually the right one. The love he offers is tender, considerate, and kind. She thought about Hilde, imagining a woman who was beautiful, charismatic, and loving, but used to getting her own way. She had betrayed Richard in the worst way, not once, but twice. First, the affair with Trevor, and then the pregnancy. Claire saw how an impulsive and impatient Hilde might have become terrified when her life began to spin out of control, and her mood became dark and desperate.

Claire moved to the rug at Richard's feet, took his hand and pressed it against her warm cheek. "Richard, none of us knows what the future holds. I couldn't predict Jake's death, the madness I felt in grief, and the bizarre happenings that I still can't really understand. I'm just trying to hold on and make sense of it all. I need your help and your patience. I love you."

Richard turned to look at her. "You're not a prophet," she continued. "You couldn't predict or control what Hilde and Trevor would do. How they might hurt and betray you, and then ask you to forgive and do the impossible in return. I'm sure you tried so hard to do what was decent and correct." She looked into his eyes, trying to coax him into forgiving himself. "Richard, I'm sorry that you're left with such a painful burden, but please don't use it as a stumbling block that gets in our way. My husband is a ghost. I don't want a relationship with a man who is part ghost and haunted by the ghost of a woman he thinks he should have saved, when that wasn't possible. For us to have a chance together, you have to forgive yourself. Take as much time as you need, but don't come to me until you've put this to rest."

The speech wasn't an ultimatum. They both knew she was right. He was stuck in self-recrimination and regret. Claire left the room without anger and with just a gentle resolve. Maybe Bodhipaksa's lecture on cause and effect had penetrated because she could see the future with Richard. His emotional turmoil and guilt would destroy their relationship. There would be no moving forward, just a slow rotting and chafing in the grip of the past.

The next morning, the couple left early to make the long drive back to Manhattan. A sad silence took hold in the car and didn't dissipate during the entire ride home. Claire could have broken the silence, with kind words and reassurances, but she knew these were momentary distractions that wouldn't thaw the frozen center of Richard's heart. He was stuck, and only he could break free.

In the days after she returned home, Claire was sure Richard would call. Two weeks dragged by, then four. How many times each day was she tempted to pick up the phone to call him? To talk him out of his funk and describe all the ways their lives together could be wonderful. After six weeks with no word from him, she started to doubt the closeness they'd shared. Their mad trek around Europe had created an intimate bubble, but sooner or later it was bound to pop. Admit it, she told herself, this thing with Richard was like an intense, short-lived summer romance. It was a sweet dream, and now it's over.

One day, there was a message from Brandt on her voicemail. Just a quick update. He was still at work in Rome, translating the scroll and studying the paintings. Kushner was working with him. He didn't go into detail, but Claire could tell that the two men had somehow done the impossible and salvaged their relationship. It gave her hope. She thought about the complicated unfolding of events. If Kushner hadn't stolen the scroll and gone after the paintings, then Lincoln Swelt would still be alive. Cause and effect. Bodhipaksa was right. Every action leads to a reaction and often unforeseeable consequences. But Brandt had put his money where his mouth was. He had forgiven one friend for causing the death of another.

She was painting again, and one day Deirdre called and said, "Instead of waiting till spring, let's do your show on Valentine's Day. People spend more money when they're feeling sexy." Come late December, her agent was already hyping the show and preparing high-end invitations. On the front was a photograph of *Absent a Miracle*, and inside a summons to attend a show called *The Miracles of Nature*, a series of nature-inspired abstract works, by celebrated artist Claire Lucas.

Claire was hard at it, working all day and sometimes into the night to turn out new canvases. She was even working in watercolor again, putting the finishing touches to the lakescapes she had done at Lake Como. The days raced by and were both happy and sad. It felt good to be absorbed in satisfying work again, pursuing her own material, and not channeling an inspired work. But, still, all her efforts felt tinged with sadness. The love that would have made her life complete had sputtered and died after such a glorious beginning.

Christmas came and went, and the Jake Lucas Fund made its first grant to provide food, clothing, and gifts to women in shelters and prisons. Then one day in mid-January, Claire answered her cell. "Claire, it's Josie McLean. I'm back in the States for two weeks and I want to see you."

They met in Midtown at a coffee shop, and Josie's wardrobe was sensible as usual, a black turtleneck with slacks, and a three-quarter-length camel coat. Claire was fashionable in a chartreuse, wool pant suit, and cream blouse. "You look wonderful," Josie exclaimed. Hard to believe that this alive, colorful, and beautiful young woman was the same pale and care-worn specimen that Richard had brought to Glastonbury Tor less than four months earlier.

The friends sipped coffee and indulged in small talk before taking a stroll up Fifth Avenue. "I got your number from Richard. We're having dinner tonight. Care to join us?" Josie asked, and Claire stiffened, although there was little or no guile in the anthropologist's request. "I'm sorry, I have plans tonight," she said, heading off the invitation and Josie changed the subject. "Richard told me about your adventures in Europe. What an amazing experience." Claire smiled wistfully. It all seemed so dreamlike and far away.

At 59th Street, the two women turned into Central Park. The weather was mild for January, as they sat on a park bench to watch joggers, cyclists, and couples shepherding kids and pushing strollers. Claire told Josie about the visions that had continued after their first meeting. "Aside from the occasional vivid dream about Jake, Sebastian, or Anselmo, they've all but stopped," she said, "and I still don't know what to make of them. Brandt believes they're iron-clad proof that the scroll's predictions are true. Bodhipaksa simply sees them as the play of my mind, illusions that I should just acknowledge and release. My doctor thinks my brain's a little injured."

Josie didn't respond right away and concentrated on the passersby who flowed in and out of the park, as Claire relaxed into the silence. "Our creative power is quite extraordinary," she said finally. "People believe that their lives just happen, but on a deep level, usually beneath awareness, we author our life and its unique course. Our beliefs drive our thoughts. Our thoughts become actions, and those actions shape our destiny."

Claire could feel Josie was watching her, gauging her reactions. "Claire, are you aware of a shaman's true purpose?" Claire shook her head. She could always count on Josie to transport her to other worlds, other cultures, other ways of being.

"The shaman or holy man in any primitive society is the one who has the big dream that gives the tribe its purpose and direction," Josie said with authority. "He knows that inner power is abundant. He uses it to shape individuals and communities. A shaman helps others change their destinies by changing their beliefs or the stories they tell themselves. Think of the Rain Dances performed by the first Americans. Consider the Buddhist monks who meditate in the snowy Himalayas and heat their bodies until their robes steam. In Haiti, where Santeria is practiced, a man will die after a death curse has been put on him, because his belief in the curse is so strong that it kills him."

"Mind over matter, is that what you are telling me?" Claire looked into Josie's pale blue eyes.

"I am telling you that you possess enormous creative power, and you can use it to create a rich, full, and meaningful life for yourself and others. We shape our waking dream like we shape our dreams when we sleep. Stay in touch with the creative function, Claire. At the deepest level of your intuition, feel for the truth." Josie stood up, reached into her large tote bag, and handed her a gift-wrapped box. "I brought you something. I picked it up years ago during my travels in India. It's beautiful, but it was meant for you not me." Claire went to untie the lavender ribbon around the package.

"Open it at home." Josie leaned down and kissed her new friend goodbye. "I have to go." She turned and walked away, looking back before disappearing down Fifth Avenue. Claire blew her a kiss. It was more than forty blocks to her apartment, a long walk through the park, but she set out with gusto.

At home, Claire set down her bag, along with Josie's gift, and made Earl Grey tea. The hot, fragrant drink reminded her of London and Richard. She eyed the box wrapped in purple paper and tied with the lilac bow. After draining her teacup, she slowly, carefully, opened the package. Inside, folded between layers of white tissue paper, was a magnificent Indian sari in lilac silk with an ornately beaded and embroidered edge. There was no vision, no shudder, or flash of light, but somewhere inside, Claire registered a coincidence. She thought of the Indian wife in a purple sari, who had haunted her dreams and become the central figure in her extraordinary painting.

The artist stood before the full-length mirror in her bedroom. She tied back her hair and wrapped the sari around her, tossing a length of fabric across her shoulder. She felt disoriented and didn't recognize herself in the glass. Her face that had looked back at her thousands of times was suddenly unfamiliar. "Was I the Indian wife? Was that me all along?" she whispered to her reflection. What's a dream? What's real life? she wondered, accepting that she would never really know.

***

Claire was not nervous. She looked around the Vetch Gallery and had to admit that here, under proper lighting, her paintings looked very beautiful. She didn't feel exposed or fear rejection. Anyway, there was no going back now. She held a glass of champagne, careful not to jostle and spill down the delicate fabric of the lilac sari. She caught people eyeing her with curiosity, and from the open landing above the main gallery, she saw Deirdre pointing at her.

"You look amazing!" her agent had gushed earlier when Claire climbed out of the cab and strolled into the gallery, resplendent in the sari, with her curls held back by two jeweled combs.

Claire had to admit that the Vetch Gallery had done an expert job hanging the show. "Miracles of Nature, Abstracts by Claire Lucas," the large sign at the gallery entrance announced, and most of her canvases were here: flowers and landscapes, raindrops, and snowfall; scenes from nature that she had deconstructed and rendered as simple shapes and colors. She wasn't anxious or self-conscious. She was simply present for this thrilling but unexpected milestone in her career. She walked through the crowd, alert to the odors of perfume, liquor, and hors d'oeuvres, the rise and fall of conversation and laughter.

Deirdre slipped her arm through Claire's and they did the rounds, meeting guests who had plenty of money to spend at places like Deirdre Vetch's gallery. The artist was confident, able to enter and exit conversations skillfully, connecting and disconnecting from groups of well-dressed Manhattanites, who had come to view her paintings and maybe even buy them.

By 8 p.m., the room was packed. Claire noticed the beautiful young man, with dark curls, dressed in jeans and a rich brown, linen shirt—Gio Monte. He maintained eye contact, as he snaked through the crowd to reach her. "Signora Markson, I didn't know you are Claire Lucas." He kissed her on both cheeks. Not up to correcting his mistake, she just smiled. He was on a routine trip to New York to check on his father's real estate holdings. "I love these works," he said, gesturing toward her paintings. "When you come back to Milan, please come to my house. My parents would love to see these."

"Friends of yours?" Claire pointed to a boisterous group of young men by the door, who were signaling in Gio's direction that it was time to move on and partake of Manhattan's rich cornucopia that awaited them.

"Maybe you would like this?" Gio reached into his wallet and handed Claire a photograph of himself with Anselmo, taken outdoors at Il Campo in Siena. Facing the sun, Anselmo squinted. He looked young and aware of his charms, his chest squared, and his arm draped around his handsome young friend. Claire took the photo and thanked Gio. He kissed her on both cheeks and was gone with a double "Ciao, ciao."

Claire thought of Sebastian and Anselmo. She could only wonder if she had shared past lives, or a fantasy of past lives with them, in a dream world or parallel universe. Who knew which metaphysical theory best summed up her strange encounters? She did know that these two painters and fellow travelers would always be important to her.

Deirdre sidled up and spoke out the side of her mouth in a stage whisper. "We sold six already." The excited painter performed a little victory shuffle and hugged her agent, who immediately took off, on the hunt for more sales. Claire felt hot in the crush of the growing crowd. Wandering into the long corridor that ran alongside the main showroom for air, she pressed her back against the wall and fanned her flushed cheeks with a program. A silky softness, cool and fragrant, brushed against her face, and turning her head, she was almost smothered by a bouquet of intoxicating yellow roses.

"Do these go with lilac?" Richard put his hand on the wall above her head and leaned over her.

"They go perfectly," Claire said. "Are they for me?" He was so handsome, such a beautiful man, no matter what he was to her now. He leaned down and kissed her, holding nothing back. "Who do I see about buying one of your paintings?"

"Talk to me later. I can get you a deal." She was rejoicing inside that he was here, bringing so much of her happiness with him.

"Don't keep your public waiting," he said. "I'm going to walk around and admire your talent."

"Entertaining the public is not my thing." Claire pulled him down until his face met hers, and she kissed him. She had no desire to be coy or play games or exact revenge because he had made her wait so long. She was just so completely and absolutely overjoyed that he was back.

"All right then, want to go for a drink?"

"Perfect. Let me tell Deirdre goodbye first."

"I'll wait for you outside." He walked toward the door.

Deirdre was disappointed. "You can't leave yet. There are so many fans of your work that you haven't met."

"But I have to go," Claire insisted. "Schedule as many lunches and private showings as you like, and I promise I'll be there."

On her way out, Claire lifted a small framed watercolor from the gallery wall, her favorite in the series she had done of Lake Como. "Please don't touch the paintings, ma'am." The stern command startled Claire who swung around, before walking over to Manny and hugging the embarrassed security guard. "Ms. Lucas, I'm sorry. I didn't realize it was you."

"It's so good to see you, Manny." She fished around in her small, beaded purse and handed him a hundred-dollar bill. He waved his hand in refusal. "Take it." Claire pressed the money into his palm. Dear, reliable Manny, always standing guard over her work. "Please tell Deirdre that I can't part with this one, so I took it."

Manuel nodded and helped her put on her wrap. Outside on the sidewalk, Richard had disappeared, and Claire's heart momentarily sank, until she saw him step out of the shadows. "This is for you." She handed him the small, exquisite watercolor of the villa, lake, and shoreline, done in vibrant jewel colors and loose simple strokes.

"It's beautiful," he said, pulling her toward him with one arm, as he ran his hand down her back.

"It's just the beginning," she whispered, and pressed her face into his shirt with its familiar smell of fresh air and a subtle cologne.

The End

ROUNDFIRE
BOOKS

FICTION

Historical fiction that lives

Put simply, we publish great stories. Whether it's literary or popular, a gentle tale or a pulsating thriller, the connecting theme in all Roundfire fiction titles is that once you pick them up you won't want to put them down.

If you have enjoyed this book, why not tell other readers by posting a review on your preferred book site.

Recent bestsellers from Roundfire are:

The Bookseller's Sonnets
Andi Rosenthal
The Bookseller's Sonnets intertwines three love stories with a
tale of religious identity and mystery spanning five hundred
years and three countries.
Paperback: 978-1-84694-342-3 ebook: 978-184694-626-4

Birds of the Nile
An Egyptian Adventure
N.E. David
Ex-diplomat Michael Blake wanted a quiet birding trip up the
Nile – he wasn't expecting a revolution.
Paperback: 978-1-78279-158-4 ebook: 978-1-78279-157-7

Blood Profit$
The Lithium Conspiracy
J. Victor Tomaszek, James N. Patrick, Sr.
The blood of the many for the profits of the few… *Blood Profit$*
will take you into the cigar-smoke-filled room where American
policy and laws are really made.
Paperback: 978-1-78279-483-7 ebook: 978-1-78279-277-2

The Burden
A Family Saga
N.E. David
Frank will do anything to keep his mother and father
apart. But he's carrying baggage – and it might just weigh
him down …
Paperback: 978-1-78279-936-8 ebook: 978-1-78279-937-5

On the Far Side, There's a Boy
Paula Coston
Martine Haslett, a thirty-something 1980s woman, plays hard on the fringes of the London drag club scene until one night which prompts her to sign up to a charity. She writes to a young Sri Lankan boy, with consequences far and long.
Paperback: 978-1-78279-574-2 ebook: 978-1-78279-573-5

Tuareg
Alberto Vazquez-Figueroa
With over 5 million copies sold worldwide, *Tuareg* is a classic adventure story from best-selling author Alberto Vazquez-Figueroa, about honour, revenge and a clash of cultures.
Paperback: 978-1-84694-192-4

Readers of ebooks can buy or view any of these bestsellers by clicking on the live link in the title. Most titles are published in paperback and as an ebook. Paperbacks are available in traditional bookshops. Both print and ebook formats are available online.

Find more titles and sign up to our readers' newsletter at
www.collectiveinkbooks.com/fiction